'I MUST MAKE AN INCISION,' HE SAID – 'IN THE HEAD THIS TIME.'
from 'The Third Drug' by Edith Nesbit

THE
DARKER
SEX

THE
DARKER
SEX

Tales of the Supernatural and Macabre
by Victorian Women Writers

Edited by
MIKE ASHLEY

PETER OWEN
London and Chester Springs, PA, USA

PETER OWEN PUBLISHERS
73 Kenway Road, London SW5 0RE

Peter Owen books are distributed in the USA by
Dufour Editions Inc., Chester Springs, PA 19425-0007

This collection first published in Great Britain 2009 by
Peter Owen Publishers

Selection and Introduction © Mike Ashley 2009

ISBN 978-0-7206-1335-3

A catalogue record for this book is available from the British Library

Printed and bound in the UK by
CPI Bookmarque, Croydon, CR0 4TD

COPYRIGHT ACKNOWLEDGEMENTS

Front cover illustration and frontispiece by Arthur Watts from *The Strand* magazine,
February 1908, accompanying the story 'The Third Drug' by Edith Nesbit.
The editor thanks Sue Lonoff de Cuevas for her permission to reprint her
translation of 'The Palace of Death' by Emily Brontë, as published in
The Belgian Essays (Yale University Press, 1997) © 1997 by Sue Lonoff.
'The Three Kisses' © 1920 by Violet Quirk. First published in *The Novel Magazine*,
February 1920. Every effort has been made to trace the current copyright holder.

CONTENTS

INTRODUCTION

IS THE FEMALE of the species really more deadly than the male? Far be it from me to say one way or the other, but there is no doubt that for many years there has been a predisposition among women writers for dark tales of the supernatural and macabre.

Women have long been natural storytellers. The double meaning of the phrase 'spinning a yarn' is far from accidental. As women spun their yarn so they would tell stories. When that cottage industry faded with the industrial revolution, women continued to spin yarns but this time as published stories. When the movement for Gothic fiction dawned in the late eighteenth century, it might have been a man who started it – Horace Walpole – but it was three women who popularized it: Clara Reeve, Mary Shelley (with *Frankenstein*) and, most notably, Ann Radcliffe. It was her novel, *The Mysteries of Udolpho*, published in 1794, that really established the Gothic theme and inspired many imitations. Her husband, William Radcliffe, encouraged her writing but could not read the stories on his own as they frightened him too much.

By the Victorian era many women, both in Britain and America, found they had a natural gift for telling stories of horror and the supernatural. In fact, it would not be too far from the truth to say that the women writers, from Catherine Crowe and Elizabeth Gaskell through to Charlotte Riddell and Mary Braddon, perfected the traditional ghost story and developed its darker features. When we think of the Gothic horrors of the early Victorian era, typified by the 'mad woman in the attic' plot, it is writers such as Jane Austen and Emily Brontë who come to mind. Austen may have lampooned the Gothic novel in *Northanger Abbey*, but in so doing she recognized the power and effect of the sensational novels. And

9

when it came to sensation, none was better than Mary Braddon, whose *Lady Audley's Secret*, published in 1862, shocked society with its theme of bigamy – not too far removed from Braddon's own life.

This anthology selects some of the best and most representative work by these Victorian and later writers, not all of them well known, to show how they developed the supernatural story. Though there are some traditional ghost stories, such as Mrs Gaskell's 'The Old Nurse's Story', I have deliberately chosen a wide range of macabre themes to show the versatility of the writers. There are some surprises. Mary Ann Evans, who wrote as George Eliot and who is best known for such books as *Silas Marner* and *Middlemarch*, also wrote a story about precognition, 'The Lifted Veil'. Edith Nesbit, best known for her children's books *The Railway Children* and *Five Children and It*, loved to tell horror stories and in 'The Third Drug', explores the idea of experimenting on humans to create a super-being – a story more science fiction than supernatural.

One aspect that binds these stories together is how they consider the extent to which either the dead might have power over the living or the living have power over death. Emily Brontë's short fable, 'The Palace of Death', which has been all but forgotten since she first wrote it in 1842, admirably serves as a prologue to that theme, while Elizabeth Stuart Phelps's powerful 'The Presence' likewise brings it to a close. In between, the stories run the full range of the supernatural, showcasing the talents of the 'darker sex'.

Mike Ashley

Emily Brontë

THE PALACE OF DEATH

We start our exploration of the battle between life and death with a little-known piece by Emily Brontë (1818–48). Renowned for Wuthering Heights *(1847), Emily was the most precocious and strong-willed of the surviving Brontë sisters, though Charlotte was the eldest. All three sisters wrote from an early age, together with their brother Branwell, setting stories in their imaginary kingdoms – Gondal in the case of Emily and Anne. By the time she turned twenty, Emily had completed many stories and poems, though none had been published. In 1842, Charlotte and Emily, now in their mid-twenties, were sent to Brussels to expand their education. While there, under the stern stewardship of Constantin Heger, the two women completed several writing assignments, one of which was 'Le Palais de la Mort' ('The Palace of Death'), written in October 1842. It was composed in French and was not translated into English for over a century. Even now it is one of Emily Brontë's least-known works. The following translation by Sue Lonoff was included in the volume* The Belgian Essays *(1997) featuring the work of both Charlotte and Emily.*

The Palace of Death

IN TIMES PAST, when men were few in number, Death lived frugally and husbanded her means. Her sole minister then was Old Age, who guarded the gate of her palace and from time to time admitted a solitary victim to appease the hunger of her mistress. This abstinence was soon recompensed; Her Majesty's prey increased prodigiously, and Old Age began to find that he had too much to do.

It was at this time that Death decided to change her way of living, to appoint new agents, and to take a prime minister.

On the day set for the nomination, the silence of the sombre palace was broken by the arrival of candidates from all quarters; the vaults, the chambers and the galleries resounded with the noise of steps that came and went, as if the bones that lay strewn about the pavement had suddenly come back to life; and Death, looking down from the height of her throne; smiled hideously to see what multitudes hastened to serve her. Amongst the first arrivals were Wrath and Vengeance, who hurried to the station themselves before Her Majesty, loudly arguing about the justice of their particular rights. Envy and Treason took their positions behind in the shadow. Famine and Plague, attended by their companions Sloth and Avarice, secured very convenient places in the crowd and cast a scornful eye over the other guests. None the less they were forced to give way when Ambition and Fanaticism appeared; the retinues of those two personages filled the council chamber, and they imperiously demanded an immediate audience.

'I doubt not,' said the former, 'that Your Majesty will be fair in her decision, but why waste time in vain disputes when a glance will suffice to determine the one who is alone worthy of the office in question? Who are all these pretenders who besiege your throne? What can they do in your service? The ablest amongst them is no more capable of governing your empire than is a soldier, with no quality other than his courage, of commanding an army. They know how to strike one victim here and another there; they know how to entrap feeble prey, the men on whom those are your mark has been visible since birth, and those are the limits of their usefulness; as for me, I will lead the elite of the race to your portals, those who are furthest from your power. I will harvest them in their flower and offer them to you as troops at the same stroke. Besides, I have so many means; it is not the sword alone that wins my victories; I have other agents, secret but powerful allies. Fanaticism himself is but an instrument that I shall employ for my profit.'

On hearing these words, Fanaticism shook his savage head, and, raising toward Death an eye burning with the fire of obsession, he began: 'I know this blusterer will happily borrow my weapons and march under my banners, but is that any reason that she should presume to compare herself with me? Not only will I be as powerful as she at overturning states and desolating realms, but I will enter into families; I will set the son against the father, the daughter against the mother; inspired by me the faithful friend will become a mortal enemy, the wife will betray her husband, the domestic his master. No sentiment can withstand me; I will banners traverse the earth beneath heaven's banners and crowns will be as stones beneath my feet. As for the other candidates, they are unworthy of attention; Wrath is barbarism; vengeance is partial; Famine can be conquered by industry; Plague is capricious. Your prime minister must be someone who is always close to men, who surrounds and possesses them. Decide then between Ambition and me; we are the only ones between whom your choice can hesitate.'

Fanaticism fell silent, and Her Majesty seemed to waver in doubt between these two rivals when the door of the hall opened, and there entered a person before whom everyone fell back in astonishment, for she had a figure that seemed to glow with joy and health, her step was as light as a zephyr, and Death herself appeared uneasy at her first approach; however, she soon reassured herself. 'You recognize me,' the stranger said to her; 'I arrive later than the others, but I know that my claim is certain. Some of my rivals are formidable, I admit, and I may perhaps be surpassed by several in striking deeds that draw the admiration of the mob, but I have a friend before whom this whole assembly will be forced to succumb. Her name is Civilization: in a few years she will come to dwell on this earth with us, and each century will amplify her power. In the end, she will divert Ambition from your service; she will put the brake of law on wrath; she will wrest the weapons from Fanaticism's hands; she will chase Famine off amongst the savages. I alone will grow and flourish under her reign; the power of all the others will expire with their partisans; mine will exist even when I am dead. If once I make acquaintance with the father, my influence will extend to the son, and before men unite to banish me from their society, I will have changed their entire nature and made the whole species an easier prey for your Majesty, so effectively, in fact, that Old Age will have almost a sinecure and your palace will be gorged with victims.' 'Say no more,' said Death, descending from her throne and embracing Intemperance (for that was the stranger's name). 'It is enough that I know you. For the others, I have lucrative and important offices; they will all be my ministers, but for you alone is reserved the honour of being my viceroy.'

Elizabeth Gaskell

The Old Nurse's Story

Though she died in 1865 of a heart attack, at the age of just fifty-five, the works of Elizabeth Gaskell continue to live on and delight each new generation. The series of sketches that make up the book Cranford *(1853) is perhaps the most lively and popular of her works, though* Mary Barton *(1848) and* North and South *(1855) were of great importance in their day for highlighting social conditions and inequalities. She was in some ways a female equivalent of Charles Dickens, who held her in very high regard. It was Dickens who encouraged her to turn her abilities to the supernatural and to write a ghost story for the first special Christmas issue of his magazine* Household Words *in 1852. The result was 'The Old Nurse's Story', which became one of the most popular and most reprinted of all Victorian ghost stories. It set the standard for the field for the next fifty years.*

The Old Nurse's Story

YOU KNOW, MY dears, that your mother was an orphan and an only child; and I dare say you have heard that your grandfather was a clergyman up in Westmorland, where I come from. I was just a girl in the village school, when, one day, your grandmother came in to ask the mistress if there was any scholar there who would do for a nurse-maid; and mighty proud I was, I can tell ye, when the mistress called me up, and spoke to my being a good girl at my needle, and a steady honest girl, and one whose parents were very respectable, though they might be poor. I thought I should like nothing better than to serve the pretty young lady, who was blushing as deep as I was, as she spoke of the coming baby, and what I should have to do with it. However, I see you don't care so much for this part of my story, as for what you think is to come, so I'll tell you at once. I was engaged and settled at the parsonage before Miss Rosamond (that was the baby, who is now your mother) was born. To be sure, I had little enough to do with her when she came, for she was never out of her mother's arms, and slept by her all night long; and proud enough was I sometimes when missis trusted her to me. There never was such a baby before or since, though you've all of you been fine enough in your turns; but for sweet, winning ways, you've none of you come up to your mother. She took after her mother, who was a real lady born; a Miss Furnivall, a granddaughter of Lord Furnivall's, in Northumberland. I believe she had neither brother nor sister, and had been brought up in my lord's family till she had married your grandfather, who was just a curate, son to a shopkeeper in Carlisle – but a clever, fine gentleman as ever was – and one who was a right-down hard worker in his parish, which was very wide, and scattered all abroad over the Westmorland Fells. When your mother, little Miss Rosamond, was about four or five years old, both her parents died in a fortnight – one after the other. Ah! that was a sad time. My pretty young mistress and me was looking for another baby, when my master came home from one of his long rides, wet, and tired, and took the fever he died of; and then she never held up her head again, but just lived to see her dead baby, and have it laid on her breast before she sighed away her life. My mistress had asked me, on her death-bed, never to leave Miss Rosamond; but if she had never spoken a word, I would have gone with the little child to the end of the world.

The next thing, and before we had well stilled our sobs, the executors and guardians came to settle the affairs. They were my poor young mistress's own cousin, Lord Furnivall, and Mr Esthwaite, my master's brother, a shopkeeper in Manchester; not so well-to-do then as he was afterwards, and with a large family rising about him. Well! I don't know if it were their settling, or because of a letter my mistress wrote on her death-bed to her cousin, my lord; but somehow it was settled that Miss Rosamond and me were to go to Furnivall Manor House, in Northumberland, and my lord spoke as if it had been her mother's wish that she should live with his family, and as if he had no objections, for that one or two more or less could make no difference in so grand a household. So, though that was not the way in which I should have wished the coming of my bright and pretty pet to have been looked at – who was like a sunbeam in any family, be it never so grand – I was well pleased that all the folks in the Dale should stare and admire, when they heard I was going to be young lady's maid at my Lord Furnivall's at Furnivall Manor.

But I made a mistake in thinking we were to go and live where my lord did. It turned out that the family had left Furnivall Manor House fifty years or more. I could not hear that my poor young mistress had ever been there, though she had been brought up in the family; and I was sorry for that, for I should have liked Miss Rosamond's youth to have passed where her mother's had been.

My lord's gentleman, from whom I asked as many questions as I durst, said that the Manor House was at the foot of the Cumberland Fells, and a very grand place; that an old Miss Furnivall, a great-aunt of my lord's, lived there, with only a few servants; but that it was a very healthy place, and my lord had thought that it would suit Miss Rosamond very well for a few years, and that her being there might perhaps amuse his old aunt.

I was bidden by my lord to have Miss Rosamond's things ready by a certain day. He was a stern proud man, as they say all the Lords Furnivall were; and he never spoke a word more than was necessary. Folk did say he had loved my young mistress; but that, because she knew that his father would object, she would never listen to him, and married Mr Esthwaite; but I don't know. He never married at any rate. But he never took much notice of Miss Rosamond; which I thought he might have done if he had cared for her dead mother. He sent his gentleman with us to the Manor House, telling him to join him at Newcastle that same evening; so there was no great length of time for him to make us known to all the strangers before he, too, shook us off; and we were left, two lonely young things (I was not eighteen), in the great old Manor House. It seems like yesterday that we drove there. We had left our own dear parsonage very early, and we had both cried as if our hearts would break, though we were travelling in my lord's carriage, which I thought so much of once. And now it was long past noon on a September day, and we stopped to change horses for the last time at a little smoky town, all full of colliers and miners. Miss Rosamond had fallen asleep, but Mr Henry told me to waken her, that she might see the park and the Manor House as we drove up. I thought it rather a pity; but I did what he bade me, for fear he should complain of me to my lord. We had left all signs of a town, or even a village, and were then inside the gates of a large wild park – not like the parks here in the south, but with rocks, and the noise of running water, and gnarled thorn-trees, and old oaks, all white and peeled with age.

The road went up about two miles, and then we saw a great and stately house, with many trees close around it, so close that in some places their branches dragged against the walls when the wind blew;

and some hung broken down; for no one seemed to take much charge of the place; – to lop the wood, or to keep the moss-covered carriage-way in order. Only in front of the house all was clear. The great oval drive was without a weed; and neither tree nor creeper was allowed to grow over the long, many-windowed front; at both sides of which a wing projected, which were each the ends of other side fronts; for the house, though it was so desolate, was even grander than I expected. Behind it rose the Fells, which seemed unenclosed and bare enough; and on the left hand of the house, as you stood facing it, was a little, old-fashioned flower-garden, as I found out afterwards. A door opened out upon it from the west front; it had been scooped out of the thick dark wood for some old Lady Furnivall; but the branches of the great forest trees had grown and overshadowed it again, and there were very few flowers that would live there at that time.

When we drove up to the great front entrance, and went into the hall I thought we should be lost – it was so large, and vast, and grand. There was a chandelier all of bronze, hung down from the middle of the ceiling; and I had never seen one before, and looked at it all in amaze. Then, at one end of the hall, was a great fire-place, as large as the sides of the houses in my country, with massy andirons and dogs to hold the wood; and by it were heavy old-fashioned sofas. At the opposite end of the hall, to the left as you went in – on the western side – was an organ built into the wall, and so large that it filled up the best part of that end. Beyond it, on the same side, was a door; and opposite, on each side of the fire-place, were also doors leading to the east front; but those I never went through as long as I stayed in the house, so I can't tell you what lay beyond.

The afternoon was closing in, and the hall, which had no fire lighted in it, looked dark and gloomy, but we did not stay there a moment. The old servant, who had opened the door for us, bowed to Mr Henry, and took us in through the door at the further side of the great organ, and led us through several smaller halls and passages into the west drawing-room, where he said that Miss Furnivall was sitting. Poor little Miss Rosamond held very tight to me, as if she were scared and lost in that great place, and as for myself, I was not much better. The west drawing-room was very cheerful-looking, with a warm fire in it, and plenty of good, comfortable furniture about. Miss Furnivall was an old lady not far from eighty, I should think, but I do not know. She was thin and tall, and had a face as full of fine wrinkles as if they had been drawn all over it with a needle's point. Her eyes were very watchful, to make up, I suppose, for her being so deaf as to be obliged to use a trumpet. Sitting with her, working at the same great piece of tapestry, was Mrs Stark, her maid and companion, and almost as old as she was. She had lived with Miss Furnivall ever since they both were young, and now she seemed more like a friend than a servant; she looked so cold and grey, and stony, as if she had never loved or cared for any one; and I don't suppose she did care for any one, except her mistress; and, owing to the great deafness of the latter, Mrs Stark treated her very much as if she were a child. Mr Henry gave some message from my lord, and then he bowed good-bye to us all – taking no notice of my sweet little Miss Rosamond's outstretched hand – and left us standing there, being looked at by the two old ladies through their spectacles.

I was right glad when they rung for the old footman who had shown us in at first, and told him to take us to our rooms. So we went out of that great drawing-room, and into another sitting-room, and out of that, and then up a great flight of stairs, and along a broad gallery – which was something like a library, having books all down one side, and windows and writing-tables all down the other – till we came to our rooms, which I was not sorry to hear were just over the kitchens; for I began to think I should be lost in that wilderness of a house. There was an old nursery, that had been used for all the little lords and ladies long ago, with a pleasant fire burning in the grate, and the kettle boiling on the hob, and tea-things spread out on the table; and out of that room was the night-nursery, with a little crib for Miss Rosamond close to my bed. And old James called up Dorothy, his wife, to bid us welcome; and both he and she were so hospitable and kind, that by and by Miss

Rosamond and me felt quite at home; and by the time tea was over, she was sitting on Dorothy's knee, and chattering away as fast as her little tongue could go. I soon found out that Dorothy was from Westmorland, and that bound her and me together, as it were; and I would never wish to meet with kinder people than were old James and his wife. James had lived pretty nearly all his life in my lord's family, and thought there was no one so grand as they. He even looked down a little on his wife; because, till he had married her, she had never lived in any but a farmer's household. But he was very fond of her, as well he might be. They had one servant under them, to do all the rough work. Agnes they called her; and she and me, and James and Dorothy, with Miss Furnivall and Mrs Stark, made up the family; always remembering my sweet little Miss Rosamond! I used to wonder what they had done before she came, they thought so much of her now. Kitchen and drawing-room, it was all the same. The hard, sad Miss Furnivall, and the cold Mrs Stark, looked pleased when she came fluttering in like a bird, playing and pranking hither and thither, with a continual murmur, and pretty prattle of gladness. I am sure, they were sorry many a time when she flitted away into the kitchen, though they were too proud to ask her to stay with them, and were a little surprised at her taste; though to be sure, as Mrs Stark said, it was not to be wondered at, remembering what stock her father had come of. The great, old rambling house was a famous place for little Miss Rosamond. She made expeditions all over it, with me at her heels; all, except the east wing, which was never opened, and whither we never thought of going. But in the western and northern part was many a pleasant room; full of things that were curiosities to us, though they might not have been to people who had seen more. The windows were darkened by the sweeping boughs of the trees, and the ivy which had overgrown them: but, in the green gloom, we could manage to see old China jars and carved ivory boxes, and great heavy books, and, above all, the old pictures!

Once, I remember, my darling would have Dorothy go with us to tell us who they all were; for they were all portraits of some of my lord's family, though Dorothy could not tell us the names of every one. We had gone through most of the rooms, when we came to the old state drawing-room over the hall, and there was a picture of Miss Furnivall; or, as she was called in those days, Miss Grace, for she was the younger sister. Such a beauty she must have been! but with such a set, proud look, and such scorn looking out of her handsome eyes, with her eyebrows just a little raised, as if she wondered how anyone could have the impertinence to look at her; and her lip curled at us, as we stood there gazing. She had a dress on, the like of which I had never seen before, but it was all the fashion when she was young: a hat of some soft white stuff like beaver, pulled a little over her brows, and a beautiful plume of feathers sweeping round it on one side; and her gown of blue satin was open in front to a quilted white stomacher.

'Well, to be sure!' said I, when I had gazed my fill. 'Flesh is grass, they do say; but who would have thought that Miss Furnivall had been such an out-and-out beauty, to see her now?'

'Yes,' said Dorothy. 'Folks change sadly. But if what my master's father used to say was true, Miss Furnivall, the elder sister, was handsomer than Miss Grace. Her picture is here somewhere; but, if I show it you, you must never let on, even to James, that you have seen it. Can the little lady hold her tongue, think you?' asked she.

I was not so sure, for she was such a little sweet, bold, open-spoken child, so I set her to hide herself; and then I helped Dorothy to turn a great picture, that leant with its face towards the wall, and was not hung up as the others were. To be sure, it beat Miss Grace for beauty; and, I think, for scornful pride, too, though in that matter it might be hard to choose. I could have looked at it an hour, but Dorothy seemed half frightened at having shown it to me, and hurried it back again, and bade me run and find Miss Rosamond, for that there were some ugly places about the house, where she should like ill for the child to go. I was a brave, high-spirited girl, and thought little of what the old woman said, for I liked hide-and-seek as well as any child in the parish; so off I ran to find my little one.

As winter drew on, and the days grew shorter, I was sometimes almost certain that I heard a noise as if someone was playing on the great organ in the hall. I did not hear it every evening; but, certainly, I did very often; usually when I was sitting with Miss Rosamond, after I had put her to bed, and keeping quite still and silent in the bedroom. Then I used to hear it booming and swelling away in the distance. The first night, when I went down to my supper, I asked Dorothy who had been playing music, and James said very shortly that I was a gowk to take the wind soughing amongst the trees for music: but I saw Dorothy look at him very fearfully, and Bessy, the kitchen-maid, said something beneath her breath, and went quite white. I saw they did not like my question, so I held my peace till I was with Dorothy alone, when I knew I could get a good deal out of her. So, the next day, I watched my time, and I coaxed and asked her who it was that played the organ; for I knew that it was the organ and not the wind well enough, for all I had kept silence before James. But Dorothy had had her lesson, I'll warrant, and never a word could I get from her. So then I tried Bessy, though I had always held my head rather above her, as I was evened to James and Dorothy, and she was little better than their servant. So she said I must never, never tell; and if I ever told, I was never to say *she* had told me; but it was a very strange noise, and she had heard it many a time, but most of all on winter nights, and before storms; and folks did say, it was the old lord playing on the great organ in the hall, just as he used to do when he was alive; but who the old lord was, or why he played, and why he played on stormy winter evenings in particular, she either could not or would not tell me. Well! I told you I had a brave heart; and I thought it was rather pleasant to have that grand music rolling about the house, let who would be the player; for now it rose above the great gusts of wind, and wailed and triumphed just like a living creature, and then it fell to a softness most complete; only it was always music, and tunes, so it was nonsense to call it the wind. I thought at first that it might be Miss Furnivall who played, unknown to Bessy; but, one day when I was in the hall by myself, I opened the organ and peeped all about it and around it, as I had done to the organ in Crosthwaite Church once before, and I saw it was all broken and destroyed inside, though it looked so brave and fine; and then, though it was noonday, my flesh began to creep a little, and I shut it up, and run away pretty quickly to my own bright nursery; and I did not like hearing the music for some time after that, any more than James and Dorothy did. All this time Miss Rosamond was making herself more and more beloved. The old ladies liked her to dine with them at their early dinner; James stood behind Miss Furnivall's chair, and I behind Miss Rosamond's all in state; and, after dinner, she would play about in a corner of the great drawing-room, as still as any mouse, while Miss Furnivall slept, and I had my dinner in the kitchen. But she was glad enough to come to me in the nursery afterwards; for, as she said, Miss Furnivall was so sad, and Mrs Stark so dull; but she and I were merry enough; and, by and by, I got not to care for that weird rolling music, which did one no harm, if we did not know where it came from.

That winter was very cold. In the middle of October the frosts began, and lasted many, many weeks. I remember, one day at dinner, Miss Furnivall lifted up her sad, heavy eyes, and said to Mrs Stark, 'I am afraid we shall have a terrible winter', in a strange kind of meaning way. But Mrs Stark pretended not to hear, and talked very loud of something else. My little lady and I did not care for the frost; not we! As long as it was dry we climbed up the steep brows, behind the house, and went up on the Fells, which were bleak, and bare enough, and there we ran races in the fresh, sharp air; and once we came down by a new path that took us past the two old gnarled holly-trees, which grew about half-way down by the east side of the house. But the days grew shorter and shorter; and the old lord, if it was he, played away more and more stormily and sadly on the great organ. One Sunday afternoon – it must have been towards the end of November – I asked Dorothy to take charge of little Missey when she came out of the drawing-room, after Miss Furnivall had had her nap; for it was too cold to take her with me to church, and yet I wanted to go. And Dorothy was glad enough to promise, and was so fond of the child that all seemed well; and Bessy and I set off very briskly, though the sky hung heavy and black over the white earth, as if the night had never fully gone away; and the air, though still, was very biting and keen.

'We shall have a fall of snow,' said Bessy to me. And sure enough, even while we were in church, it came down thick, in great large flakes, so thick it almost darkened the windows. It had stopped snowing before we came out, but it lay soft, thick, and deep beneath our feet, as we tramped home. Before we got to the hall the moon rose, and I think it was lighter then – what with the moon, and what with the white dazzling snow – than it had been when we went to church, between two and three o'clock. I have not told you that Miss Furnivall and Mrs Stark never went to church: they used to read the prayers together, in their quiet gloomy way; they seemed to feel the Sunday very long without their tapestry-work to be busy at. So when I went to Dorothy in the kitchen, to fetch Miss Rosamond and take her upstairs with me, I did not much wonder when the old woman told me that the ladies had kept the child with them, and that she had never come to the kitchen, as I had bidden her, when she was tired to behaving pretty in the drawing-room. So I took off my things and went to find her, and bring her to her supper in the nursery. But when I went into the best drawing-room, there sat the two old ladies, very still and quiet, dropping out a word now and then, but looking as if nothing so bright and merry as Miss Rosamond had ever been near them. Still I thought she might be hiding from me; it was one of her pretty ways; and that she had persuaded them to look as if they knew nothing about her; so I went softly peeping under this sofa, and behind that chair, making believe I was sadly frightened at not finding her.

'What's the matter, Hester?' said Mrs Stark, sharply. I don't know if Miss Furnivall had seen me, for, as I told you, she was very deaf, and she sat quite still, idly staring into the fire, with her hopeless face. 'I'm only looking for my little Rosy-Posy,' replied I, still thinking that the child was there, and near me, though I could not see her.

'Miss Rosamond is not here,' said Mrs Stark. 'She went away

more than an hour ago to find Dorothy.' And she too turned and went on looking into the fire.

My heart sank at this, and I began to wish I had never left my darling. I went back to Dorothy and told her. James was gone out for the day, but she and me and Bessy took lights and went up into the nursery first, and then we roamed over the great large house, calling and entreating Miss Rosamond to come out of her hiding-place, and not frighten us to death in that way. But there was no answer; no sound.

'Oh!' said I at last, 'Can she have got into the east wing and hidden there?'

But Dorothy said it was not possible, for that she herself had never been in there; that the doors were always locked, and my lord's steward had the keys, she believed; at any rate, neither she nor James had ever seen them: so I said I would go back, and see if, after all, she was not hidden in the drawing-room, unknown to the old ladies; and if I found her there, I said, I would whip her well for the fright she had given me; but I never meant to do it. Well, I went back to the west drawing-room, and I told Mrs Stark we could not find her anywhere, and asked for leave to look all about the furniture there, for I thought now, that she might have fallen asleep in some warm hidden corner; but no! we looked, Miss Furnivall got up and looked, trembling all over, and she was nowhere there; then we set off again, everyone in the house, and looked in all the places we had searched before, but we could not find her. Miss Furnivall shivered and shook so much that Mrs Stark took her back into the warm drawing-room; but not before they had made me promise to bring her to them when she was found. Well-a-day! I began to think she never would be found, when I be-thought me to look out into the great front court, all covered with snow. I was upstairs when I looked out; but, it was such clear moonlight, I could see, quite plain, two little footprints, which might be traced from the hall door, and round the corner of the east wing. I don't know how I got down, but I tugged open the great, stiff hall door; and, throwing the skirt of my gown over my head for a cloak, I ran out. I turned the east corner, and there a black shadow fell on the snow; but when I came again into the moonlight, there were the little footmarks going up – up to the Fells. It was bitter cold; so cold that the air almost took the skin off my face as I ran, but I ran on, crying to think how my poor little darling must be perished, and frightened. I was within sight to the holly-trees when I saw a shepherd coming down the hill, bearing something in his arms wrapped in his maud. He shouted to me, and asked me if I had lost a bairn; and, when I could not speak for crying, he bore towards me, and I saw my wee bairnie lying still, and white, and stiff, in his arms, as if she had been dead. He told me he had been up the Fells to gather in his sheep, before the deep cold of night came on, and that under the holly-trees (black marks on the hill-side, where no other bush was for miles around) he had found my little lady – my lamb – my queen – my darling – stiff and cold, in the terrible sleep which is frost-begotten. Oh! the joy, and the tears of having her in my arms once again! for I would not let him carry her; but took her, maud and all, into my own arms, and held her near my own warm neck and heart, and felt the life stealing slowly back again into her little gentle limbs. But she was still insensible when we reached the hall, and I had no breath for speech. We went in by the kitchen door.

'Bring the warming-pan,' said I; and I carried her upstairs and began undressing her by the nursery fire, which Bessy had kept up. I called my little lammie all the sweet and playful names I could think of – even while my eyes were blinded by my tears; and at last, oh! at length she opened her large blue eyes. Then I put her into her warm bed, and sent Dorothy down to tell Miss Furnivall that all was well; and I made up my mind to sit by my darling's bedside the live-long night. She fell away into a soft sleep as soon as her pretty head had touched the pillow, and I watched by her till morning light; when she wakened up bright and clear – or so I thought at first – and, my dears, so I think now.

She said that she had fancied that she should like to go to Dorothy, for that both the old ladies were asleep, and it was very dull in the drawing-room; and that, as she was going through the west lobby, she saw the snow through the high window falling – falling – soft and steady; but she wanted to see it lying pretty and white on the ground; so she made her way into the great hall; and then, going to the window, she saw it bright and soft upon the drive; but while she stood there she saw a little girl, not so old as she was, 'but so pretty,' said my darling, 'and this little girl beckoned to me to come out; and oh, she was so pretty and so sweet, I could not choose but go'. And then this other little girl had taken her by the hand, and side by side the two had gone round the east corner.

'Now, you are a naughty little girl, and telling stories,' said I. 'What would your good mamma, that is in heaven, and never told a story in her life, say to her little Rosamond, if she heard her – and I dare say she does – telling stories!'

'Indeed, Hester,' sobbed out my child, 'I'm telling you true. Indeed I am.'

'Don't tell me!' said I, very stern. 'I tracked you by your foot-marks through the snow; there were only yours to be seen: and if you had had a little girl to go hand in hand with you up the hill, don't you think the footprints would have gone along with yours?'

'I can't help it, dear, dear Hester,' said she, crying, 'if they did not; I never looked at her feet, but she held my hand fast and tight in her little one, and it was very, very cold. She took me up the Fell-path, up to the holly trees; and there I saw a lady weeping and cry-ing; but when she saw me, she hushed her weeping, and smiled very proud and grand, and took me on her knee, and began to lull me to sleep; and that's all, Hester – but that is true; and my dear mamma knows it is,' said she, crying. So I thought the child was in a fever, and pretended to believe her, as she went over her story – over and over again, and always the same. At last Dorothy knocked at the door with Miss Rosamond's breakfast; and she told me the old ladies were down in the eating parlour, and that they wanted to speak to me. They had both been into the night-nursery the evening before, but it was after Miss Rosamond was asleep; so they had only looked at her – not asked me any questions.

I shall catch it, thought I to myself, as I went along the north gallery. And yet, I thought, taking courage, it was in their charge I left her; and it's they that's to blame for letting her steal away unknown and unwatched. So I went in boldly, and told my story. I told it all to Miss Furnivall, shouting it close to her ear; but when I came to the mention of the other little girl out in the snow, coaxing and tempting her out, and willing her up to the grand and beautiful lady by the holly-tree, she threw her arms up – her old and withered arms – and cried aloud, 'Oh! Heaven, forgive! Have mercy!'

Mrs Stark took hold of her; roughly enough, I thought; but she was past Mrs Stark's management, and spoke to me, in a kind of wild warning and authority.

'Hester! Keep her from that child! It will lure her to her death! That evil child! Tell her it is a wicked, naughty child.' Then Mrs Stark hurried me out of the room; where, indeed, I was glad enough to go; but Miss Furnivall kept shrieking out, 'Oh! have mercy! Wilt Thou never forgive! It is many a long year ago . . .'

I was very uneasy in my mind after that. I durst never leave Miss Rosamond, night or day, for fear lest she might slip off again, after some fancy or other; and all the more, because I thought I could make out that Miss Furnivall was crazy, from their odd ways about her; and I was afraid lest something of the same kind (which might be in the family, you know) hung over my darling. And the great frost never ceased all this time; and, whenever it was a more stormy night than usual, between the gusts, and through the wind, we heard the old lord playing on the great organ. But, old lord, or not, wherever Miss Rosamond went, there I followed; for my love for her, pretty, helpless orphan, was stronger than my fear for the grand and terrible sound. Besides, it rested with me to keep her cheerful and merry, as beseemed her age. So we played together, and wandered together, here and there, and everywhere; for I never dared to lose sight of her again in that large and rambling house. And so it happened, that one afternoon, not long before Christmas Day, we were playing together on the billiard-table in the great hall (not that we knew the right way of playing, but she liked to roll the smooth ivory balls with her pretty hands, and I liked to do whatever she did);

and, by and by, without our noticing it, it grew dusk indoors, though it was still light in the open air, and I was thinking of taking her back into the nursery, when, all of a sudden, she cried out:

'Look, Hester! Look! there is my poor little girl out in the snow!'

I turned towards the long narrow windows, and there, sure enough, I saw a little girl, less than my Miss Rosamond – dressed all unfit to be out of doors such a bitter night – crying, and beating against the window-panes, as if she wanted to be let in. She seemed to sob and wail, till Miss Rosamond could bear it no longer, and was flying to the door to open it, when, all of a sudden, and close upon us, the great organ pealed out so loud and thundering, it fairly made me tremble; and all the more, when I remembered me that, even in the stillness of that dead-cold weather, I had heard no sound of little battering hands upon the window-glass, though the Phantom Child had seemed to put forth all its force; and, though I had seen it wail and cry, no faintest touch of sound had fallen upon my ears. Whether I remembered all this at the very moment, I do not know; the great organ sound had so stunned me into terror. But this I know: I caught up Miss Rosamond before she got the hall-door opened, and clutched her, and carried her away, kicking and screaming, into the large bright kitchen, where Dorothy and Agnes were busy with their mince-pies.

'What is the matter with my sweet one?' cried Dorothy, as I bore in Miss Rosamond, who was sobbing as if her heart would break.

'She won't let me open the door for my little girl to come in; and she'll die if she is out on the Fells all night. Cruel, naughty Hester,' she said, slapping me; but she might have struck harder, for I had seen a look of ghastly terror on Dorothy's face, which made my very blood run cold.

'Shut the back-kitchen door fast, and bolt it well,' said she to Agnes. She said no more; she gave me raisins and almonds to quiet Miss Rosamond: but she sobbed about the little girl in the snow, and would not touch any of the good things. I was thankful when she cried herself to sleep in bed. Then I stole down to the kitchen, and told Dorothy I had made up my mind. I would carry my darling back to my father's house in Applethwaite; where, if we lived humbly, we lived at peace. I said I had been frightened enough with the old lord's organ-playing; but now, that I had seen for myself this little moaning child, all decked out as no child in the neighbourhood could be, beating and battering to get in, yet always without any sound or noise – with the dark wound on its right shoulder; and that Miss Rosamond had known it again for the phantom that had nearly lured her to her death (which Dorothy knew was true); I would stand it no longer.

I saw Dorothy change colour once or twice. When I had done, she told me she did not think I could take Miss Rosamond with me, for that she was my lord's ward, and I had no right over her; and she asked me, would I leave the child that I was so fond of, just for sounds and sights that could do me no harm; and that they had all had to get used to in their turns? I was all in a hot, trembling passion; and I said it was very well for her to talk, that knew what these sights and noises betokened, and that had, perhaps, had something to do with the Spectre-Child while it was alive. And I taunted her so, that she told me all she knew, at last; and then I wished I had never been told, for it only made me more afraid than ever.

She said she had heard the tale from old neighbours that were alive when she was first married; when folks used to come to the hall sometimes, before it had got such a bad name on the countryside; it might not be true, or it might, what she had been told.

The old lord was Miss Furnivall's father – Miss Grace, as Dorothy called her, for Miss Maude was the elder, and Miss Furnivall by rights. The old lord was eaten up with pride. Such a proud man was never seen or heard of; and his daughters were like him. No one was good enough to wed them, though they had choice enough; for they were the great beauties of their day, as I had seen by their portraits, where they hung in the state drawing-room. But, as the old saying is, 'Pride will have a fall'; and these two haughty beauties fell in love with the same man, and he no better than a foreign musician, whom their father had down from London to play music with him at the Manor House. For, above all things, next to his pride, the old lord loved music. He could play on nearly every instrument that ever was heard of: and it was a strange thing it did not soften him; but he was a fierce dour old man, and had broken his poor wife's heart with his cruelty, they said. He was mad after music, and would pay any money for it. So he got this foreigner to come; who made such beautiful music that they said the very birds on the trees stopped their singing to listen. And, by degrees, this foreign gentleman got such a hold over the old lord that nothing would serve him but that he must come every year; and it was he that had the great organ brought from Holland, and built up in the hall, where it stood now. He taught the old lord to play on it; but many and many a time, when Lord Furnivall was thinking of nothing but his fine organ, and his finer music, the dark foreigner was walking abroad in the woods with one of the young ladies; now Miss Maude and then Miss Grace.

Miss Maude won the day and carried off the prize, such as it was; and he and she were married, all unknown to any one; and before he made his next yearly visit, she had been confined of a little girl at a farmhouse on the Moors, while her father and Miss Grace thought she was away at Doncaster Races. But, though she was a wife and a mother, she was not a bit softened but as haughty and as passionate as ever; and perhaps more so, for she was jealous of Miss Grace, to whom her foreign husband paid a deal of court – by way of blinding her – as he told his wife. But Miss Grace triumphed over Miss Maude, and Miss Maude grew fiercer and fiercer, both with her husband and with her sister; and the former – who could easily shake off what was disagreeable, and hide himself in foreign countries – went away a month before his usual time that summer, and half threatened that he would never come back again. Meanwhile, the little girl was left at the farm-house, and her mother used to have her horse saddled and gallop wildly over the hills to see her once every week, at the very least – for where she loved, she loved; and where she hated, she hated. And the old lord went on playing – playing on his organ; and the servants thought the sweet music he made had soothed down his awful temper, of which (Dorothy said) some terrible tales could be told. He grew infirm, too, and had to walk with a crutch; and his son – that was the present Lord Furnivall's father – was with the army in America, and the other son at sea; so Miss Maude had it pretty much her own way, and she and Miss Grace grew colder and bitterer to each other every day; till at last they hardly ever spoke, except when the old lord was by. The foreign musician came again the next summer, but it was for the last time; for they led him such a life with their jealousy and their passions that he grew weary, and went away, and never was heard of again. And Miss Maude, who had always meant to have her marriage acknowledged when her father should be dead, was left now a deserted wife – whom nobody knew to have been married – with a child that she dared not own, though she loved it to distraction; living with a father whom she feared, and a sister whom she hated. When the next summer passed over and the dark foreigner never came, both Miss Maude and Miss Grace grew gloomy and sad; they had a haggard look about them, though they looked handsome as ever. But by and by Miss Maude brightened; for her father grew more and more infirm, and more than ever carried away by his music; and she and Miss Grace lived almost entirely apart, having separate rooms, the one on the west side, Miss Maude on the east – those very rooms which were now shut up. So she thought she might have her little girl with her, and no one need ever know except those who dared not speak about it, and were bound to believe that it was, as she said, a cottager's child she had taken a fancy to. All this, Dorothy said, was pretty well known; but what came afterwards no one knew, except Miss Grace, and Mrs Stark, who was even then her maid, and much more of a friend to her than ever her sister had been. But the servants supposed, from words that were dropped, that Miss Maude had triumphed over Miss Grace, and told her that all the time the dark foreigner had been mocking her with pretended love – he was her own husband; the colour left Miss Grace's cheek and lips that very day for ever, and she was heard to say many a time that sooner or later she would have her revenge; and Mrs Stark was forever spying about the east rooms.

One fearful night, just after the New Year had come in, when the snow was lying thick and deep, and the flakes were still falling – fast enough to blind anyone who might be out and abroad – there was a great and violent noise heard, and the old lord's voice above all, cursing and swearing awfully – and the cries of a little child – and the proud defiance of a fierce woman – and the sound of a blow – and a dead stillness – and moans and wailings dying away on the hill-side! Then the old lord summoned all his servants, and told them, with terrible oaths, and words more terrible, that his daughter had disgraced herself, and that he had turned her out of doors – her, and her child – and that if ever they gave her help – or food – or shelter – he prayed that they might never enter Heaven. And, all the while, Miss Grace stood by him, white and still as any stone; and when he had ended she heaved a great sigh, as much as to say her work was done, and her end was accomplished. But the old lord never touched his organ again, and died within the year; and no wonder! for, on the morrow of that wild and fearful night, the shepherds, coming down the Fell side, found Miss Maude sitting, all crazy and smiling, under the holly-trees, nursing a dead child – with a terrible mark on its right shoulder. 'But that was not what killed it,' said Dorothy; 'it was the frost and the cold; every wild creature was in its hole, and every beast in its fold – while the child and its mother were turned out to wander on the Fells! And now you know all! and I wonder if you are less frightened now?'

I was more frightened than ever; but I said I was not. I wished Miss Rosamond and myself well out of that dreadful house for ever; but I would not leave her, and I dared not take her away. But oh! how I watched her, and guarded her! We bolted the doors, and shut the window-shutters fast, an hour or more before dark, rather than leave them open five minutes too late. But my little lady still heard the weird child crying and mourning; and not all we could do or say could keep her from wanting to go to her, and let her in from the cruel wind and the snow. All this time, I kept away from Miss Furnivall and Mrs Stark, as much as ever I could; for I feared them – I knew no good could be about them, with their grey hard faces and their dreamy eyes, looking back into the ghastly years that were gone. But, even in my fear, I had a kind of pity – for Miss Furnivall, at least. Those gone down to the pit can hardly have a more hopeless look than that which was ever on her face. At last I even got so sorry for her – who never said a word but what was quite forced from her – that I prayed for her; and I taught Miss Rosamond to pray for one who had done a deadly sin; but often when she came to those words, she would listen, and start up from her knees, and say, 'I hear my little girl plaining and crying very sad – Oh! let her in, or she will die!'

One night – just after New Year's Day had come at last, and the long winter had taken a turn, as I hoped – I heard the west drawing-room bell ring three times, which was the signal for me. I would not leave Miss Rosamond alone, for all she was asleep – for the old lord had been playing wilder than ever – and I feared lest my darling should waken to hear the spectre child; see her I knew she could not. I had fastened the windows too well for that. So I took her out of her bed and wrapped her up in such outer clothes as were most handy, and carried her down to the drawing-room, where the old ladies sat at their tapestry work as usual. They looked up when I came in, and Mrs Stark asked, quite astounded, 'Why did I bring Miss Rosamond there, out of her warm bed?' I had begun to whisper, 'Because I was afraid of her being tempted out while I was away, by the wild child in the snow,' when she stopped me short (with a glance at Miss Furnivall), and said Miss Furnivall wanted me to undo some work she had done wrong, and which neither of them could see to unpick. So I laid my pretty dear on the sofa, and sat down on a stool by them, and hardened my heart against them, as I heard the wind rising and howling.

Miss Rosamond slept on sound, for all the wind blew so; and Miss Furnivall said never a word, nor looked round when the gusts shook the windows. All at once she started up to her full height, and put up one hand, as if to bid us listen.

'I hear voices!' said she. 'I hear terrible screams – I hear my father's voice!'

Just at that moment my darling wakened with a sudden start: 'My little girl is crying, oh, how she is crying!' and she tried to get up and go to her, but she got her feet entangled in the blanket, and I caught her up; for my flesh had begun to creep at these noises, which they heard while we could catch no sound. In a minute or two the noises came, and gathered fast, and filled our ears; we, too, heard voices and screams, and no longer heard the winter's wind that raged abroad. Mrs Stark looked at me, and I at her, but we dared not speak. Suddenly Miss Furnivall went towards the door, out into the ante-room, through the west lobby, and opened the door into the great hall. Mrs Stark followed, and I durst not be left, though my heart almost stopped beating for fear. I wrapped my darling tight in my arms, and went out with them. In the hall the screams were louder than ever; they sounded to come from the east wing – nearer and nearer – close on the other side of the locked-up doors – close behind them. Then I noticed that the great bronze chandelier seemed all alight, though the hall was dim, and that a fire was blazing in the vast hearth-place, though it gave no heat; and I shuddered up with terror, and folded my darling closer to me. But as I did so, the east door shook, and she, suddenly struggling to get free from me, cried, 'Hester! I must go! My little girl is there; I hear her; she is coming! Hester, I must go!'

I held her tight with all my strength; with a set will, I held her. If I had died, my hands would have grasped her still, I was so resolved in my mind. Miss Furnivall stood listening, and paid no regard to my darling, who had got down to the ground, and whom I, upon my knees now, was holding with both my arms clasped round her neck; she still striving and crying to get free.

All at once the east door gave way with a thundering crash, as if torn open in a violent passion, and there came into that broad and mysterious light, the figure of a tall old man, with grey hair and gleaming eyes. He drove before him, with many a relentless gesture of abhorrence, a stern and beautiful woman, with a little child cling-ing to her dress.

'O Hester! Hester!' cried Miss Rosamond. 'It's the lady! the lady below the holly-trees; and my little girl is with her. Hester! Hester! let me go to her; they are drawing me to them. I feel them – I feel them. I must go!'

Again she was almost convulsed by her efforts to get away; but I held her tighter and tighter, till I feared I should do her a hurt; but rather that than let her go towards those terrible phantoms. They passed along towards the great hall-door, where the winds howled and ravened for their prey; but before they reached that, the lady turned; and I could see that she defied the old man with a fierce and proud defiance; but then she quailed – and then she threw up her arms wildly and piteously to save her child – her little child – from a blow from his uplifted crutch.

And Miss Rosamond was torn as by a power stronger than mine, and writhed in my arms, and sobbed (for by this time the poor darling was growing faint).

'They want me to go with them on to the Fells – they are drawing me to them. Oh, my little girl! I would come, but cruel, wicked Hester holds me very tight.' But when she saw the uplifted crutch she swooned away, and I thanked God for it. Just at this moment – when the tall old man, his hair streaming as in the blast of a furnace, was going to strike the little shrinking child – Miss Furnivall, the old woman by my side, cried out, 'Oh, Father! Father! Spare the little innocent child!' But just then I saw – we all saw – another phantom shape itself, and grow clear out of the blue and misty light that filled the hall; we had not seen her till now, for it was another lady who stood by the old man, with a look of relentless hate and triumphant scorn. That figure was very beautiful to look upon, with a soft white hat drawn down over the proud brows, and a red and curling lip. It was dressed in an open robe of blue satin. I had seen that figure before. It was the likeness of Miss Furnivall in her youth; and the terrible phantoms moved on, regardless of old Miss Furnivall's wild entreaty – and the uplifted crutch fell on the right shoulder of the little child, and the younger sister looked on, stony and deadly serene. But at that moment, the dim lights, and the fire that gave no heat, went out of themselves, and Miss Furnivall lay at our feet stricken down by the palsy – death-stricken.

Yes! she was carried to her bed that night never to rise again. She lay with her face to the wall, muttering low but muttering always: 'Alas! alas! what is done in youth can never be undone in age! What is done in youth can never be undone in age!'

Mary E. Braddon

THE SHADOW IN THE CORNER

Mary Braddon was one of the most popular Victorian writers, known as the Queen of the Circulating Libraries. She had a long, prolific career, spreading over fifty years from her first sales in 1856 until incapacitated by a stroke in 1907, though she still produced occasional stories up to her death in 1915, aged seventy-nine. Braddon's early life had been scandalous, especially when she set up house with publisher John Maxwell, whose wife was still alive but confined to a mental asylum. Braddon and Maxwell feigned marriage and had five children, though they could not formally marry until after Maxwell's wife's death in 1874. No stranger to controversy, Braddon used the themes of bigamy and deceit in her best-known novel, Lady Audley's Secret, *which has never been out of print since it first appeared in 1862. In her long career she wrote over eighty novels, many of the later ones achieving a literary respectability with her growing fascination for social issues. She earned a fortune, her estate at the time of her death being valued at over £68,000, the equivalent of over £5 million today.*

Some aspects of Braddon's radicalism emerge in the following story, first published in All the Year Round *in 1879. It shows the rise of scientific understanding over superstition, and yet even the most ardent realist sometimes stumbles upon the inexplicable.*

The Shadow in the Corner

WILDHEATH GRANGE STOOD a little way back from the road, with a barren stretch of heath behind it, and a few tall fir-trees, with straggling wind-tossed heads, for its only shelter. It was a lonely house on a lonely road, little better than a lane, leading across a desolate waste of sandy fields to the sea-shore; and it was a house that bore a bad name amongst the natives of the village of Holcroft, which was the nearest place where humanity might be found.

It was a good old house, nevertheless, substantially built in the days when there was no stint of stone and timber – a good old grey stone house with many gables, deep window-seats, and a wide staircase, long dark passages, hidden doors in queer corners, closets as large as some modern rooms, and cellars in which a company of soldiers might have lain *perdu*.

This spacious old mansion was given over to rats and mice, loneliness, echoes, and the occupation of three elderly people: Michael Bascom, whose forebears had been landowners of importance in the neighbourhood, and his two servants, Daniel Skegg and his wife, who had served the owner of that grim old house ever since he left the university, where he had lived fifteen years of his life – five as student, and ten as professor of natural science.

At three-and-thirty Michael Bascom had seemed a middle-aged man; at fifty-six he looked and moved and spoke like an old man. During that interval of twenty-three years he had lived alone in Wildheath Grange, and the country people told each other that the house had made him what he was. This was a fanciful and superstitious notion on their part, doubtless, yet it would not have been difficult to have traced a certain affinity between the dull grey building and the man who lived in it. Both seemed alike remote from the common cares and interests of humanity; both had an air of settled melancholy, engendered by perpetual solitude; both had the same faded complexion, the same look of slow decay.

Yet lonely as Michael Bascom's life was at Wildheath Grange, he would not on any account have altered its tenor. He had been glad to exchange the comparative seclusion of college rooms for the unbroken solitude of Wildheath. He was a fanatic in his love of scientific research, and his quiet days were filled to the brim with labours that seldom failed to interest and satisfy him. There were periods of depression, occasional moments of doubt, when the goal towards which he strove seemed unattainable, and his spirit fainted within him. Happily such times were rare with him. He had a dogged power of continuity which ought to have carried him to the highest pinnacle of achievement, and which perhaps might ultimately have won for him a grand name and a world-wide renown, but for a catastrophe which burdened the declining years of his harmless life with an unconquerable remorse.

One autumn morning – when he had lived just three-and-twenty years at Wildheath, and had only lately begun to perceive that his faithful butler and body servant, who was middle-aged when he first employed him, was actually getting old – Mr Bascom's breakfast meditations over the latest treatise on the atomic theory were interrupted by an abrupt demand from that very Daniel Skegg. The man was accustomed to wait upon his master in the most absolute silence, and his sudden breaking out into speech was almost as startling as if the bust of Socrates above the bookcase had burst into human language.

'It's no use,' said Daniel; 'my missus must have a girl!'

'A what?' demanded Mr Bascom, without taking his eyes from the line he had been reading.

'A girl – a girl to trot about and wash up, and help the old lady. She's getting weak on her legs, poor soul. We've none of us grown younger in the last twenty years.'

'Twenty years!' echoed Michael Bascom scornfully. 'What is

twenty years in the formation of a strata – what even in the growth of
an oak – the cooling of a volcano!'

'Not much, perhaps, but it's apt to tell upon the bones of a
human being.'

'The manganese staining to be seen upon some skulls would
certainly indicate — ' began the scientist dreamily.

'I wish my bones were only as free from rheumatics as they were
twenty years ago,' pursued Daniel testily; 'and then, perhaps, I
should make light of twenty years. Howsoever, the long and the
short of it is, my missus must have a girl. She can't go on trotting up
and down these everlasting passages, and standing in that stone
scullery year after year, just as if she was a young woman. She must
have a girl to help.'

'Let her have twenty girls,' said Mr Bascom, going back to his
book.

'What's the use of talking like that, sir. Twenty girls, indeed! We
shall have rare work to get one.'

'Because the neighbourhood is sparsely populated?' interrogated
Mr Bascom, still reading.

'No, sir. Because this house is known to be haunted.'

Michael Bascom laid down his book, and turned a look of grave
reproach upon his servant.

'Skegg,' he said in a severe voice, 'I thought you had lived long
enough with me to be superior to any folly of that kind.'

'I don't say that I believe in ghosts,' answered Daniel with a semi-
apologetic air; 'but the country people do. There's not a mortal
among 'em that will venture across our threshold after nightfall.'

'Merely because Anthony Bascom, who led a wild life in London,
and lost his money and land, came home here broken-hearted, and
is supposed to have destroyed himself in this house – the only remnant of property that was left him out of a fine estate.'

'Supposed to have destroyed himself!' cried Skegg. 'Why the fact
is as well known as the death of Queen Elizabeth, or the great fire
of London. Why, wasn't he buried at the cross-roads between here
and Holcroft?'

'An idle tradition, for which you could produce no substantial proof,' retorted Mr Bascom.

'I don't know about proof; but the country people believe it as firmly as they believe their Gospel.'

'If their faith in the Gospel was a little stronger they need not trouble themselves about Anthony Bascom.'

'Well,' grumbled Daniel, as he began to clear the table, 'a girl of some kind we must get, but she'll have to be a foreigner, or a girl that's hard driven for a place.'

When Daniel Skegg said a foreigner, he did not mean the native of some distant clime, but a girl who had not been born and bred at Holcroft. Daniel had been raised and reared in that insignificant hamlet, and, small and dull as it was, he considered the world beyond it only margin.

Michael Bascom was too deep in the atomic theory to give a second thought to the necessities of an old servant. Mrs Skegg was an individual with whom he rarely came in contact. She lived for the most part in a gloomy region at the north end of the house, where she ruled over the solitude of a kitchen that looked like a cathedral, and numerous offices of the sculler, larder, and pantry class, where she carried on a perpetual warfare with spiders and beetles, and wore her old life out in the labour of sweeping and scrubbing. She was a woman of severe aspect, dogmatic piety, and a bitter tongue. She was a good plain cook, and ministered diligently to her master's wants. He was not an epicure, but liked his life to be smooth and easy, and the equilibrium of his mental power would have been disturbed by a bad dinner.

He heard no more about the proposed addition to his household for a space of ten days, when Daniel Skegg again startled him amidst his studious repose by the abrupt announcement: 'I've got a girl!'

'Oh,' said Michael Bascom; 'have you?' and he went on with his book.

This time he was reading an essay on phosphorus and its functions in relation to the human brain.

'Yes,' pursued Daniel in his usual grumbling tone; 'she was a waif and stray, or I shouldn't have got her. If she'd been a native she'd never have come to us.'

'I hope she's respectable,' said Michael.

'Respectable! That's the only fault she has, poor thing. She's too good for the place. She's never been in service before, but she says she's willing to work, and I daresay my old woman will be able to break her in. Her father was a small tradesman at Yarmouth. He died a month ago, and left this poor thing homeless. Mrs Midge, at Holcroft, is her aunt, and she said to the girl, Come and stay with me till you get a place; and the girl has been staying with Mrs Midge for the last three weeks, trying to hear of a place. When Mrs Midge heard that my missus wanted a girl to help, she thought it would be the very thing for her niece Maria. Luckily Maria had heard nothing about this house, so the poor innocent dropped me a curtsy, and said she'd be thankful to come, and would do her best to learn her duty. She'd had an easy time of it with her father, who had educated her above her station, like a fool as he was,' growled Daniel.

'By your own account I'm afraid you've made a bad bargain,' said Michael. 'You don't want a young lady to clean kettles and pans.'

'If she was a young duchess my old woman would make her work,' retorted Skegg decisively.

'And pray where are you going to put this girl?' asked Mr Bascom, rather irritably; 'I can't have a strange young woman tramping up and down the passages outside my room. You know what a wretched sleeper I am, Skegg. A mouse behind the wainscot is enough to wake me.'

'I've thought of that,' answered the butler, with his look of ineffable wisdom. 'I'm not going to put her on your floor. She's to sleep in the attics.'

'Which room?'

'The big one at the north end of the house. That's the only ceiling that doesn't let water. She might as well sleep in a shower-bath as in any of the other attics.'

'The room at the north end,' repeated Mr Bascom thoughtfully; 'isn't that — ?'

'Of course it is,' snapped Skegg; 'but she doesn't know anything about it.'

Mr Bascom went back to his books, and forgot all about the orphan from Yarmouth, until one morning on entering his study he was startled by the appearance of a strange girl, in a neat black and white cotton gown, busy dusting the volumes which were stacked in blocks upon his spacious writing-table – and doing it with such deft and careful hands that he had no inclination to be angry at this unwonted liberty. Old Mrs Skegg had religiously refrained from all such dusting, on the plea that she did not wish to interfere with the master's ways. One of the master's ways, therefore, had been to inhale a good deal of dust in the course of his studies.

The girl was a slim little thing, with a pale and somewhat old-fashioned face, flaxen hair, braided under a neat muslin cap, a very fair complexion and light-blue eyes. They were the lightest-blue eyes Michael Bascom had ever seen, but there was a sweetness and gentleness in their expression which atoned for their insipid colour.

'I hope you do not object to my dusting your books, sir,' she said, dropping a curtsy.

She spoke with a quaint precision which struck Michael Bascom as a pretty thing in its way.

'No; I don't object to cleanliness, so long as my books and papers are not disturbed. If you take a volume off my desk, replace it on the spot you took it from. That's all I ask.'

'I will be very careful, sir.'

'When did you come here?'

'Only this morning, sir.'

The student seated himself at his desk, and the girl withdrew, drifting out of the room as noiselessly as a flower blown across the threshold. Michael Bascom looked after her curiously. He had seen very little of youthful womanhood in his dry-as-dust career, and he wondered at this girl as at a creature of a species hitherto unknown to him. How fairly and delicately she was fashioned; what a translucent skin; what soft and pleasing accents issued from those rose-tinted lips. A pretty thing, assuredly, this kitchen wench! A pit that in all this busy world there could be no better work found for her than the scouring of pots and pans.

Absorbed in considerations about dry bones, Mr Bascom thought no more of the pale-faced handmaiden. He saw her no more about his rooms. Whatever work she did there was done early in the morning, before the scholar's breakfast.

She had been a week in the house, when he met her one day in the hall. He was struck by the change in her appearance.

The girlish lips had lost their rose-bud hue; the pale-blue eyes had a frightened look, and there were dark rings round them, as in one whose nights had been sleepless, or troubled by evil dreams.

Michael Bascom was so startled by an undefinable look in the girl's face that, reserved as he was by habit and nature, he expanded so far as to ask her what ailed her.

'There is something amiss, I am sure,' he said. 'What is it?'

'Nothing, sir,' she faltered, looking still more scared at his question. 'Indeed, it is nothing; or nothing worth troubling you about.'

'Nonsense. Do you suppose, because I live among books, I have no sympathy with my fellow-creatures? Tell me what is wrong with you, child. You have been grieving about the father you have lately lost, I suppose.'

'No, sir; it is not that. I shall never leave off being sorry for that. It is a grief which will last me all my life.'

'What, there is something else then?' asked Michael impatiently. 'I see; you are not happy here. Hard work does not suit you. I thought as much.'

'Oh, sir, please don't think that,' cried the girl, very earnestly. 'Indeed, I am glad to work – glad to be in service; it is only . . .'

She faltered and broke down, the tears rolling slowly from her sorrowful eyes, despite her effort to keep them back.

'Only what?' cried Michael, growing angry. 'The girl is full of secrets and mysteries. What do you mean, wench?'

'I – I know it is very foolish, sir; but I am afraid of the room where I sleep.'

'Afraid! Why?'

'Shall I tell you the truth, sir? Will you promise not to be angry?'

'I will not be angry if you will only speak plainly; but you provoke me by these hesitations and suppressions.'

'And please, sir, do not tell Mrs Skegg that I have told you. She would scold me; or perhaps even send me away.'

'Mrs Skegg shall not scold you. Go on, child.'

'You may not know the room where I sleep, sir; it is a large room at one end of the house, looking towards the sea. I can see the dark line of water from the window, and I wonder sometimes to think that it is the same ocean I used to see when I was a child at Yarmouth. It is very lonely, sir, at the top of the house. Mr and Mrs Skegg sleep in a little room near the kitchen, you know, sir, and I am quite alone on the top floor.'

'Skegg told me you had been educated in advance of your position in life, Maria. I should have thought the first effect of a good education would have been to make you superior to any foolish fancies about empty rooms.'

'Oh, pray, sir, do not think it is any fault in my education. Father took such pains with me; he spared no expense in giving me as good an education as a tradesman's daughter need wish for. And he was a religious man, sir. He did not believe' – here she paused, with a suppressed shudder – 'in the spirits of the dead appearing to the living, since the days of miracles, when the ghost of Samuel appeared to Saul.

He never put any foolish ideas into my head, sir. I hadn't a thought of fear when I first lay down to rest in the big lonely room upstairs.'

'Well, what then?'

'But on the very first night,' the girl went on breathlessly, 'I felt weighed down in my sleep as if there were some heavy burden laid upon my chest. It was not a bad dream, but it was a sense of trouble that followed me all through my sleep; and just at daybreak – it begins to be light a little after six – I woke suddenly, with the cold perspiration pouring down my face, and knew that there was something dreadful in the room.'

'What do you mean by something dreadful. Did you see anything?'

'Not much, sir; but it froze the blood in my veins, and I knew it was this that had been following me and weighing upon me all through my sleep. In the corner, between the fire-place and the wardrobe, I saw a shadow – a dim, shapeless shadow . . .'

'Produced by an angle of the wardrobe, I daresay.'

'No, sir; I could see the shadow of the wardrobe, distinct and sharp, as if it had been painted on the wall. This shadow was in the corner – a strange, shapeless mass; or, if it had any shape at all, it seemed . . .'

'What?' asked Michael eagerly.

'The shape of a dead body hanging against the wall!'

Michael Bascom grew strangely pale, yet he affected utter incredulity.

'Poor child,' he said kindly; 'you have been frett ing about your father until your nerves are in a weak state, and you are full of fancies. A shadow in the corner, indeed; why, at daybreak, every corner is full of shadows. My old coat, flung upon a chair, will make you as good a ghost as you need care to see.'

'Oh, sir, I have tried to think it is my fancy. But I have had the same burden weighing me down every night. I have seen the same shadow every morning.'

'But when broad daylight comes, can you not see what stuff your shadow is made of?'

'No, sir: the shadow goes before it is broad daylight.'

'Of course, just like other shadows. Come, come, get these silly notions out of your head, or you will never do for the work-a-day world. I could easily speak to Mrs Skegg, and make her give you another room, if I wanted to encourage you in your folly. But that would be about the worst thing I could do for you. Besides, she tells me that all the other rooms on that floor are damp; and, no doubt, if she shifted you into one of them, you would discover another shadow in another corner, and get rheumatism into the bargain. No, my good girl, you must try to prove yourself the better for a superior education.'

'I will do my best, sir,' Maria answered meekly, dropping a curtsy.

Maria went back to the kitchen sorely depressed. It was a dreary life she led at Wildheath Grange – dreary by day, awful by night; for the vague burden and the shapeless shadow, which seemed so slight a matter to the elderly scholar, were unspeakably terrible to her. Nobody had told her that the house was haunted, yet she walked about those echoing passages wrapped round with a cloud of fear. She had no pity from Daniel Skegg and his wife. Those two pious souls had made up their minds that the character of the house should be upheld, so far as Maria went. To her, as a foreigner, the Grange should be maintained to be an immaculate dwelling, tainted by no sulphurous blast from the under world. A willing, biddable girl had become a necessary element in the existence of Mrs Skegg. That girl had been found, and that girl must be kept. Any fancies of a supernatural character must be put down with a high hand.

'Ghosts, indeed!' cried the amiable Skegg. 'Read your Bible, Maria, and don't talk no more about ghosts.'

'There are ghosts in the Bible,' said Maria, with a shiver at the recollection of certain awful passages in the Scripture she knew so well.

'Ah, they was in their right place, or they wouldn't ha' been there,' retorted Mrs Skegg. 'You ain't a-goin' to pick holes in your Bible, I hope, Maria, at your time of life.'

Maria sat down quietly in her corner by the kitchen fire, and turned over the leaves of her dead father's Bible till she came to the chapters they two had loved best and oftenest read together. He had been a simple-minded, straightforward man, the Yarmouth cabinet-maker – a man full of aspirations after good, innately refined, instinctively religious. He and his motherless girl had spent their lives alone together, in the neat little home which Maria had so soon learnt to cherish and beautify; and they had loved each other with an almost romantic love. They had had the same tastes, the same ideas. Very little had sufficed to make them happy. But inexorable death parted father and daughter, in one of those sharp, sudden partings which are like the shock of an earthquake – instantaneous ruin, desolation and despair.

Maria's fragile form had bent before the tempest. She had lived through a trouble that might have crushed a stronger nature. Her deep religious convictions, and her belief that this cruel parting would not be for ever, had sustained her. She faced life, and its cares and duties, with a gentle patience which was the noblest form of courage.

Michael Bascom told himself that the servant-girl's foolish fancy about the room that had been given her was not a matter of serious consideration. Yet the idea dwelt in his mind unpleasantly, and disturbed him at his labours. The exact sciences require the complete power of a man's brain, his utmost attention; and on this particular evening Michael found that he was only giving his work a part of his attention. The girl's pale face, the girl's tremulous tones, thrust themselves into the foreground of his thoughts.

He closed his book with a fretful sigh, wheeled his large armchair round to the fire, and gave himself up to contemplation. To attempt study with so disturbed a mind was useless. It was a dull grey evening, early in November; the student's reading-lamp was lighted, but the shutters were not yet shut, nor the curtains drawn. He could see the leaden sky outside his windows, the fir-tree tops tossing in the angry wind. He could hear the wintry blast whistling amidst the gables, before it rushed off seaward with a savage howl that sounded like a war-whoop.

Michael Bascom shivered, and drew nearer the fire.

'It's childish, foolish nonsense,' he said to himself, 'yet it's strange she should have that fancy about the shadow, for they say Anthony Bascom destroyed himself in that room. I remember hearing it when I was a boy, from an old servant whose mother was housekeeper at the great house in Anthony's time. I never heard how he died, poor fellow – whether he poisoned himself, or shot himself, or cut his throat; but I've been told that was the room. Old Skegg has heard it too. I could see that by his manner when he told me the girl was to sleep there.'

He sat for a long time, till the grey of evening outside his study windows changed to the black of night, and the war-whoop of the wind died away to a low complaining murmur. He sat looking into the fire, and letting his thoughts wander back to the past and the traditions he had heard in his boyhood.

That was a sad, foolish story of his great-uncle, Anthony Bascom: the pitiful story of a wasted fortune and a wasted life. A riotous collegiate career at Cambridge, a racing-stable at Newmarket, an imprudent marriage, a dissipated life in London, a runaway wife; an estate forfeited to Jew money-lenders, and then the fatal end.

Michael had often heard that dismal story: how, when Anthony Bascom's fair false wife had left him, when his credit was exhausted, and his friends had grown tired of him, and all was gone except Wildheath Grange, Anthony, the broken-down man of fashion, had come to that lonely house unexpectedly one night, and had ordered his bed to be got ready for him in the room where he used to sleep when he came to the place for the wild duck shooting, in his boyhood. His old blunderbuss was still hanging over the mantelpiece, where he had left it when he came into the property, and could afford to buy the newest thing in fowling-pieces. He had not been to Wildheath for fifteen years; nay, for a good many of those years he had almost forgotten that the drear; old house belonged to him.

The woman who had been housekeeper at Bascom Park, till house and lands had passed into the hands of the Jews, was at this time the sole occupant of Wildheath. She cooked some supper for her master, and made him as comfortable as she could in the long untenanted dining-room; but she was distressed to find, when she cleared the table after he had gone upstairs to bed, that he had eaten hardly anything.

Next morning she got his breakfast ready in the same room, which she managed to make brighter and cheerier than it had looked overnight. Brooms, dusting-brushes, and a good fire did much to improve the aspect of things. But the morning wore on to noon, and the old housekeeper listened in vain for her master's foot-fall on the stairs. Noon waned to late afternoon. She had made no attempt to disturb him, thinking that he had worn himself out by a tedious journey on horseback, and that he was sleeping the sleep of exhaustion. But when the brief November day clouded with the first shadows of twilight, the old woman grew seriously alarmed, and went upstairs to her master's door, where she waited in vain for any reply to her repeated calls and knockings.

The door was locked on the inside, and the housekeeper was not strong enough to break it open. She rushed downstairs again full of fear, and ran bare-headed out into the lonely road. There was no habitation nearer than the turnpike on the old coach road, from which this side road branched off to the sea. There was scanty hope of a chance passer-by. The old woman ran along the road, hardly knowing whither she was going or what she was going to do, but with a vague idea that she must get somebody to help her.

Chance favoured her. A cart, laden with sea-weed, came lumber-ing slowly along from the level line of sands yonder where the land melted into water. A heavy lumbering farm-labourer walked beside the cart.

'For God's sake, come in and burst open my master's door!' she entreated, seizing the man by the arm. 'He's lying dead, or in a fit, and I can't get to help him.'

'All right, missus,' answered the man, as if such an invitation were a matter of daily occurrence. 'Whoa, Dobbin; stond still, horse, and be donged to thee.'

Dobbin was glad enough to be brought to anchor on the patch of waste grass in front of the Grange garden. His master followed the housekeeper upstairs, and shattered the old-fashioned box-lock with one blow of his ponderous fist.

The old woman's worst fear was realized. Anthony Bascom was dead. But the mode and manner of his death Michael had never been able to learn. The housekeeper's daughter, who told him the story, was an old woman when he was a boy. She had only shaken her head, and looked unutterable things, when he questioned her too closely. She had never even admitted that the old squire had committed suicide. Yet the tradition of his self-destruction was rooted in the minds of the natives of Holcroft: and there was a settled belief that his ghost, at certain times and seasons, haunted Wildheath Grange.

Now Michael Bascom was a stern materialist. For him the universe with all its inhabitants, was a great machine, governed by inexorable laws. To such a man the idea of a ghost was simply absurd – as absurd as the assertion that two and two make five, or that a circle can be formed of a straight line. Yet he had a kind of dilettante interest in the idea of a mind which could believe in ghosts. The subject offered an amusing psychological study. This poor little pale girl, now, had evidently got some supernatural terror into her head, which could only be conquered by rational treatment.

'I know what I ought to do,' Michael Bascom said to himself suddenly. 'I'll occupy that room myself tonight, and demonstrate to this foolish girl that her notion about the shadow is nothing more than a silly fancy, bred of timidity and low spirits. An ounce of proof is better than a pound of argument. If I can prove to her that I have spent a night in the room, and seen no such shadow, she will understand what an idle thing superstition is.'

Daniel came in presently to shut the shutters.

'Tell your wife to make up my bed in the room where Maria has been sleeping, and to put her into one of the rooms on the first floor for to-night, Skegg,' said Mr Bascom.

'Sir?'

Mr Bascom repeated his order.

'That silly wench has been complaining to you about her room,' Skegg exclaimed indignantly. 'She doesn't deserve to be well fed and cared for in a comfortable home. She ought to go to the workhouse.'

'Don't be angry with the poor girl, Skegg. She has taken a foolish fancy into her head, and I want to show her how silly she is,' said Mr Bascom.

'And you want to sleep in his – in that room yourself,' said the butler.

'Precisely.'

'Well,' mused Skegg, 'if he does walk – which I don't believe – he was your own flesh and blood; and I don't suppose he'll do you any hurt.'

When Daniel Skegg went back to the kitchen he railed mercilessly at poor Maria, who sat pale and silent in her corner by the hearth, darning old Mrs Skegg's grey worsted stockings, which were the roughest and harshest armour that ever human foot clothed itself withal. 'Was there ever such a whimsical, fine, lady-like miss,' demanded Daniel, 'to come into a gentleman's house, and drive him out of his own bedroom to sleep in an attic, with her nonsenses and vagaries.' If this was the result of being educated above one's station, Daniel declared that he was thankful he had never got so far in his schooling as to read words of two syllables without spelling. Education might be hanged for him, if this was all it led to.

'I am very sorry,' faltered Maria, weeping silently over her work. 'Indeed, Mr Skegg, I made no complaint. My master questioned me, and I told him the truth. That was all.'

'All!' exclaimed Mr Skegg irately; 'all, indeed! I should think it was enough.'

Poor Maria held her peace. Her mind, fluttered by Daniel's unkindness, had wandered away from that bleak big kitchen to the lost home of the past – the snug little parlour where she and her father had sat beside the cosy hearth on such a night as this; she with her smart work-box and her plain sewing, he with the newspaper he loved to read; the petted cat purring on the rug, the kettle singing on the bright brass trivet, the tea-tray pleasantly suggestive of the most comfortable meal in the day.

Oh, those happy nights, that dear companionship! Were they really gone for ever, leaving nothing behind them but unkindness and servitude?

*

Michael Bascom retired later than usual that night. He was in the habit of sitting at his books long after every other lamp but his own had been extinguished. The Skeggs had subsided into silence and darkness in their drear ground-floor bed-chamber. Tonight his studies were of a peculiarly interesting kind, and belonged to the order of recreative reading rather than of hard work. He was deep in the history of that mysterious people who had their dwelling-place in the Swiss lakes, and was much exercised by certain speculations and theories about them.

The old eight-day clock on the stairs was striking two as Michael slowly ascended, candle in hand, to the hitherto unknown region of the attics. At the top of the staircase he found himself facing a dark narrow passage which led northwards, a passage that was in itself sufficient to strike terror to a superstitious mind, so black and uncanny did it look.

'Poor child,' mused Mr Bascom, thinking of Maria; 'this attic floor is rather dreary, and for a young mind prone to fancies . . .'

He had opened the door of the north room by this time, and stood looking about him.

It was a large room, with a ceiling that sloped on one side, but was fairly lofty upon the other; an old-fashioned room, full of old-fashioned furniture – big, ponderous, clumsy – associated with a day that was gone and people that were dead. A walnut-wood wardrobe stared him in the face – a wardrobe with brass handles, which gleamed out of the darkness like diabolical eyes. There was a tall four-post bedstead, which had been cut down on one side to accommodate the slope of the ceiling, and which had a misshapen and deformed aspect in consequence. There was an old mahogany bureau that smelt of secrets. There were some heavy old chairs with rush bottoms, mouldy with age, and much worn. There was a corner washstand, with a big basin and a small jug – the odds and ends of past years. Carpet there was none, save a narrow strip beside the bed.

'It is a dismal room,' mused Michael, with the same touch of pity for Maria's weakness which he had felt on the landing just now.

To him it mattered nothing where he slept; but having let himself down to a lower level by his interest in the Swiss lake-people, he was in a manner humanized by the lightness of his evening's reading, and was even inclined to compassionate the weaknesses of a foolish girl.

He went to bed, determined to sleep his soundest. The bed was comfortable, well supplied with blankets, rather luxurious than otherwise, and the scholar had that agreeable sense of fatigue which promises profound and restful slumber.

He dropped off to sleep quickly, but woke with a start ten minutes afterwards. What was this consciousness of a burden of care that had awakened him – this sense of all-pervading trouble that weighed upon his spirits and oppressed his heart – this icy horror of some terrible crisis in life through which he must inevitably pass? To him these feelings were as novel as they were painful. His life had flowed on with smooth and sluggish tide, unbroken by so much as a ripple of sorrow. Yet to-night he felt all the pangs of unavailing remorse; the agonizing memory of a life wasted; the stings of humiliation and disgrace, shame, ruin; a hideous death, which he had doomed himself to die by his own hand. These were the horrors that pressed him round and weighed him down as he lay in Anthony Bascom's room.

Yes, even he, the man who could recognize nothing in nature, or in nature's God, better or higher than an irresponsible and invariable machine governed by mechanical laws, was fain to admit that here he found himself face to face with a psychological mystery. This trouble, which came between him and sleep, was the trouble that had pursued Anthony Bascom on the last night of his life. So had the suicide felt as he lay in that lonely room, perhaps striving to rest his wearied brain with one last earthly sleep before he passed to the unknown intermediate land where all is darkness and slumber. And that troubled mind had haunted the room ever since. It was not the ghost of the man's body that returned to the spot where he had suffered and perished, but the ghost of his mind – his very self; no meaningless simulacrum of the clothes he were, and the figure that filled them.

Michael Bascom was not the man to abandon his high ground of sceptical philosophy without a struggle. He tried his hardest to conquer this oppression that weighed upon mind and sense. Again and again he succeeded in composing himself to sleep, but only to wake again and again to the same torturing thoughts, the same remorse, the same despair. So the night passed in unutterable weariness; for though he told himself that the trouble was not his trouble, that there was no reality in the burden, no reason for the remorse, these vivid fancies were as painful as realities, and took as strong a hold upon him.

The first streak of light crept in at the window – dim, and cold, and grey; then came twilight, and he looked at the corner between the wardrobe and the door.

Yes; there was the shadow: not the shadow of the wardrobe only – that was clear enough, but a vague and shapeless something which darkened the dull brown wall; so faint, so shadow, that he could form no conjecture as to its nature, or the thing it represented. He determined to watch this shadow till broad daylight; but the weariness of the night had exhausted him, and before the first dimness of dawn had passed away he had fallen fast asleep, and was tasting the blessed balm of undisturbed slumber. When he woke the winter sun was shining in at the lattice, and the room had lost its gloomy aspect. It looked old-fashioned, and grey, and brown, and shabby; but the depth of its gloom had fled with the shadows and the darkness of night.

Mr Bascom rose refreshed by a sound sleep, which had lasted nearly three hours. He remembered the wretched feelings which had gone before that renovating slumber; but he recalled his strange sensations only to despise them, and he despised himself for having attached any importance to them.

Indigestion very likely, he told himself; or perhaps mere fancy, engendered of that foolish girl's story. The wisest of us is more under the dominion of imagination than he would care to confess. Well, Maria shall not sleep in this room any more. There is no particular reason why she should, and she shall not be made unhappy to please old Skegg and his wife.

When he had dressed himself in his usual leisurely way, Mr Bascom walked up to the corner where he had seen or imagined the shadow, and examined the spot carefully.

At first sight he could discover nothing of a mysterious character. There was no door in the papered wall, no trace of a door that had been there in the past. There was no trap-door in the worm-eaten boards. There was no dark ineradicable stain to hint at murder. There was not the faintest suggestion of a secret or a mystery.

He looked up at the ceiling. That was sound enough, save for a dirty patch here and there where the rain had blistered it.

Yes; there was something – an insignificant thing, yet with a suggestion of grimness which startled him.

About a foot below the ceiling he saw a large iron hook projecting from the wall, just above the spot where he had seen the shadow of a vaguely defined form. He mounted on a chair the better to examine this hook, and to understand, if he could, the purpose for which it had been put there.

It was old and rusty. It must have been there for many years. Who could have placed it there, and why? It was not the kind of hook upon which one would hang a picture or one's garments. It was placed in an obscure corner. Had Anthony Bascom put it there on the night he died; or did he find it there ready for a fatal use?

If I were a superstitious man, thought Michael, I should be inclined to believe that Anthony Bascom hung himself from that rusty old hook.

*

'Sleep well, sir?' asked Daniel, as he waited upon his master at breakfast.

'Admirably,' answered Michael, determined not to gratify the man's curiosity.

He had always resented the idea that Wildheath Grange was haunted.

'Oh, indeed, sir. You were so late that I fancied —'

'Late, yes! I slept so well that I overshot my usual hour for waking. But, by-the-way, Skegg, as that poor girl objects to the room, let her sleep somewhere else. It can't make any difference to us, and it may make some difference to her.'

'Humph!' muttered Daniel in his grumpy way. 'You didn't see anything queer up there, did you?'

'See anything? Of course not.'

'Well, then, why should she see things? It's all her silly fiddle-faddle.'

'Never mind, let her sleep in another room.'

'There ain't another room on the top floor that's dry.'

'Then let her sleep on the floor below. She creeps about quietly enough, poor little timid thing. She won't disturb me.'

Daniel grunted, and his master understood the grunt to mean obedient assent; but here Mr Bascom was unhappily mistaken. The proverbial obstinacy of the pig family is as nothing compared with the obstinacy of a cross-grained old man, whose narrow mind has never been illuminated by education. Daniel was beginning to feel jealous of his master's compassionate interest in the orphan girl. She was a sort of gentle clinging thing that might creep into an elderly bachelor's heart unawares, and make herself a comfortable nest there.

'We shall have fine carryings-on, and me and my old woman will be nowhere, if I don't put down my heel pretty strong upon this nonsense,' Daniel muttered to himself, as he carried the breakfast-tray to the pantry.

Maria met him in the passage.

'Well, Mr Skegg, what did my master say?' she asked breath-lessly.

'Did he see anything strange in the room?'

'No, girl. What should he see? He said you were a fool.'

'Nothing disturbed him? And he slept there peacefully?' faltered Maria.

'Never slept better in his life. Now don't you begin to feel ashamed of yourself?'

'Yes,' she answered meekly; 'I am ashamed of being so full of fancies. I will go back to my room tonight, Mr Skegg, if you like, and I will never complain of it again.'

'I hope you won't,' snapped Skegg; 'you've given us trouble enough already.'

Maria sighed, and went about her work in saddest silence. The day wore slowly on, like all other days in that lifeless old house. The scholar sat in his study; Maria moved softly from room to room, sweeping and dusting in the cheerless solitude. The mid-day sun faded into the grey of afternoon, and evening came down like a blight upon the dull old house.

Throughout that day Maria and her master never met. Anyone who had been so far interested in the girl as to observe her appearance would have seen that she was unusually pale, and that her eyes had a resolute look, as of one who was resolved to face a painful ordeal. She ate hardly anything all day. She was curiously silent. Skegg and his wife put down both these symptoms to temper.

'She won't eat and she won't talk,' said Daniel to the partner of his joys. 'That means sulkiness, and I never allowed sulkiness to master me when I was a young man, and you tried it on as a young woman, and I'm not going to be conquered by sulkiness in my old age.'

Bed-time came, and Maria bade the Skeggs a civil good-night, and went up to her lonely garret without a murmur.

The next morning came, and Mrs Skegg looked in vain for her patient hand-maiden, when she wanted Maria's services in preparing the breakfast.

'The wench sleeps sound enough this morning,' said the old woman. 'Go and call her, Daniel. My poor legs can't stand them stairs.'

'Your poor legs are getting uncommon useless,' muttered Daniel testily, as he went to do his wife's behest.

He knocked at the door, and called Maria – once, twice, thrice, many times; but there was no reply. He tried the door, and found it locked. He shook the door violently, cold with fear.

Then he told himself that the girl had played him a trick. She had stolen away before daybreak, and left the door locked to frighten him. But, no; this could not be, for he could see the key in the lock when he knelt down and put his eye to the keyhole. The key prevented his seeing into the room.

She's in there, laughing in her sleeve at me, he told himself; but I'll soon be even with her.

There was a heavy bar on the staircase, which was intended to secure the shutters of the window that lighted the stairs. It was a detached bar, and always stood in a corner near the window, which it was but rarely employed to fasten. Daniel ran down to the landing, and seized upon this massive iron bar, and then ran back to the garret door.

One blow from the heavy bar shattered the old lock, which was the same lock the carter had broken with his strong fist seventy years before. The door flew open, and Daniel went into the attic which he had chosen for the stranger's bed-chamber.

Maria was hanging from the hook in the wall. She had contrived to cover her face decently with her handkerchief. She had hanged herself deliberately about an hour before Daniel found her, in the early grey of morning. The doctor, who was summoned from Holcroft, was able to declare the time at which she had slain herself, but there was no one who could say what sudden access of terror had impelled her to the desperate act, or under what slow torture of nervous apprehension her mind had given way. The coroner's jury returned the customary merciful verdict of 'Temporary insanity'.

The girl's melancholy fate darkened the rest of Michael Bascom's life. He fled from Wildheath Grange as from an accursed spot, and from the Skeggs as from the murderers of a harmless innocent girl. He ended his days at Oxford, where he found the society of congenial minds and the books he loved. But the memory of Maria's sad face, and sadder death, was his abiding sorrow. Out of that deep shadow his soul was never lifted.

Charlotte Riddell

NUT BUSH FARM

Charlotte Riddell's career almost paralleled Mary Braddon's, though her circumstances were very different. Born in Ireland in 1832, she was the daughter of the High Sheriff, but on his death in 1851 most of his money and property went to the children of his first marriage, leaving young Charlotte to look after her mother, whose health was frail, with only a small allowance. The two moved to London and to support her mother Charlotte turned to writing, selling her first book in 1856 to Thomas Newby, who had bought Emily Brontë's Wuthering Heights *ten years earlier. Charlotte also became a favourite of the Braddon-style sensation novels with her own version of a bigamous relationship in* George Geith of Fen Court *(1864). Charlotte's mother died in 1856 and though Charlotte married the following year her husband, Joseph Riddell, later became a bankrupt and an invalid, so Charlotte – now writing almost entirely as Mrs J.H. Riddell – continued to write at a prolific pace to support herself and her husband. She had no children and died, almost penniless, in 1906, a week before her seventy-fourth birthday.*

Charlotte Riddell produced a number of stories of the weird and supernatural. In fact these are regarded as among the best such tales during the second half of Victoria's reign. Some, including the following, were collected in Weird Stories *(1882), but most were scattered through various books and magazines, and her full contribution to the field was not fully appreciated until E.F. Bleiler assembled* The Collected Ghost Stories *in 1977. Her longer supernatural stories were only recently collected as* The Haunted River *in 2001.*

Nut Bush Farm

I

WHEN I ENTERED upon the tenancy of Nut Bush Farm almost the first piece of news which met me, in the shape of a whispered rumour, was that 'something' had been seen in the 'long field'.

Pressed closely as to what he meant, my informant reluctantly stated that the 'something' took the 'form of a man', and that the wood and the path leading thereto from Whittleby were supposed to be haunted.

Now, all this annoyed me exceedingly. I do not know when I was more put out than by this intelligence. It is unnecessary to say I did not believe in ghosts or anything of that kind, but my wife being a very nervous, impressionable woman, and our only child a delicate weakling, in the habit of crying himself into fits if left alone at night without a candle, I really felt at my wits' end to imagine what I should do if a story of this sort reached their ears.

And reach them I knew it must if they came to Nut Bush Farm, so the first thing I did when I heard people did not care to venture down the Beech Walk or through the copse, or across the long field after dark, or indeed by day, was to write to say I thought they had both better remain on at my father-in-law's till I could get the house thoroughly to rights.

After that I lit my pipe and went out for a stroll; when I knocked the ashes out of my pipe and re-entered the sitting-room I had made up my mind. I could not afford to be frightened away from my tenancy. For weal or for woe I must stick to Nut Bush Farm.

It was quite by chance I happened to know anything of the place at first. When I met with that accident in my employers' service, which they rated far too highly and recompensed with a liberality I never can feel sufficiently grateful for, the doctors told me plainly if I could not give up office work and leave London altogether, they would not give a year's purchase for my life.

Life seemed very sweet to me then – it always has done – but just at period I felt the pleasant hopes of convalescence; and with that thousand pounds safely banked, I *could* not let it slip away from me.

'Take a farm,' advised my father-in-law. 'Though people say a farmer's is a bad trade, I know many a man who is making money out of it. Take a farm, and if you want a helping hand to enable you to stand the racket for a year or two, why, you know I am always ready.'

I had been bred and born on a farm. My father held something like fifteen hundred acres under the principal landowner in his county, and though it so happened I could not content myself at home but must needs come up to London to see the lions and seek my fortune, still I had never forgotten the meadows and the corn-fields, and the cattle, and the orchards, and the woods and the streams, amongst which my happy boyhood had been spent. Yes, I thought I should like a farm – one not too far from London; and 'not too big', advised my wife's father.

'The error people make nowadays,' he went on, 'is spreading their butter over too large a surface. It is the same in business as in land – they stretch their arms out too far – they will try to wade in deep waters – and the consequence is they know a day's peace, and end mostly in the bankruptcy court.'

He spoke as one having authority, and I knew what he said was quite right. He had made his money by a very different course of procedure, and I felt I could not follow a better example.

I knew something about farming, though not very much. Still, agriculture is like arithmetic: when once one knows the multiplication table the rest is not so difficult. I had learnt unconsciously the alphabet of soils and crops and stock when I was an idle young dog, and liked nothing better than talking to the labourers and accompanying the woodman when he went out felling trees; and so I did not feel much afraid of what the result would be, more especially as

I had a good business head on my shoulders, and enough money to 'stand the racket', as my father-in-law put it, till the land began to bring in her increase.

When I got strong and well again after my long illness – I mean strong and well enough to go about – I went down to look at a farm which was advertised as to let in Kent.

According to the statement in the newspaper, there was no charm that farm lacked; when I saw it I discovered the place did not possess one virtue, unless, indeed, an old Tudor house fast falling to ruins, which would have proved invaluable to an artist, could be so considered. Far from a railway, having no advantages of water carriage, remote from a market, apparently destitute of society. Nor could these drawbacks be accounted the worst against it. The land, poor originally, seemed to have been totally exhausted. There were fields on which I do not think a goose could have found subsistence – nothing grew luxuriantly save weeds; it would have taken all my capital to get the ground clean. Then I saw the fences were dilapidated, the hedges in a deplorable condition, and the farm buildings in such a state of decay I would not have stabled a donkey in one of them.

Clearly, the King's Manor, which was the modest name of the place, would not do at any price, and yet I felt sorry, for the country around was beautiful, and already the sweet, pure air seemed to have braced up my nerves and given me fresh energy. Talking to mine host at the Bunch of Hops in Whittleby, he advised me to look over the local paper before returning to London.

'There be a many farms vacant,' he said; 'mayhap you'll light on one to suit.' To cut a long story short, I did look in the local paper and found many farms to let, but not one to suit. There was a drawback to each – a drawback at least so far as I was concerned. I felt determined I would not take a large farm. My conviction was then what my conviction still remains, that it is better to cultivate fifty acres thoroughly than to crop, stock, clean, and manure a hundred insufficiently. Besides, I did not want to spend my strength on wages or take a place so large I could not oversee the workmen on foot.

For all these reasons and many more I came reluctantly to the conclusion that there was nothing in that part of the country to suit a poor unspeculative plodder like myself.

It was a lovely afternoon in May when I turned my face towards Whittleby, as I thought, for the last time. In the morning I had taken train for a farm some ten miles distant and worked my way back on foot to a 'small cottage with land' a local agent thought might suit me. But neither the big place not the little answered my requirements, much to the disgust of the auctioneer, who had himself accompanied us to the cottage under the impression I would immediately purchase it and so secure his commission.

Somewhat sulkily he told me a short cut back to Whittleby, and added, as a sort of rider to all previous statements, the remark: 'You had best look out for what you want in Middlesex. You'll find nothing of that sort hereabouts.'

As to the last part of the foregoing sentence I was quite of his opinion, but I felt so oppressed with the result of all my wanderings that I thought upon the whole I had better abandon my search altogether, or else pursue it in some county very far away indeed – perhaps in the land of dreams for that matter!

As has been said, it was a lovely afternoon in May – the hedges were snowy with hawthorn blossom, the chestnuts were bursting into flower, the birds were singing fit to split their little throats, the lambs were dotting the hillsides, and I – ah, well, I was a boy again, able to relish all the rich banquet God spreads out day by day for the delight and nourishment of His too often thankless children.

When I came to a point halfway up some rising ground where four lanes met and then wound off each on some picturesque diverse way, I paused to look around regretfully.

As I did so – some distance below me – along what appeared to be a never-before-traversed lane, I saw the gleam of white letters on a black board.

Come, I thought, I'll see what this is at all events, and bent my steps towards the place, which might, for all I knew about it, have been a ducal mansion or a cockney's country villa.

The board appeared modestly conspicuous in the foreground of a young fir plantation, and simply bore this legend:

TO BE LET, HOUSE AND LAND,
Apply at the White Dragon.

It is a mansion, I thought, and I walked on slowly, disappointed. All of a sudden the road turned a sharp corner, and I came in an instant upon the prettiest place I had ever seen or ever desire to see.

I looked at it over a low laurel hedge growing inside an open paling about four feet high. Beyond the hedge there was a strip of turf, green as emeralds, smooth as a bowling green – then came a sunk fence, the most picturesque sort of protection the ingenuity of man ever devised; beyond that, a close-cut lawn which sloped down to the sunk fence from a house with projecting gables in the front, the recessed portion of the building having three windows on the first floor. Both gables were covered with creepers, the lawn was girt in by a semicircular sweep of forest trees; the afternoon sun streamed over the grass and tinted the swaying foliage with a thousand tender lights. Hawthorn bushes, pink and white, mingled with their taller and grander brothers. The chestnuts here were in flower, the copper beech made a delightful contrast of colour, and a birch rose delicate and graceful close beside.

It was like a fairy scene. I passed my hand across my eyes to assure myself it was all real. Then I thought 'if this place be even nearly within my means I will settle here. My wife will grow stronger in this paradise – my boy get more like other lads. Such things as nerves must be unknown where there is not a sight or sound to excite them. Nothing but health, purity, and peace.'

Thus thinking, I tore myself away in search of the White Dragon, the landlord of which small public-house sent a lad to show me over the farm.

'As for the rent,' he said, 'you will have to speak to Miss Gostock herself – she lives at Chalmont, on the road between here and Whittleby.'

In every respect the place suited me; it was large enough, but not too large; had been well farmed, and was amply supplied with water – a stream indeed flowing through it; a station was shortly to be opened, at about half a mile's distance; and most of the produce could be disposed of to dealers and tradesmen at Crayshill, a town to which the communication by rail was direct.

I felt so anxious about the matter it was quite a disappointment to find Miss Gostock from home. Judging from the look of her house, I did not suppose she could afford to stick out for a long rent, or to let a farm lie idle for any considerable period. The servant who appeared in answer to my summons was a singularly red-armed and rough-handed Phyllis. There was only a strip of carpeting laid down in the hall, the windows were bare of draperies, and the avenue gate, set a little back from the main road, was such as I should have felt ashamed to put in a farmyard.

Next morning I betook myself to Chalmont, anxiously wondering, as I walked along, what the result of my interview would prove.

When I neared the gate, to which uncomplimentary reference has already been made, I saw standing on the other side a figure wearing a man's broad-brimmed straw hat, a man's coat and a woman's skirt.

I raised my hat in deference to the supposed sex of this stranger. She put up one finger to the brim of hers and said, 'Servant, sir.'

Not knowing exactly what to do, I laid my hand upon the latch of the gate and raised it, but she did not alter her position in the least.

She only asked, 'What do you want?'

'I want to see Miss Gostock,' was my answer.

'I am Miss Gostock,' she said. 'What is your business with me?'

I replied meekly that I had come to ask the rent of Nut Bush Farm.

'Have you viewed it?' she enquired.

'Yes.' I told her I had been over the place on the previous afternoon.

'And have you a mind to take it?' she persisted. 'For I am not going to trouble myself answering a lot of idle enquiries.'

So far from my being an idle enquirer, I assured the lady that if we could come to terms about the rent I should be very glad indeed to take the farm. I said I had been searching the neighbourhood within a circuit of ten miles for some time unsuccessfully, and added, somewhat unguardedly, I suppose, Nut Bush Farm was the only place I had met with which at all met my views.

Standing in an easy attitude, with one arm resting on the top bar of the gate and one foot crossed over the other, Miss Gostock surveyed me, who had unconsciously taken up a similar position, with an amused smile.

'You must think me a very honest person, young man,' she remarked. I answered that I hoped she was, but I had not thought at all about the matter. 'Or else,' proceeded this extraordinary lady, 'you fancy I am a much greater flat than I am.'

'On the contrary,' was my reply. 'If there be one impression stronger than another which our short interview has made upon me it is that you are a wonderfully direct and capable woman of business.'

She looked at me steadily, and then closed one eye, which performance, done under the canopy of that broad-brimmed straw hat, had the most ludicrous effect imaginable.

'You won't catch me napping,' she observed, 'but, however, as you seem to mean dealing, come in; I can tell you my terms in two minutes', and opening the gate-a trouble she would not allow me to take off her hands – she gave me admission.

The Miss Gostock took off her hat, and swinging it to and fro began slowly walking up the ascent leading to Chalmont, I beside her.

'I have quite made up my mind,' she said, 'not to let the farm again without a premium. My last tenant treated me abominably.'

I intimated I was sorry to hear that, and waited for further information.

'He had the place at a low rent – a very low rent. He should not have got it so cheap but for his covenanting to put so much money in the soil; and, well, I'm bound to say he acted fair so far as that –

he fulfilled that part of his contract. Nearly two years ago we had a bit of a quarrel about – well, it's no matter what we fell out over – only the upshot of the affair was he gave me due notice to leave at last winter quarter. At that time he owed about a year and a half's rent – for he was a man who never could bear parting with money – and like a fool I did not push him for it. What trick do you suppose he served me for my pains?'

It was simply impossible for me to guess, so I did not try. 'On the twentieth of December,' went on Miss Gostock, turning her broad face and curly grey hair – she wore her hair short like a man – towards me, 'he went over to Whittleby, drew five thousand pounds out of the bank, was afterwards met going towards home by a gentleman named Waite, a friend of his. Since then he has never been seen nor heard of.'

'Bless my soul!' I exclaimed involuntarily.

'You may be very sure I did not bless his soul,' she snarled out angrily. 'The man bolted with the five thousand pounds, having previously sold off all his stock and the bulk of his produce, and when I distrained for my rent, which I did pretty smart, I can tell you, there was scarce enough on the premises to pay the levy.'

'But what in the world made him bolt?' I asked, quite unconsciously adopting Miss Gostock's expressive phrase. 'As he had so much money, why did he not pay you your rent?'

'Ah! Why, indeed?' mocked Miss Gostock. 'Young sir, I am afraid you are a bit of a humbug, or you would have suggested at once there was a pretty girl at the bottom of the affair. He left his wife and children, and me – all in the lurch – and went off with a slip of a girl, whom I once took, thinking to train up as a better sort of servant, but was forced to discharge. Oh, the little hussy!'

Somehow I did not fancy I wanted to hear anything more about her late tenant and the pretty girl, and consequently ventured to enquire how that gentleman's defalcations bore upon the question of the rent I should have to pay.

'I tell you directly,' she said, and as we had by this time arrived at the house, she invited me to enter, and led the way into an old-fashioned parlour that must have been furnished about the time chairs and tables were first invented and which did not contain a single feminine belonging – not even a thimble.

'Sit down,' she commanded, and I sat. 'I have quite made up my mind,' she began, 'not to let the farm again, unless I get a premium sufficient to insure me against the chances of possible loss. I mean to ask a very low rent and – a premium.'

'And what amount of premium do you expect?' I enquired, doubtfully.

'I want –' and here Miss Gostock named a sum which fairly took my breath away.

'In that case,' I said as soon as I got it again, 'it is useless to prolong this interview. I can only express my regret for having intruded, and wish you good morning.' And arising, I was bowing myself out when she stopped me.

'Don't be so fast,' she cried, 'I only said what I wanted. Now what are you prepared to give?'

'I can't be buyer and seller too,' I answered, repeating a phrase the precise meaning of which, it may here be confessed, I have never been able exactly to understand.

'Nonsense,' exclaimed Miss Gostock – I am really afraid the lady used a stronger term – 'if you are anything of a man of business, fit at all to commence farming, you must have an idea on the subject. You shall have the land at a pound an acre, and you will give me for premium – come, how much?'

By what mental process I instantly jumped to an amount it would be impossible to say, but I did mention one which elicited from Miss Gostock the remark: 'That won't do at any price.'

'Very well, then,' I said, 'we need not talk any more about the matter.'

'But what *will* you give?' asked the lady.

'I have told you,' was my answer, 'and I am not given either to haggling or beating down.'

'You won't make a good farmer,' she observed.

'If a farmer's time were of any value, which it generally seems as

if it were not,' I answered, 'he would not waste it in splitting a six-
pence.'

She laughed, and her laugh was not musical. 'Come now,' she
said, 'make another bid.'

'No,' I replied, 'I have made one and that is enough. I won't offer
another penny.'

'Done then,' cried Miss Gostock. 'I accept your offer – we'll just
sign a little memorandum of agreement, and the formal deeds can
be prepared afterwards. You'll pay a deposit, I suppose?'

I was so totally taken aback by her acceptance of my offer I could
only stammer out I was willing to do anything that might be usual.

'It does not matter much whether it is usual or not,' she said;
'either pay it or I won't keep the place for you. I am not going to
have my land lying idle and my time taken up for your pleasure.'

'I have no objection to paying you a deposit,' I answered.

'That's right,' she exclaimed. 'Now if you will just hand me over
the writing-desk we can settle the matter, so far as those thieves of
lawyers will let us, in five minutes.

Like one in a dream I sat and watched Miss Gostock while she
wrote. Nothing about the transaction seemed to me real. The farm
itself resembled nothing I had ever before seen with my waking eyes,
and Miss Gostock appeared to me but as some monstrous figure in a
story of giants and hobgoblins. The man's coat, the woman's skirt,
the hobnailed shoes, the grisly hair, the old straw hat, the bare, unfur-
nished room, the bright sunshine outside, all struck me as mere
accessories in a play – as nothing which had any hold on the outside, everyday world.

It was drawn – we signed our names. I handed Miss Gostock
over a cheque. She locked one document in an iron box let into the
wall, and handed me the other, adding, as a rider, a word of caution
about 'keeping it safe and taking care it was not lost'.

Then she went to a corner cupboard, and producing a square
decanter half full of spirits, set that and two tumblers on the table.

'You don't like much water, I suppose,' she said, pouring out a
measure which frightened me.

'I could not touch it, thank you, Miss Gostock,' I exclaimed. 'I dare not do so; I should never get back to Whittleby.'

For answer she only looked at me contemptuously and said, 'D——d nonsense.

'No nonsense, indeed,' I persisted; 'I am not accustomed to anything of that sort.'

Miss Gostock laughed again, then crossing to the sideboard she returned with a jug of water, a very small portion of the contents of which she mixed with the stronger liquor, and raised the glass to her lips. 'To your good health and prosperity,' she said, and in one instant the fiery potion was swallowed.

'You'll mend of all that,' she remarked, as she laid down her glass, and wiped her lips in the simplest manner by passing the back of her hand over them.

'I hope not, Miss Gostock,' I ventured to observe.

'Why, you look quite shocked,' she said. 'Did you never see a lady take a mouthful of brandy before?'

I ventured to hint that I had not, more particularly so early in the morning.

'Pooh!' she said. 'Early in the morning or late at night, where's the difference? However, there was a time when I – but that was before I had come through so much trouble. Good-bye for the present, and I hope we shall get on well together.'

I answered I trusted we should, and was half-way to the hall-door, when she called me back.

'I forgot to ask you if you were married,' she said.

'Yes, I have been married some years,' I answered.

'That's a pity,' she remarked, and dismissed me with a wave of her hand.

What on earth would have happened had I not been married? I considered as I hurried down the drive. Surely she never contemplated proposing to me herself? But nothing she could do would surprise me.

II

There were some repairs I had mentioned it would be necessary to have executed before I came to live at Nut Bush Farm, but when I found Miss Gostock intended to do them herself – nay, was doing them all herself – I felt thunderstruck.

On one memorable occasion I came upon her with a red hand-kerchief tied round her head, standing at a carpenter's bench in a stable yard, planing away, under a sun which would have killed anybody but a negro or my landlady.

She painted the gates, and put sash lines in some of the windows; she took off the locks, oiled, and replaced them; she mowed the lawn, and offered to teach me how to mow; and, lastly, she showed me a book where she charged herself and paid herself for every hour's work done.

'I've made at least twenty pounds out of your place,' she said triumphantly. 'Higgs at Whittleby would not have charged me a halfpenny less for the repairs. The tradesmen here won't give me a contract – they say it is just time thrown away, but I know that would have been about his figure. Well, the place is ready for you now, and if you take my advice, you'll get your grass up as soon as possible. It's a splendid crop, and, if you hire hands enough, not a drop of rain need spoil it. If this weather stands you might cut one day and carry the next.'

I took her advice, and stacked my hay in magnificent condition. Miss Gostock was good enough to come over and superintend the building of the stack, and threatened to split one man's head open with the pitchfork, and proposed burying another – she called him a 'lazy blackguard' – under a pile of hay.

'I will say this much for Hascot,' she remarked, as we stood together beside the stream; 'he was a good farmer. Where will you see better or cleaner land? A pattern I call it – and to lose his whole future for the sake of a girl like Sally Powner; leaving his wife and children on the parish, too!'

'You don't mean that?' I said.

'Indeed I do. They are all at Crayshill. The authorities did talk of shifting them, but I know nothing about what they have done.'

I stood appalled. I thought of my own poor wife and the little lad, and wondered if any Sally on the face of the earth could make me desert them.

'It has given the place a bad sort of name,' remarked Miss Gostock, looking at me sideways; 'but, of course, that does not signify anything to you.'

'Oh, of course not,' I agreed.

'And don't you be minding any stories; there are always a lot of stories going about places.'

I said I did not mind stories. I had lived too long in London to pay much attention to them.

'That's right,' remarked Miss Gostock, and negativing my offer to see her home she started off to Chalmont.

It was not half an hour after her departure when I happened to be walking slowly round the meadows, from which the newly mown hay had been carted, that I heard the rumour which vexed me – 'Nut Bush Farm haunted.' I thought: I said the whole thing was too good to last.

'What, Jack, lost in reverie?' cried my sister, who had come up from Devonshire to keep me company, and help to get the furniture a little to rights, entering at the moment, carrying lights. 'Supper will be ready in a minute, and you can dream as much as you like after you have had something to eat.'

I did not say anything to her about my trouble, which was then indeed no bigger than a man's hand, but which grew and grew till it attained terrible proportions.

What was I to do with my wife and child? I never could bring them to a place reputed to be haunted. All in vain I sauntered up and down the Beech Walk night after night; walked through the wood – as a rule selected that route when I went to Whittleby. It did not produce the slightest effect. Not a farm servant but eschewed that path townward; not a girl but preferred spending her Sunday at home rather than venture under the interlacing branches of the beech trees, or through the dark recesses of the wood.

It was becoming serious – I did not know what to do.

One wet afternoon Lolly came in draggled but beaming.

'I've made a new acquaintance, Jack,' she said. 'A Mrs Waite – such a nice creature, but in dreadfully bad health. It came on to rain when I was coming home, and so I took refuge under a great tree at the gate of a most picturesque old house. I had not stood there long before a servant with an umbrella appeared at the porch to ask if I would not please to walk in until the storm abated. I waited there ever so long, and we had such a pleasant talk. She is a most delightful woman, with a melancholy, pathetic sort of expression that has been haunting me ever since. She apologized for not having called – said she was not strong and could not walk so far. They keep no conveyance she can drive. Mr Waite, who is not at home at present, rides into Whittleby when anything is wanted.

'I hoped she would not think of standing on ceremony with me. I was only a farmer's daughter, and accustomed to plain, homely ways, and I asked her if I might walk round and bid her good-bye before I went home.'

'You must not go home yet, Lolly,' I cried, alarmed. 'What in the world should I do without you?'

'Well, you would be a lonely boy,' she answered, complacently, 'with no one to sew on a button or darn your socks, or make you eat or go to bed, or do anything you ought to do.'

I had not spoken a word to her about the report which was troubling me, and I knew there must be times when she wondered why I did not go up to London and fetch my wife and child to enjoy the bright summer-time; but Lolly was as good as gold, and never asked me a question, or even indirectly enquired if Lucy and I had quarrelled, as many another sister might.

She was as pleasant and fresh to look upon as a spring morning, with her pretty brown hair smoothly braided, her cotton or muslin dresses never soiled or crumpled, but as nice as though the laundress had that moment sent them home – a rose in her belt and her hands never idle – forever busy with curtain or blind, or something her housewifely eyes thought had need of making or mending.

About ten days after that showery afternoon when she found shelter under Mr Waite's hospitable roof, I felt surprised when, entering the parlour a few minutes before our early dinner, I found Lolly standing beside one of the windows apparently hopelessly lost in the depths of a brown study.

'Why, Lolly,' I exclaimed, finding she took no notice of me, 'where have you gone to now? A penny for your thoughts, young lady.'

'They are not worth a penny,' she said, and turning from the window took some work and sat down at a little distance from the spot where I was standing.

I was so accustomed to women, even the best and gayest of them, having occasional fits of temper or depression – times when silence on my part seemed the truest wisdom – that, taking no notice of my sister's manner, I occupied myself with the newspaper till dinner was announced.

During the progress of that meal she talked little and ate still less, but when I was leaving the room, in order to go out to a field of barley where the reapers were at work, she asked me to stop a moment.

'I want to speak to you, Jack,' she said.

'Speak, then,' I answered, with that lack of ceremony which obtains amongst brothers and sisters.

She hesitated for a moment, but did not speak.

'What on earth is the matter with you, Lolly?' I exclaimed. 'Are you sick, or cross, or sorry, or what?'

'If it must be one of the four,' she answered, with a dash of her usual manner, 'it is "or what", Jack,' and she came close up to where I stood and took me sorrowfully by the button-hole.

'Well?' I said, amused, for this had always been a favourite habit of Lolly's when she wanted anything from one of the males of her family.

'Jack, you won't laugh at me?'

'I feel much more inclined to be cross with you,' I answered. 'What are you beating about the bush for, Lolly?'

She lifted her fair face a moment and I saw she was crying. 'Lolly, Lolly!' I cried, clasping her to my heart, 'what is it, dear? Have you bad news from home, or have you heard anything about Lucy or the boy? Don't keep me in suspense, there's a darling. No matter what has happened, let me know the worst.'

She smiled through her tears, and Lolly has the rarest smile! It quieted my anxious heart in a moment, even before she said: 'No, Jack – it is nothing about home, or Lucy, or Teddy, but – but – but –' and then she relinquished her hold on the button-hole and fingered each button on the front of my coat carefully and lingeringly. 'Did you ever hear – Jack – anybody say anything about this place?'

I knew in a moment what she meant; I knew the cursed tattle had reached her ears, but I only asked: 'What sort of thing, Lolly?'

She did not answer me; instead, she put another question. 'Is that the reason you have not brought Lucy down?'

I felt vexed – but I had so much confidence in her good sense, I could not avoid answering without a moment's delay.

'Well, yes; I do not want her to come till this foolish report has completely died away.'

'Are you quite sure it is a foolish report?' she enquired.

'Why, of course; it could not be anything else.'

She did not speak immediately, then all at once:

'Jack,' she said, 'I must tell you something. Lock the door that we may not be interrupted.'

'No,' I answered; 'come into the barley field. Don't you remember Mr Fenimore Cooper advised: If you want to talk secrets, choose the middle of a plain?'

I tried to put a good face on the matter, but the sight of Lolly's tears, the sound of Lolly's doleful voice, darkened my very heart. What had she to tell me which required locked doors or the greater privacy of a half-reaped barley field? I could trust my sister – she was no fool – and I felt perfectly satisfied that no old woman's story had wrought the effect produced on her.

'Now, Lolly,' I said, as we paced side by side along the top of the barley field in a solitude all the more complete because life and plenty of it was close at hand.

'You know what they say about the place, Jack?'

This was interrogative, and so I answered. 'Well, no, Lolly, I can't say that I do, for the very good reason that I have always refused to listen to the gossip. What do they say?'

'That a man haunts the Beech Walk, the long meadow, and the wood.'

'Yes, I have heard that,' I replied.

'And they say, further, the man is Mr Hascot, the late tenant.'

'But he is not dead,' I exclaimed. 'How, then, can they see his ghost?'

'I cannot tell. I know nothing but what I saw this morning. After breakfast I went to Whittleby, and as I came back I observed a man before me on the road. Following him, I noticed a curious thing, that none of the people he met made way for him or he for them. He walked straight on, without any regard to the persons on the side path, and yet no one seemed to come into collision with him. When I reached the field path I saw him going on still at the same pace. He did not look to right or left, and did not seem to walk – the motion was gliding . . .'

'Yes, dear.'

'He went on, and so did I, till we reached the hollow where the nut-bushes grow, then he disappeared from sight. I looked down amongst the trees, thinking I should be able to catch a glimpse of his figure through the underwood, but, no, I could see no signs of him, neither could I hear any. Everything was as still as death; it seemed to me that my ear had a spell of silence laid upon it.'

'And then?' I asked hoarsely, as she paused.

'Why, Jack, I walked on and crossed the little footbridge and was just turning into the Beech Walk when the same man bustled suddenly across my path, so close to me if I had put out my hands I could have touched him. I drew back, frightened for a minute, then, as he had not seemed to see me, I turned and looked at him as he sped along down the little winding path to the wood. I thought he must be some silly creature, some harmless sort of idiot, to be running here and there without any apparent object. All at once, as he neared the wood, he stopped, and, half wheeling round, beckoned to me to follow him.'

'You did not, Lolly?'

'No, I was afraid. I walked a few steps quietly till I got amongst the beech trees and so screened from sight, and then I began to run. I could not run fast, for my knees trembled under me; but still I did run as far nearly as that seat round the Priest's Tree. I had not got quite up to the seat when I saw a man rise from it and stand upright as if waiting for me. *It was the same person, Jack!* I recognized him instantly, though I had not seen his face clearly before. He stood quiet for a moment, and then, with the same gliding motion, silently disappeared.'

'Someone must be playing a very nice game about Nut Bush Farm,' I exclaimed.

'Perhaps so, dear,' she said doubtfully.

'Why, Lolly, you don't believe it was a ghost you met in the broad daylight?' I cried incredulously.

'I don't think it was a living man, Jack,' she answered.

'Living or dead, he dare not bring himself into close quarters with me,' was my somewhat braggart remark. 'Why, Lolly, I have walked the ground day after day and night after night in the hope of seeing your friend, and not a sign of an intruder, in the flesh or out of it, could I find. Put the matter away, child, and don't ramble in that direction again. If I can ascertain the name of the person who is trying to frighten the household and disgust me with Nut Bush Farm he shall go to gaol if the magistrates are of my way of thinking. Now, as you have told me this terrible story, and we have reduced your great mountain to a molehill, I will walk back with you to the house.'

She did not make any reply. We talked over indifferent matters as we paced along. I went with her into the pleasant sunshiny drawing-room and looked her out a book and made her promise to read something amusing; then I was going, when she put up her lips for me to kiss her, and said: 'Jack, you won't run any risks?'

'Risks – pooh, you silly little woman!' I answered; and so left my sister and repaired to the barley field once more.

When it was time for the men to leave off work I noticed that one after another began to take a path leading immediately to the main road, which was a very circuitous route to the hamlet, where most of them had either cottages or lodgings.

I noticed this for some time, and then asked a brawny young fellow.

'Why don't you go home through the Beech Walk? It is not above half the distance.' He smiled and made some almost unintelligible answer.

'Why are you all afraid of taking the shortest way,' I remarked, 'seeing there are enough of you to put half-a-dozen ghosts to the rout?'

'Likely, sir,' was the answer; 'but the old master was a hard man living, and there is not many would care to meet him dead.'

'What old master?' I enquired.

'Mr Hascot: it's him as walks. I saw him as plain as I see you now, sir, one moonlight night, just this side of the wood, and so did Nat Tyler and James Monsey, and James Monsey's father – wise Ben.'

'But Mr Hascot is not dead. How can he "walk", as you call it?' was my natural exclamation.

'If he is living, then, sir, where is he?' asked the man. 'There is nobody can tell that, and there is a many, especially just lately, think he must have been made away with. He had a cruel lot of money about him. Where is all that money gone to?'

The fellow had waxed quite earnest in his interrogations, and really for the first time the singularity of Mr Hascot's disappearance seemed to strike me.

I said, after an instant's pause, 'The money is wherever he is. He went off with some girl, did he not?'

'It suited the old people to say so,' he answered; 'but there is many a one thinks they know more about the matter than is good for them. I can't help hearing, and one of the neighbours did say Mrs Ockfield was seen in church last Sunday with a new dress on and a shawl any lady might have worn.'

'And who is Mrs Ockfield?' I enquired.

'Why, Sally Powner's grandmother. The old people treated the girl shameful while she was with them, and now they want to make her out no better than she should be.'

And with a wrathful look the young man, who I subsequently discovered had long been fond of Sally, took up his coat and his tin bottle and his sickle, and with a brief 'I think I'll be going, sir; good night' departed.

It was easy to return to the house, but I found it impossible to shake the effect produced by this dialogue off my mind.

For the first time I began seriously to consider the manner of Mr Hascot's disappearance, and more seriously still commenced trying to piece together the various hints I had received as to his character.

A hard man – a hard master, all I ever heard speak considered him, but just, and in the main not unkind. He had sent coals to one widow, kept a poor old labourer off the parish, and then in a minute, for the sake of a girl's face, left his own wife and children to the mercy of nearest Union.

As I paced along it seemed to me monstrous, and yet how did it happen that till a few minutes previously I had never heard even a suspicion of foul play?

Was it not more natural to conclude the man must have been made away with, than that, in one brief day, he should have changed his nature and the whole current of his former life?

Upon the other hand, people must have had some strong reason for imagining he was gone off with Miss Powner. The notion of a man disappearing in this way – vanishing as if the earth had opened to receive him and closed again – for the sake of any girl, however attractive, was too unnatural an idea for anyone to have evolved out of his internal consciousness. There must have been some substratum of fact, and then, upon the other hand, there seemed to me more than a substratum of possibility in the theory started of his having been murdered.

Supposing he had been murdered, I went on to argue, what then? Did I imagine he 'walked'? Did I believe he could not rest wherever he was laid?

Pooh – nonsense! It might be that the murderer haunted the place of his crime – that he hovered about to see if his guilt were still undetected, but as to anything in the shape of a ghost tenanting the Beech Walk, long meadow, and wood, I did not believe it – I could not, and I added, 'If I saw it with my own eyes, I would not.'

Having arrived at which decided and sensible conclusion, I went in to supper. Usually a sound sleeper, I found it impossible that night when I lay down to close my eyes. I tossed and turned, threw off the bedclothes under the impression I was too hot and drew them tight up round me the next instant, feeling cold. I tried to think of my crops, of my land, of my wife, of my boy, of my future – all in vain. A dark shadow, a wall-like night stood between me and all the ordinary interests of my life – I could not get the notion of Mr Hascot's strange disappearance out of my mind. I wondered if there was anything about the place which made it in the slightest degree probable I should ever learn to forget the wife who loved, the boy who was dependent on me. Should I ever begin to think I might have done better as regards my choice of a wife, that it would be nicer to have healthy, merry children than my affectionate, delicate lad?

When I got to this point, I could stand it no longer. I felt as though some mocking spirit were taking possession of me, which eventually would destroy all my peace of mind, if I did not cast it out promptly and effectually.

I would not lie there supine to let any demon torment me; and, accordingly, springing to the floor, I dressed in hot haste, and flinging wide the window, looked out over a landscape bathed in the clear light of a most lovely moon

'How beautiful! I thought. I have never yet seen the farm by night, I'll just go and take a stroll round it and then turn in again – after a short walk I shall likely be able to sleep.

So saying to myself, I slipped downstairs, closed the hall door softly after me, and went out into the moonlight.

III

As I stood upon the lawn, looking around with a keen and subtle pleasure, I felt, almost for the first time in my life, the full charm and beauty of night. Every object was as clearly revealed as though the time had been noon instead of an hour past midnight, but there lay a mystic spell on tree and field and stream the garish day could never equal. It was a fairy light and a fairy scene, and it would scarcely have astonished me to see fantastic elves issue from the fox-glove's flowers or dart from the shelter of concealing leaves and dance a measure on the emerald sward.

For a minute I felt – as I fancy many and many a commonplace man must have done when first wedded to some miracle of grace and beauty – a sense of amazement and unreality.

All this loveliness was mine – the moonlit lawn – the stream murmuring through the fir plantation, singing soft melodies as it pursued its glittering way – the trees with a silvery gleam tinting their foliage – the roses giving out their sweetest, tenderest perfumes – the wonderful silence around – the fresh, pure air – the soft night wind – the prosperity with which God had blessed me. My heart grew full, as I turned and gazed first on this side and then on that, and I felt vexed and angry to remember I had ever suffered myself to listen to idle stories and to be made uncomfortable by reason of village gossip.

On such a night it really seemed a shame to go to bed, and, though the restlessness which first induced me to rise had vanished, and in doing so left the most soothing calm behind, I wandered on away from the house, now beside the stream, and again across a meadow, where faint odours from the lately carried hay still lingered.

Still the same unreal light over field and copse – still the same

witching glamour – still the same secret feeling. I was seeing something and experiencing some sensation I might never again recall on
this side of the grave!

A most lovely night – one most certainly not for drawn curtains
and closed eyelids – one rather for lovers' tête-a-tête or a dreamy
reverie – for two young hearts to reveal their secrets to each other or
one soul to commune alone with God.

Still rambling, I found myself at last beside a stile, opening upon a
path, which, winding upwards, led past the hollow where the nut trees
grew, and then joined the footway leading through the long field
to Whittleby. The long field was the last in that direction belonging to
Nut Bush Farm. It joined upon a portion of the land surrounding
Chalmont, and the field path continued consequently to pass through
Miss Gostock's property till the main road was reached. It cut off a
long distance and had been used generally by the inhabitants of the
villages and hamlets dotted about my place until the rumour being
circulated that something might be 'seen' or 'met' deterred people
from venturing by a route concerning which such evil things were
whispered. I had walked it constantly, both on account of the time it
saved and also in order to set a good example to my labourers and my
neighbours, but I might as well have saved my pains.

I was regarded merely as foolhardy, and I knew people generally
supposed I should one day have cause to repent my temerity.

As I cleared the stile and began winding my upward way to the
higher ground beyond, the thought did strike me what a likely place
for a murder Nut Bush Hollow looked. It was a deep excavation,
out of which, as no one supposed it to be natural, hundreds and
thousands of loads of earth must at some time or other have been
carted. From top to bottom it was clothed with nut trees – they grew
on every side, and in thick, almost impenetrable masses. For years
and years they seemed to have had no care bestowed on them, the
Hollow forming in this respect a remarkable contrast to the rest of
Mr Hascot's careful farming, and, as a fir plantation ran along the
base of the Hollow, while the moon's light fell clear and full on some
of the bushes, the others lay in densest shadow.

The road that once led down into the pit was now completely overgrown with nut bushes which grew luxuriantly to the very edge of the Beech Walk, and threatened ere long to push their way between the trunks of the great trees, which were the beauty and the pride of my lovely farm.

At one time, so far as I could understand, the nut bushes had the whole place almost to themselves, and old inhabitants told me that formerly, in the days when their parents were boys and girls, the nuts used to pay the whole of the rent. As years passed, however, whether from want of care or some natural cause, they gradually ceased to bear, and had to be cut down and cleared off the ground – those in the dell, however, being suffered to remain, the hollow being useless for husbandry, and the bushes which flourished there producing a crop of nuts sufficient for the farmer's family.

All this recurred to my mind as I stood for a moment and looked down into the depths of rustling green below me. I thought of the boys who must have gone nutting there, of all the nests birds had built in the branches so closely interlaced, of the summers' suns which had shone full and strong upon that mass of foliage, of the winters' snows which had lain heavy on twig and stem and wrapped the strong roots in a warm coveting of purest white.

And then the former idea again asserted itself – what a splendid place for a tragedy; a sudden blow – a swift stab – even a treacherous push – and the deed could be done. A man might be alive and well one minute and dead the next!

False friend or secret enemy; rival or thief, it was competent for either in such a place at any lonely hour to send a man upon his last long journey. Had Mr Hascot been so served? Down, far down, was he lying in a quiet, dreamless sleep? At that very moment, was there anyone starting from fitful slumber to grapple with his remorse for crime committed, or shrink with horror from the dread of detection?

Where was my fancy leading me? I suddenly asked myself. This was worse than in my own chamber preventing the night watches. Since I had been standing there my heart felt heavier than when tossing from side to side in bed, and wooing unsuccessfully the slumber which refused to come for my asking.

What folly! what nonsense! and into what an insane course of speculation had I not embarked. I would leave the eerie place and get once again into the full light of the moon's bright beams.

Hush! Hark! What was that? Deep down amongst the underwood – a rustle, a rush, and a scurry – then silence – then a stealthy movement amongst the bushes – then whilst I was peering down into the abyss lined with waving green below, SOMETHING passed by me swiftly, something which brought with it a cold chill as though the hand of one dead had been laid suddenly on my heart.

Instantly I turned and looked around. There was not a living thing in sight – neither on the path, nor on the sward, nor on the hillside, nor skirting the horizon as I turned my eyes upward.

For a moment I stood still in order to steady my nerves. Then, reassuring myself with the thought it must have been an animal of some kind, I completed the remainder of the ascent without further delay.

The ghost, I suspect, I said to myself as I reached the long field and the path leading back to the farm, will resolve itself into a hare or pheasant. Is not the whirr of a cock pheasant rising, for instance, enough, when coming unexpectedly, to frighten any nervous person out of his wits? And might not a hare, or a cat, or, better still, a stoat – yes, a stoat, with its gliding, almost noiseless, movements – mimic the footfall of a suppositious ghost?

By this time I had gained the summit of the incline, and slightly out of breath with breasting the ascent, stood for a moment contemplating the exquisite panorama stretched out beneath me. I linger on that moment because it was the last time I ever saw beauty in the moonlight. Now I cannot endure the silvery gleam of the queen of night – weird, mournful, fantastic if you like, but to be desired – no.

Whenever possible I draw the blinds and close the shutters, yet withal on moonlight nights I cannot sleep, the horror of darkness is to my mind nothing in comparison to the terror of a full moon. But I drivel. Let me hasten on.

From the crest of the hill I could see lying below a valley of dreamlike beauty – woods in the foreground – a champagne country spreading away into the indefinite distance – a stream winding in and out, dancing and glittering under the moon's beams – a line of hills dimly seen against the horizon, and already a streak of light appearing above them the first faint harbinger of dawn.

'It is morning, then, already,' I said, and with the words turned my face homewards. As I did so I saw before me on the path – *clearly* – the figure of a man.

He was walking rapidly and I hurried my pace in order to over-take him. Now to this part of the story I desire to draw particular attention. *Let me hurry as I might, I never seemed able to get a foot nearer to him.*

At intervals he paused, as if on purpose to assist my desire, but the moment I seemed gaining upon him the distance between us suddenly increased. I could not tell how he did it; the fact only remained – it was like pursuing some phantom in a dream.

All at once when he reached the bridge he stood quite still. He did not move hand or limb as I drew near – the way was so narrow I knew I should have to touch him in passing; nevertheless, I pressed forward. My foot was on the bridge – I was close to him – I felt my breath coming thick and fast – I clasped a stick I had picked up in the plantation firmly in my hand – I stopped, intending to speak – I opened my mouth, intending to do so – and then – then – without any movement on his part – I was alone!

Yes, as totally alone as though he had never stood on the bridge – never preceded me along the field path – never loitered upon my footsteps – never paused for my coming. I was appalled

'Lord, what is this? I thought. Am I going mad? I felt as if I were. On my honour, I know I was as nearly insane at that moment as a man ever can be who is still in the possession of his senses.

Beyond lay the farm of which in my folly I had felt so proud to be the owner, where I once meant to be so happy and win health for my wife and strength for my boy. I saw the Beech Walk I had gloried in –

the ricks of hay it seemed so good to get thatched geometrically as only one man in the neighbourhood was said to be able to lay the straw.

What was farm, or riches, or beech trees, or anything, to me now? Over the place there seemed a curse – better the meanest cottage than a palace with such accessories.

If I had been incredulous before, I was not so now – I could not distrust the evidence of my own eyes – and yet as I walked along, I tried after a minute or two to persuade myself imagination had been playing some juggler's trick with me. The moon, I argued, always lent herself readily to a game of hide-and-seek. She is always open to join in fantastic gambols with shadows – with thorn bushes – with a waving branch – aye, even with a clump of gorse. I must have been mistaken – I had been thinking weird thoughts as I stood by that dismal dell – I had seen no man walking – beheld no figure disappear.

Just as I arrived at this conclusion I beheld someone coming towards me down the Beech Walk. It was a man walking leisurely with a firm, free step. The sight did me good. Here was something tangible – something to question. I stood still, in the middle of the path – the Beech Walk being rather a grassy glade with a narrow footway dividing it, than anything usually understood by the term walk – so that I might speak to the intruder when he drew near and ask him what he meant by trespassing on my property, more especially at such an hour. There were no public rights on my land except as regarded the path across the long field and through the wood. No one had any right or business to be in the Beech Walk, by day or night, save those employed about the farm, and this person was a gentleman; even in the distance I could distinguish that. As he came closer I saw he was dressed in a loose Palmerston suit, that he wore a low-crowned hat, and that he carried a light cane. The moonbeams dancing down amongst the branches and between the leaves fell full upon his face and, catching sight of a ring he had on his right hand, made it glitter with as many different colours as a prism.

A middle-aged man, so far as I could judge, with a set, determined expression of countenance, dark hair, no beard or whiskers, only a small moustache. A total stranger to me. I had never seen him nor any one like him in the neighbourhood. Who could he be, and what in the wide world was he doing on my premises at that unearthly hour of the morning?

He came straight on, never moving to right or left – taking no more notice of me than if he had been blind. His easy indifference, his contemptuous coolness, angered me, and planting myself a little more in his way, I began: 'Are you aware, sir — ?'

I got no further. Without swerving in the slightest degree from the path, he passed me! I felt something like a cold mist touch me for an instant, and the next I saw him pursuing his steady walk down the centre of the glade. I was sick with fear, but for all that I ran after him faster than I had ever done since boyhood.

All to no purpose! I might as well have tried to catch the wind. Just where three ways joined I stood still and looked around. I was quite alone! Neither sign nor token of the intruder could I discover. On my left lay the dell where the nut trees grew, and above it the field path to Whittleby showing white and clear in the moonlight; close at hand was the bridge; straight in front the wood looked dark and solemn. Between me and it lay a little hollow, down which a narrow path wound tortuously. As I gazed I saw that, where a moment before no one had been, a man was walking now. But I could not follow. My limbs refused their office. He turned his head, and, lifting his hand on which the ring glittered, beckoned me to come. He might as well have asked one seized with paralysis. On the confines of the wood he stood motionless as if awaiting my approach; then, when I made no sign of movement, he wrung his hands with a despairing gesture, and disappeared.

At the same moment, moon, dell, bridge, and stream faded from my sight – and I fainted.

IV

It was not much past eight o'clock when I knocked at Miss Gostock's hall door, and asked if I could see that lady.

After that terrible night vision I had made up my mind. Behind Mr Hascot's disappearance I felt sure there lurked some terrible tragedy – living, no man should have implored my help with such passionate earnestness without avail, and if indeed one had appeared to me from the dead I would right him if I could.

But never for a moment did I then think of giving up the farm. The resolve I had come to seemed to have braced up my courage – let what might come or go, let crops remain unreaped and men neglect their labour, let monetary loss and weary, anxious days be in store if they would, I meant to go on to the end.

The first step on my road clearly led in the direction of Miss Gostock's house. She alone could give me all the information I required – her alone could I speak freely and fully about what I had seen.

I was instantly admitted, and found the lady, as I had expected, at breakfast. It was her habit, I knew, to partake of that meal while the labourers she employed were similarly engaged. She was attired in an easy *negligé* of a white skirt and a linen coat which had formerly belonged to her brother. She was not taking tea or coffee like any other woman – but was engaged upon about a pound of smoking steak which she ate covered with mustard and washed down with copious draughts of home-brewed beer.

She received me cordially and invited me to join in the banquet – a request I ungallantly declined, eliciting in return the remark I should never be good for much till I ceased living on 'slops' and took to 'good old English' fare.

After these preliminaries I drew my chair near the table and said: 'I want you to give me some information, Miss Gostock, about my predecessor.'

'What sort of information?' she asked, with a species of frost at once coming over her manner.

'Can you tell me anything of his personal appearance?'

'Why do you ask?'

I did not immediately answer, and seeing my hesitation she went on: 'Because if you mean to tell me you or anyone else has seen him about your place I would not believe it if you swore it – there!'

'I do not ask you to believe it, Miss Gostock,' I said.

'And I give you fair warning, it is of no use coming here and asking me to relieve you of your bargain, because I won't do it. I like you well enough – better than I ever liked a tenant; but I don't intend to be a shilling out of pocket by you.'

'I hope you never may be,' I answered meekly.

'I'll take very good care I never am,' she retorted; 'and so don't come here talking about Mr Hascot. He served me a dirty turn, and I would not put it one bit past him to try and get the place a bad name.'

'Will you tell me what sort of looking man he was?' I asked determinedly.

'No, I won't,' she snapped, and while she spoke she rose, drained the last drop out of a pewter measure and after tossing on the straw hat with a defiant gesture thumped its crown well down on her head.

I took the hint, and rising, said I must endeavour to ascertain the particulars I wanted elsewhere.

'You won't ascertain them from me,' retorted Miss Gostock, and we parted as we had never done before – on bad terms.

Considerably perplexed, I walked out of the house. A rebuff of this sort was certainly the last thing I could have expected, and as I paced along I puzzled myself by trying to account for Miss Gostock's extraordinary conduct and anxiously considering what I was to do under present circumstances. All at once the recollection of mine host of the Bunch of Hops flashed across my mind. He must have seen Mr Hascot often, and I could address a few casual questions to him without exciting his curiosity.

No sooner thought than done. Turning my face towards Whittleby, I stepped briskly on.

'Did I ever see Mr Hascot?' repeated the landlord – when after some general conversation about politics, the weather, the crops, and many other subjects, I adroitly turned it upon the late tenant of Nut Bush Farm. 'Often, sir. I never had much communication with him, for he was one of your stand-aloof, keep-your-distance sort of gentlemen – fair dealing and honourable – but neither free nor generous. He has often sat where you are sitting now, sir, and not so much as said "It is a fine day", or "I am afraid we shall have rain."

'You had but to see him walking down the street to know what he was. As erect as a grenadier, with a firm easy sort of marching step, he looked every inch a gentleman – just in his everyday clothes, a Palmerston suit and a round hat, he was, as many a one said, fit to go to court. His hands were not a bit like a farmer's but white and delicate as any lady's, and the diamond ring he wore flashed like a star when he stroked the slight bit of a moustache that was all the hair he had upon his face. No – not a handsome gentleman but fine-looking, with a presence – bless and save us all to think of his giving up everything for the sake of that slip of a girl.'

'She was very pretty, wasn't she?' I enquired.

'Beautiful – we all said she was too pretty to come to any good. The old grandmother, you see, had serious cause for keeping so tight a hold over her, but it was in her, and "what's bred in bone", you know, sir.'

'And you really think they did go off together?'

'Oh, yes, sir; nobody had ever any doubt about that.' On this subject his tone was so decided I felt it was useless to continue the conversation, and having paid him for the modest refreshment of which I had partaken I sauntered down the High Street and turned into the bank, where I thought of opening an account.

When I had settled all preliminaries with the manager he saved me the trouble of beating about the bush by breaking cover himself and asking if anything had been heard of Mr Hascot.

'Not that I know of,' I answered.

'Curious affair, wasn't it?' he said.

'It appears so, but I have not heard the whole story.'

'Well, the whole story is brief,' returned the manager. 'He comes over here one day and without assigning any reason withdraws the whole of his balance, which was very heavy – is met on the road homeward but never returns home – the same day the girl Powner is also missing. What do you think of all that?'

'It is singular,' I said. 'Very.'

'Yes, and to leave his wife and family totally unprovided for.'

'I cannot understand that at all.'

'Nor I – it was always known he had an extreme partiality for the young person – he and Miss Gostock quarrelled desperately on the subject – but no one could have imagined an attachment of that sort would have led a man so far astray – Hascot more especially. If I had been asked to name the last person in the world likely to make a fool of himself for the sake of a pretty face I should have named the late tenant of Nut Bush Farm.'

'There never was a suspicion of foul play?' I suggested.

'Oh dear no! It was broad daylight when he was last seen on the Whittleby road. The same morning it is known he and the girl were talking earnestly together beside the little wood on your property, and two persons answering to their description were traced to London; that is to say, a gentleman came forward to say he believed he had travelled up with them as far as New Cross on the afternoon in question.'

'He was an affectionate father I have heard,' I said.

'A *most* affectionate parent – a most devoted husband. Dear, dear! It is dreadfully sad to think how a bad woman may drag the best of men down to destruction. It is terrible to think of his wife and family being inmates of the Union.'

'Yes, and it is terrible to consider not a soul has tried to get them out of it,' I answered, a little tartly.

'H'm, perhaps so; but we all know we are contributing to their support,' he returned with an effort at jocularity, which, in my then frame of mind, seemed singularly *mal à propos*.

'There is something in that,' I replied with an effort, and leaving the bank next turned my attention to the poorhouse at Crayshill.

At that time many persons thought what I did quixotic. It is so much the way of the world to let the innocent suffer for the guilty, that I believe Mr Hascot's wife might have ended her days in Crayshill Union but for the action I took in the matter.

Another night I felt I could not rest till I had arranged for a humble lodging she and her family could occupy till I was able to form some plan for their permanent relief. I found her a quiet, lady-like woman, totally unable to give me the slightest clue as to where her husband might be found. 'He was just at the stile on the Chalmont fields,' she said, 'when Mr Waite met him; no one saw him afterwards, unless it might be the Ockfields, but, of course, there is no information to be got them. The guardians have tried every possible means to discover his whereabouts without success. My own impression is he and Sally Powner have gone to America, and that some day we may hear from him. He cannot harden his heart for ever and forget . . .' Here Mrs Hascot's sentence trailed off into passionate weeping.

'It is too monstrous!' I considered. 'The man never did such a thing as desert his wife and children. Someone knows all about the matter', and then in a moment I paused in the course of my meditations.

Was that person Miss Gostock?

It was an ugly idea, and yet it haunted me. When I remembered the woman's masculine strength, when I recalled her furious impetuosity when I asked her a not very exasperating question, as I recalled the way she tossed off that brandy, when I considered her love of money, her eagerness to speak ill of her late tenant, her semi-references to some great trouble prior to which she was more like other women, or, perhaps, to speak more correctly, less unlike them – doubts came crowding upon my mind.

It was when entering her ground Mr Hascot was last seen. He had a large sum of money in his possession. She was notoriously fond of rambling about Nut Bush Farm, and what my labouring men called 'spying around', which had been the cause of more than one pitched battle between herself and Mr Hascot.

'The old master could not a-bear her,' said one young fellow.

I hated myself for the suspicion; and yet, do what I would, I could not shake it off. Not for a moment did I imagine Miss Gostock had killed her former tenant in cold blood; but it certainly occurred to me that the dell was deep and the verge treacherous, that it would be easy to push a man over, either by accident or design, that the nut-bushes grew thick, that a body might lie amongst them till it rotted, ere even the boys who went nutting there, season after season, happened to find it.

Should I let the matter drop? No, I decided. With that mute appeal haunting my memory, I should know no rest or peace till I had solved the mystery of Mr Hascot's disappearance, and cleared his memory from the shameful stain circumstances had cast upon it.

What should I do next? I thought the matter over for a few days, and then decided to call on Mr Waite, who never yet had called on me. As usual, he was not at home; but I saw his wife, whom I found just the sort of woman Lolly described – a fair, delicate creature who seemed fading into the grave.

She had not much to tell me. It was her husband who saw Mr Hascot at the Chalmont stile; it was he also who had seen Mr Hascot and the girl Powner talking together on the morning of their disappearance. It so happened he had often chanced to notice them together before. 'She was a very, very pretty girl,' Mrs Waite added, 'and I always thought a modest one. She had a very sweet way of speaking – quite above her station – inherited, no doubt, for her father was a gentleman. Poor little Sally!'

The words were not much, but the manner touched me sensibly. I felt drawn to Mrs Waite from that moment, and told her more of what I had beheld and what I suspected than I had mentioned to anyone else.

As to my doubts concerning Miss Gostock, I was, of course, silent, but I said quite plainly I did not believe Mr Hascot had gone off with any girl or woman either, that I thought he had come to an unfair end, and that I was of opinion the stories circulated, concerning a portion of Nut Bush Farm being haunted, had some foundation in fact.

'Do you believe in ghosts then?' she asked, with a curious smile.

'I believe in the evidence of my senses,' I answered, 'and I declare to you, Mrs Waite, that one night, not long since, I saw as plainly as I see you what I can only conclude to have been the semblance of Mr Hascot.'

She did not make any reply, she only turned very pale, and blaming myself for having alarmed one in her feeble state of health, I hastened to apologize and take my leave.

As we shook hands, she retained mine for a moment, and said, 'When you hear anything more, if you should, that is, you will tell us, will you not? Naturally we feel interested in the matter. He was such a neighbour, and – we knew him.'

I assured her I would not fail to do so, and left the room. Before I reached the front door I found I had forgotten one of my gloves, and immediately retraced my steps. The drawing-room door was ajar, and, somewhat unceremoniously perhaps, I pushed it open and entered.

To my horror and surprise, Mrs Waite, whom I had left apparently in her ordinary state of languid health, lay full length on the sofa sobbing as if her heart would break. What I said so indiscreetly had brought on an attack of violent hysterics – a malady with the signs and tokens of which I was not altogether unacquainted.

Silently I stole out of the room without my glove, and left the house, closing the front door noiselessly behind me.

A couple of days elapsed, and then I decided to pay a visit to Mrs Ockfield. If she liked to throw any light on the matter, I felt satisfied he could. It was, to say the least of it, most improbable her granddaughter, whether she had been murdered or gone away with Mr Hascot, should disappear and not leave a clue by which her relatives could trace her.

The Ockfields were not liked, I found, and I flattered myself if they had any hand in Mr Hascot's sudden disappearance I should soon hit on some weak spot in their story.

I found the old woman, who was sixty-seven and who looked two hundred, standing over her washing tub.

'Can I tell you where my granddaughter is,' she repeated, drawing her hands out of the suds and wiping them on her apron. 'Surely, sir, and very glad I am to be able to tell everybody, gentle and simple, where to find our Sally. She is in a good service down in Cheshire. Mr Hascot got her the place, but we knew nothing about it till yesterday; she left us in a bit of a pet, and said she wouldn't have written me only something seemed to tell her she must. Ah, I she'll have a sore heart when she gets my letter and hears how it has been said that the master and she went off together. She thought a deal of the master, did Sally; he was always kind and stood between her and her grandfather.'

'Then do you mean to say,' I asked, 'that she knows nothing of Mr Hascot's disappearance?'

'Nothing, sir, thank God for all His mercies; the whole of the time since the day she left here she has been in service with a friend of his. You can read her letter if you like.'

Though I confess old Mrs Ockfield neither charmed nor inspired me with confidence, I answered that I should like to see the letter very much indeed.

When I took it in my hand I am bound to say I thought it had been written with a purpose, and intended less for a private than for the public eye, but as I read I fancied there was a ring of truth about the epistle, more especially as the writer made passing reference to a very bitter quarrel which had preceded her departure from the grandpaternal roof.

'It is very strange,' I said, as I returned the letter; 'it is a most singular coincidence that your granddaughter and Mr Hascot should have left Whittleby on the same day, and yet that she should know nothing of his whereabouts, as judging from her letter seems to be the case.

'Are you quite sure Mr Hascot ever did leave Whittleby, sir?' asked the old woman with a vindictive look in her still bright old eyes. 'There are those as think he never went very far from home, and that the whole truth will come out some day.'

'What do you mean?' I exclaimed, surprised.

'Least said soonest mended,' she answered shortly; 'only I hopes if ever we do know the rights of it, people as do hold their heads high enough, and have had plenty to say about our girl, and us, too, for that matter, will find things not so pleasant as they find them at present. The master had a heap of money about him, and we know that often those as has are those as wants more!'

'I cannot imagine what you are driving at,' I said, for I feared every moment she would mention Miss Gostock, and bring her name into the discussion. 'If you think Mr Hascot met with any foul play you ought to go to the police about the matter.'

'Maybe I will some time,' she answered, 'but just now I have my washing to do.'

'This will buy you some tea to have afterwards,' I said, laying down half a crown, and feeling angry with myself for this momentary irritation. After all, the woman had as much right to her suspicions as I to mine.

Thinking over Miss Powner's letter, I came to the conclusion it might be well to see the young lady for myself. If I went to the address she wrote from I could ascertain at all events whether her statement regarding her employment was correct. Yes, I would take train and travel into Cheshire. I had commenced the investigation and I would follow it to the end.

I travelled so much faster than Mrs Ockfield's letter – which, indeed, that worthy woman had not then posted – that when I arrived at my journey's end I found the fair Sally in total ignorance of Mr Hascot's disappearance and the surmises to which her own absence had given rise.

Appearances might be against the girl's truth and honesty, yet I felt she was dealing fairly with me.

'A better gentleman, sir,' she said, 'than Mr Hascot never drew breath. And so they set it about he had gone off with me – they little know – they little know! Why, sir, he thought of me and was careful for me as he might for a daughter. The first time I ever saw him grandfather was beating me, and he interfered to save me. He knew they treated me badly, and it was after a dreadful quarrel I had at home he advised me to go away. He gave me a letter to the lady I am now with, and a ten-pound note to pay my travelling expenses and keep something in my pocket. "You'll be better away from the farm, little girl," he said the morning I left. "People are beginning to talk, and we can't shut their mouths if you come running to me every time your grandmother speaks sharply to you."

'But why did you not write sooner to your relatives?' I asked.

'Because I was angry with my grandmother, sir, and I thought I would give her a fright. I did not bring any clothes or anything and I hoped – it was a wicked thing I know, sir – but I hoped she would believe I had made away with myself. Just lately, however, I began to consider that if she and grandfather had not treated me well, I was treating them worse, so I made up a parcel of some things my mistress gave me and sent it to them with a letter. I am glad it reached them safely.'

'What time was it when you saw Mr Hascot last?' I enquired.

'About two o'clock, sir, I know that, because he was in a hurry. He had got some news about the bank at Whittleby not being quite safe, and he said he had too much money there to run any risk of loss. "Be a good girl" were the last words he said, and he walked off sharp and quick by the field path to Whittleby. I stood near the bridge crying for a while. Oh, sir, I do you think anything ill can have happened to him?'

For answer, I only said the whole thing seemed most mysterious.

'He'd never have left his wife and children, sir,' she went on; 'never. He must have been made away with.'

'Had he any enemies, do you think?' I asked.

'No, sir; not to say enemies. He was called hard because he would have a day's work for a day's wage, but no one that ever I heard of had a grudge against him. Except Miss Gostock and Mr Waite, he agreed well with all the people about. He did not like Miss Gostock, and Mr Waite was always borrowing money from him. Now Mr Hascot did not mind giving, but he could not bear lending.'

I returned to Nut Bush Farm perfectly satisfied that Mr Hascot had been, as the girl expressed the matter, 'made away with'. On the threshold of my house I was met with a catalogue of disasters. The female servants had gone in a body; the male professed a dislike to be in the stable-yard in the twilight. Rumour had decided that Nut Bush Farm was an unlucky place even to pass. The cattle were out of condition because the men would not go down the Beech Walk, or turn a single sheep into the long field. Reapers wanted higher wages. The labourers were looking out for other service.

'Poor fellow! This is a nice state of things for you to come home to,' said Lolly compassionately. 'Even the poachers won't venture into the wood, and the boys don't go nutting.'

'I will clear away the nut trees and cut down the wood,' I declared savagely.

'I don't know who you are going to get to cut them,' answered Lolly, 'unless you bring men down from London.'

As for Miss Gostock, she only laughed at my dilemma, and said, 'You're a pretty fellow to be frightened by a ghost. If he was seen at Chalmont I'd ghost him.'

While I was in a state of the most cruel perplexity, I bethought me of my promise to Mrs Waite, and walked over one day to tell her the result of my enquiries.

I found her at home and Mr Waite, for a wonder, in the drawing-room. He was not a bad-looking fellow, and welcomed my visit with a heartiness which ill accorded with the discourtesy he had shown in never calling upon me.

Very succinctly I told what I had done, and where I had been. I mentioned the, terms in which Sally Powner spoke of her bene-factor. We discussed the whole matter fully – the *pros* and *cons* of anyone knowing Mr Hascot had such a sum of money on his per-son, and the possibility of his having been murdered. I mentioned what I had done about Mrs Hascot, and begged Mr Waite to afford me his help and co-operation in raising such a sum of money as might start the poor lady in some business.

'I'll do all that lies in my power,' he said heartily, shaking hands at the same time, for I had risen to go.

'And for my part,' I remarked, 'it seems to me there are only two things more I can do to elucidate the mystery, and those are – root every nut tree out of the dell and set the axe to work in the wood.'

There was a second's silence. Then Mrs Waite dropped to the floor as if she had been shot. As he stooped over her he and I exchanged glances, and then *I knew*. Mr Hascot *had* been murdered, and Mr Waite was the murderer!

*

That night I was smoking and Lolly was at needlework. The parlour windows were wide open, for it was warm, and not a breath of air seemed stirring.

There was a stillness on everything which betokened a coming thunderstorm; and we both were silent, for my mind was busy and Lolly's heart anxious. She did not see, as she said, how I was to get on at all, and for my part I could not tell what I ought to do.

All at once something whizzed through the window furthest from where we sat, and fell noisily to the floor.

'What is that?' Lolly cried, springing to her feet. 'Oh, Jack! What is it?' Surprised and shaken myself, I closed the windows and drew down the blinds before I examined the cause of our alarm. It proved to be an oblong package weighted with a stone. Unfastening it cautiously, for I did not know whether it might not contain some explosive, I came at length to a pocket book. Opening the pocket book, I found it stuffed full of bank notes.

'What are they? Where can they have come from?' exclaimed Lolly.

'They are the notes Mr Hascot drew from Whittleby bank the day he disappeared,' I answered with a sort of inspiration, but I took no notice of Lolly's last question.

For good or for evil that was a secret which lay between myself and the Waites, and which I have never revealed till now. If the vessel in which they sailed for New Zealand had not gone to the bottom I should have kept the secret still.

When they were out of the country and the autumn well advanced, I had the wood thoroughly examined, and there in a gully, covered with a mass of leaves and twigs and dead branches, we found Mr Hascot's body. His watch was in his waistcoat pocket – his ring on his finger; save for these possessions no one could have identified him.

His wife married again about a year afterwards and my brother took Nut Bush Farm off my hands. He says the place never was haunted – that I never saw Mr Hascot except in my own imagination – that the whole thing originated in a poor state of health and a too credulous disposition!

I leave the reader to judge between us.

Mary E. Penn

THE TENANT OF THE CEDARS

Though she shared the same Christian names as Mary Braddon, Mary Elizabeth Penn achieved neither the financial nor critical success. Indeed, until some of her fiction was resurrected by Richard Dalby as In the Dark and Other Ghost Stories *in 1999 she was, to all intents, forgotten. We still know nothing of her personal life, though we may judge from her stories that she travelled around Europe and may have been reasonably affluent. Her stories are among the core of Victorian ghostly tales which explore supernatural revenge and retribution.*

The Tenant of The Cedars

I

'TO BE LET, furnished, by the month or year, The Cedars, a pretty rustic cottage, delightfully situated in Ranstone Park, Berkshire, with right of fishing in the trout stream. For particulars, apply to Mr Newton, House Agent, Reading.'

This advertisement arrested my attention as I, Percival Wilford, barrister-at-law, glanced over the columns of *The Times* one August morning ten or twelve years ago.

It seemed like an answer to the question I had been deliberating as I sat at breakfast in my dull Temple chambers – namely, where should I spend the Long Vacation? I had reached that sedate period of life when one begins to realize that 'there is no joy but calm', and my ideal of a holiday retreat was some quiet, leafy nook where I could read and dream, and 'go a-fishing' and forget for a time that such things as briefs existed. I may add that I had only my own tastes to consult in the matter, having the misfortune (to which I am perfectly resigned) to be a bachelor. I made a note of the advertisement, and resolved to run down to the place next day and see whether it answered to its attractive description.

Accordingly, on the following afternoon I took the train to Reading, and walked thence to the village of Ranstone, which consisted of one long, uphill street, beginning with a blacksmith's forge and ending with a barn. Midway between them stood an inn: the Golden Sheaf. Feeling somewhat fatigued by a five-mile walk along dusty country roads, I turned into this hostelry to refresh myself with a glass of ale, and enquire my way. The landlord, a red-faced burly man, in shirt-sleeves and a white apron, seemed puzzled by my question.

'The Cedars!' he repeated; 'oh – I understand, sir. You mean the little thatched house in the park. We call it "Ranstone's Folly".'

'Why "Folly"?' I queried.

'Well, sir, because it's a fanciful sort of place, and was built for a whim. Sir Richard Ranstone, the father of the present baronet, designed it himself when a young man, and used to shut himself up there to scribble poetry. Since his death it has been let from time to time, but not often. Such a lonesome, out-of-the-way place don't suit everyone.'

'I fancy it will just suit me,' I remarked.

My host scanned me curiously as he set down the glass at my elbow. 'Perhaps you're in the poetical line yourself, sir?' he suggested.

I laughed, and assured him that my 'line' was nothing half so agreeable; and, when I had finished, paid for my modest refreshment and set off hopefully on my way.

It led through the village and along the high road, and in about ten minutes I came to the ivy-covered park wall, which was pleasantly shaded by trees.

Presently I found myself opposite the lodge-gates, my summons at which was answered by a neat, comely woman of middle age, to whom I explained my errand, and exhibited my credentials in the shape of the house agent's card.

'The cottage is right on the other side of the park, sir, close to the stream,' she said, as she admitted me. 'I'm sorry I can't show you the way, but Foster's out, and I've no one to leave. However, you can't miss it if you keep to that path', pointing to one which branched off to the right of the main avenue. 'There's a man living in charge who will show you over the house.'

'Has it been long unlet?' I enquired.

'Nigh upon three years. The last tenant only lived there six months – a lady named Lestelle.'

'That is a French name?'

'Yes, sir, she was French, and had been a singer, I believe.'

'Lestelle,' I repeated thoughtfully. 'Was it Léonie Lestelle, I wonder, who took the town by storm a few seasons ago? But that is hardly probable.'

'What was she like, sir?' my companion enquired, looking interested. 'Young and pretty?'

'More than pretty. She had one of the loveliest faces I ever saw, and a voice that matched it.'

'It must be the same,' Mrs Foster exclaimed. 'That's just her description. A beautiful young lady she was, and so gentle and sweet-spoken it was a pleasure to serve her.'

'But what brought her to The Cedars?' I questioned. 'When she disappeared from London society about four years ago, it was supposed that she had returned to France. Was she living alone?'

'Quite alone, except for the servants – an elderly woman who did the housework, and a man named Underwood who attended to the garden and went on errands. It's him that's been living in charge of the house for the last two years. He used to be one of the under-gardeners at the Hall, but was dismissed because he was always quarrelling with the other men. A sullen, ill-conditioned fellow he is – though I ought not to say so, perhaps, as he's a cripple and deformed,' she added, with compunction. 'He has a hard life of it.'

'How came Mademoiselle Lestelle to take him into her service?'

'It was out of kindness, sir, because no one else would employ him. Her patience and sweetness conquered even him. I believe he worshipped the ground she trod upon, and he was like one frantic when she was – when she died.'

I started. 'What – is she dead?' I asked.

My companion looked at me in surprise. 'Didn't you know, sir? Did you never hear?'

'I have heard nothing of her since she gave up her profession. What was the cause of her death?'

Before she could reply the sound of a horse approaching rapidly up the road made her glance towards the gates. 'It's Sir Philip,' she said, hurriedly, and ran forward to open them.

The baronet was a tall, distinguished-looking man, of two or three and thirty, with handsome, haughty features, bold dark eyes and full red lips half hidden by a sweeping moustache. A striking face but scarcely an attractive one. There was something at once hard and sensual about it that repelled me. He was mounted on a handsome chestnut mare, whose panting, foam-flecked sides showed that she had been mercilessly ridden. Apparently the exercise had not improved her owner's temper. Slight as was the delay in admitting him, he abused the woman for keeping him waiting. He was riding on when, perceiving me, he drew rein.

'The gentleman has called to see the cottage,' Mrs Foster explained.

'What cottage?' he asked, absently.

'The Cedars, Sir Philip.'

He slightly nodded, and, acknowledging my salute by touching the brim of his hat with his whip, jerked the bridle, and rode on up the avenue, followed by his dogs. Mrs Foster looked after her master's retreating figure with no great favour.

'He needn't have sworn at me,' she muttered, resentfully. 'I was as quick as I could be. But he's in one of his moods today, and makes everyone suffer for it. Ah – I wouldn't be in my lady's shoes for all her grandeur. They've only been married a couple of years, but already . . .'

A significant shake of the head finished the sentence.

'Who was Lady Ranstone?' I asked.

'She was the daughter and heiress of Mr Goldney, the great banker. She's a nice lady, but no beauty, and several years older than Sir Philip. It's pretty well known that he married her for her money, being over head and ears in debt, thanks to his . . . But I really beg your pardon, sir,' she broke off, becoming suddenly conscious of her indiscretion. 'I ought not to detain you with my gossip. If Underwood is not indoors, you'll find him somewhere in the garden – reading, most likely. He's quite a scholar, in his way. Good afternoon, sir, and a pleasant walk.'

I nodded to her, and went my way down the path she had indicated, which traversed the whole width of the park; winding across sunny glades, and ferny hollows, and under the shade of 'immemorial elms', between whose branches I caught glimpses of the hall, a stately modern building in the Italian style.

At length, emerging from a young oak plantation, I came unexpectedly upon the stream – which at this point was both broad and deep – and on the slope of the opposite bank stood The Cedars.

It was a picturesque rustic pavilion, with a high, thatched roof, whose overhanging ledge, supported on pillars, formed a veranda, on to which the lower windows opened. Behind it the trees clustered closely, and the garden in front sloped to the edge of the stream, which was spanned by a light rustic bridge. I crossed it, and passed through a wicket gate into the garden, which was in beautiful order; the parterres a mass of brilliant bloom, the grass-plot like green velvet.

It was not till I was close to the house that I perceived the figure of the custodian, who was seated in the veranda.

He was a man of from thirty-five to forty, with rugged strongly marked features, and melancholy dark eyes. His figure, though mis-shapen, was vigorous and muscular, and there was a look of sup-pressed power about him which suggested hidden reserves of force, both mental and physical. I had ample time to make these observ-ations, for he did not seem to notice my approach, nor did he reply when I addressed him.

There was a book in his hand, a well-worn volume of Shakespeare, but he was not reading. He sat in a listening attitude, with head upraised and lips apart, his foot gently beating on the ground, as if in time to music. Involuntarily I listened, too, but heard nothing except the lonely murmur of the breeze and the dis-tant forlorn note of a wood-pigeon. At length I touched his arm. He sprang to his feet, staring at me with vague alarm.

'I am sorry I startled you, but you did not hear me speak,' I said. 'Will you —'

'How long have you been watching me?' he interrupted, brusquely.

'I have but this moment come,' I returned. 'I wish to look over the house.'

He hesitated; and seemed half inclined to refuse me admission, but, thinking better of it, nodded, and limped on before me to the door, drawing back to allow me to pass in. I found myself in a small tiled entrance hall, with doors on either hand. He threw open the one to the left, and ushered me into a dusky, low room, furnished in a style of quaint simplicity, which suited the character of the house.

'This is what they call Sir Richard's study,' he explained. 'The parlour across the hall is the same size, but better furnished. I can't show it you, for the door's locked, and – and I've mislaid the key.'

His hesitation convinced me that he was telling an untruth; for some reason of his own he did not wish me to see the room. However, I only said quietly: 'I think I noticed that the window was open; we can go in that way.'

He reluctantly followed me, and stood outside as I entered through the long window, which opened, like a door, upon the veranda.

The room in which I found myself was as great a contrast to the one I had just quitted as could well be imagined. With its polished floor and panelled walls, its light but elegant furniture, its crowd of dainty ornaments, and general look of airy brightness, it might have been transported bodily from a Parisian 'Appartement'. But I noticed with surprise, that it seemed to have been recently occupied by a lady. There were fresh flowers in the vases; music on the open piano, books on the table, and a work-basket, with a strip of embroidery, which seemed to have been just thrown down. I hastily drew back, and turned to my companion.

'I understood that the house was unoccupied,' I said. 'Why did you not tell me —'

'There is no one here except myself,' he interrupted.

'Then, to whom do these belong?' I enquired, pointing to the books and music.

'To no one in particular. They did belong to a lady who lived here for a time three years ago, but she's dead.'

'You mean Mademoiselle Lestelle?'

He nodded, slowly passing his hand across his forehead.

'But how came they to be left here? Did no one claim them, after her death – no friend or relative?'

'She had no near relations, and few friends in this country. I have heard her say that she would leave no one to regret her. But she was mistaken there,' he muttered.

I looked at him curiously. There was something in his face that attracted me, in spite of its harsh lines.

'You, at least, will not soon forget her, I am sure?' I said, after a pause. His lips curved in a smile half sad, half bitter.

'I have not so many friends that I can afford to forget that one. I suppose I may claim the dog's virtue – fidelity, if no other. I know that I would gladly have died upon her grave,' he added, in a low tone of suppressed but passionate feeling which was a revelation to me. The next moment, however, he broke into a short laugh. 'You may well look astonished to hear such a romantic sentiment from "Caliban", as Sir Philip calls me. Sounds grotesque from my lips, doesn't it, sir?'

'You need not fear ridicule from me,' I said, quietly. 'I understand your feeling, and respect it.'

He gave me a half-incredulous look, as if sympathy were something new to him. Then his face changed and softened, and with a quick impulsive movement he put out his hand.

'Thank you, sir – that's kindly spoken,' he said, earnestly. 'I'm sorry I told you a falsehood about the key – for it was a falsehood. I have it in my pocket. But – but this room, where she spent so many hours, is sacred to me; so sacred, that it seems sacrilege for a stranger to enter it.' He paused, looking round reverently, as if it were indeed a sanctuary.

'I have kept it just as it was when – when last she used it,' he continued, in a low, dreamy tone, speaking to himself more than to me. 'I can almost fancy I see her bending over her book, or singing softly to herself as she worked. What a voice she had! It seemed to draw the heart out of my body. She used to let me sit in the veranda when she was singing, and she'd talk to me between whiles in her pretty broken English. She'd always a word and a smile for "Jacques", as she called me – always as gentle and courteous she was as if I'd been her friend and equal, instead of her servant. Ah! She was the sweet . . .'

His voice broke; he hastily turned his head aside.

'I've got her portrait – the last she had taken, if you would like to see it,' he resumed, after a moment, and took it from a worn leather pocket-book. It was the vignette photograph of a lovely girl of one or two and twenty, with a delicate, spiritual face, framed in cloudy dark hair; a sweet sorrowful mouth, and soft steadfast dark eyes.

'It is very like her' was my comment.

'Ah – you knew her?' he questioned eagerly.

'No, but I have heard her sing more than once. Her face had not this sorrowful look when I saw her last. What was her trouble, I wonder? Did she ever speak of her past life?'

'No – yes. She sometimes talked of her childhood, when her parents were living.'

'But not of her later years? She did not tell you why she gave up her profession?'

'She was not likely to take me into her confidence,' he rejoined evasively, and added, as if to avoid further questions, 'Perhaps you would like to see the other rooms now?' And without waiting for my reply, he crossed the hall and led the way upstairs.

Before my tour of inspection was over, I had resolved to become the temporary tenant of The Cedars. Underwood received the announcement of my decision in silence.

'I suppose I shall have to turn out when you take possession?' he said at last, glancing at me half-wistfully.

'Not unless you are disinclined to remain as my servant,' I replied.

'I shall be only too glad to stay, sir, and I'll do my best to please you,' he responded. 'I don't know whether you intend to bring a woman-servant with you; but, if not, I dare say Mrs Foster, at the lodge, could recommend one.'

'I will speak to her on my way back, and you may expect to see me this day week.'

I slipped a coin into his hand, and we parted.

II

A week later I found myself once more entering the gates of Ranstone Park, having left my 'traps' to be sent after me from Reading.

The evening was grey, moist and cool. Rain had fallen in the morning, and the air was still charged with the sweet pastoral scent of wet earth and grass. 'Autumn's fiery finger' had not yet touched the leaves, and the woods wore a green as fresh and rich as if the month had been June instead of August.

To come straight from the dust and turmoil of town to these sylvan solitudes was almost like being transported to another planet. The walk was so pleasant that I was half sorry when it was over, and I saw before me the solitary pavilion, with the woods behind it and the stream at its feet. I was received at the door by Mrs Foster and a pleasant, fresh-faced young woman, whom she introduced as her niece.

'Martha can't be spared from home altogether, sir,' she explained, 'but she'll be here early every morning, and I think you'll find her a good cook. She's given the house a thorough cleaning, all but the drawing-room. Underwood has fastened the window and locked the door, and won't let her set foot in it. I really think the man is going out of his mind,' she continued, following me into the study, where the cloth was laid for my solitary dinner. 'Just look at him now, sir.'

She pointed through the window to where the gardener was standing in the side-walk. He had paused in the act of pruning a rosebush, and seemed to be listening intently to some sound proceeding from the lower end of the walk.

'He'll stand in that way for ten minutes together, listening to nothing,' she whispered. 'It gives me a creepy feeling to look at him. People do say that the cottage is haunted, and that he —'

'Nonsense!' I interrupted; 'he is evidently subject to some delusion. Have you any idea what it is?'

She shook her head, and was silent a moment, thoughtfully

watching him. 'He has never been the same man since that dreadful affair three years ago,' she resumed, at length.

'What are you speaking of?'

She coloured and bit her lips. 'I ought not to have mentioned it, as it may set you against the house – however, I dare say you would have heard of it from someone else. I mean the murder of Mademoiselle Lestelle.'

'What!' I exclaimed, in horror. 'Do you mean to say that she was murdered?'

'In this very house, on the night of the first of September, three years ago.'

'Good heavens! – By whom?'

'That is a mystery to this hour. She was in the habit of sitting up rather late to practise her music, and that night Underwood, who was in bed but not asleep, noticed that she broke off suddenly in the middle of a song. He thought it strange, and after waiting a few moments, threw on his clothes, and hurried downstairs. He found the poor young lady lying in a pool of her own blood – dead. She had been stabbed in the back as she sat at the piano. The window was open, and there were footprints in the garden, but the murderer, whoever it was, had had time to get clear away, and has never been traced from that day to this.'

'What was supposed to be the motive of the crime? Robbery?'

'No, nothing was stolen. That's the mysterious part of it. You may think that Sir Philip was dreadfully shocked at such a thing happening on his estate. He himself offered a reward for information, but –'

'Was no one even suspected at the time?' I interrupted.

My companion hesitated. 'Well – one person was, sir.'

'Who was that?'

She pointed to the gardener. I looked at her incredulously.

'Impossible!' I exclaimed. 'Underwood – who was so devotedly attached to her!'

'Many people think he has madness in his blood,' she whispered; 'and it's well known that madmen often turn against the very person they love best when in their right senses. You see we have only his own account of what took place that night, for the housekeeper neither saw nor heard anything. The footprints may have been a cunning device to avert suspicion. Heaven forbid that I should accuse him wrongfully,' she added in conclusion, 'but everyone has noticed that since it happened he has been like a man bewitched.'

When she had left the room I stood for a moment, watching the gardener; then opened the window, and crossed the lawn to his side. He stood in the same attitude, with a rapt, ecstatic look on his face, as if he were listening to the 'music of the spheres'. He turned towards me as I approached, but did not appear to recognize me till I spoke.

'Day-dreaming again, Underwood?' I said. 'It seems to be a habit of yours.'

He passed his hand over his forehead, as if to rouse himself, and pushed back his cap.

'A very stupid one. I must try to cure myself of it,' he replied with a constrained smile.

'What were you listening to just now?' I asked point-blank.

He resumed his task, and made no reply.

'Why will you not tell me?'

'Because, if I did, you would think me mad.'

'Delusion is not necessarily a sign of insanity,' I said after a moment's pause. 'Your delusion – if you have one – may arise from disordered nerves, or —'

'I have no delusion,' he interrupted. 'My senses are quickened to hear a sound which is inaudible to others – that's all.'

'What is the sound?' I persisted; but again there was no reply. I changed the subject.

'I hear that you have the key of the drawing-room. Please give it to me.'

He took it from his pocket at once, and handed it to me, muttering something about not wishing the things to be 'meddled with'.

'Nothing need be moved, for I don't intend to use that room,' I replied; 'but I should prefer to keep the key.'

He looked up quickly. 'Ah! they have told you, I see.'

'Yes, I have been told what happened there,' I assented, looking him full in the face. He met my eyes steadily, his lips curving in a slow, sardonic smile.

'Perhaps you know that I was suspected of the crime?'

'Unjustly, I am sure,' I replied, speaking my conviction; for I could detect no shadow of guilty consciousness in the man's face: only bitterness and melancholy.

'How can you be sure of it? I may be a madman and a murderer for all you know to the contrary,' he retorted with a short, brusque laugh. Then, with one of his sudden changes of manner, he threw down his knife, and turned upon me almost fiercely.

'Does a man destroy what he adores? I worshipped her – I would have died for her. And it was me – me! they accused of taking her innocent life. Fools that they were!'

With a passionate gesture of his clenched hands he turned from me and limped hurriedly away down the path. I saw no more of him that evening, but he occupied a large share of my thoughts, both then and in the days which followed. His presence seemed to add to the uncanny sort of fascination which the place possessed for me – something which at once repelled and attracted my imagination.

Yet if the place were haunted, it seemed haunted by nothing more terrible than the gracious memory of its late tenant, which pervaded every room, like a lingering echo, or a sweet faint perfume, giving it a melancholy and mysterious charm.

A fortnight passed away in uneventful tranquillity. I took long walks in the pleasant Berkshire lanes; angled in the stream, lounged in the garden, and spent quiet evenings with my books.

I had seen nothing more of my landlord (a circumstance which I hardly regretted), and my only connection with the outer world was through my cheerful and obliging little maid, who brought my letters and papers every morning, and regaled me with scraps of village gossip. I should thoroughly have enjoyed this 'lotus-eating' existence but for the feeling of languor and depression which clung to me. For the first time in my life I was conscious of 'nerves'. I felt restless and ill at ease, and my sleep was disturbed by troubled dreams from which I woke, 'in the dead waste and middle of the night', trembling with some nameless fear.

One night when I had started awake in this uncomfortable fashion, finding it impossible to compose myself to sleep again, I half dressed, lighted a cigar, and took my seat near the open window. The night was sultry and still. The moon had set, but the sky was full of stars, and their faint, diffused light showed me the garden, the stream, and the shadowy park beyond. The murmur of running water, scarcely heard by day, was distinctly audible in the silence, and now and then a languid breeze charged with the sweet aromatic odour which the sleeping earth breathes forth, just stirred the leaves and died away. Was it in the magical stillness of such a night as this, I wondered, that Léonie Lestelle had sung her last song – that song which was never finished?

Her face rose up before me with strange distinctness, and I seemed to be listening once more to the clear, silvery sweet tones of her exquisite voice, which had a tender thrill, like the wooing note of a dove. I recollected that when last I heard her sing – it was a private concert at Lady A—'s – she had chosen Beethoven's *'Per pietà non dirmi addio!'* The words haunted me, their musical syllables setting themselves to the murmur of the breeze and the ripple of the stream.

I do not know how long I had been sitting thus when I was roused from my reverie by another sound, coming from the room beneath – the key of which had been in my own possession since the day of my arrival. It did not at once arrest my attention, but stole upon me so gradually that I could not have told at what moment I first heard it. I turned from the window and listened.

Was I dreaming, I asked myself bewilderedly, or did I hear the faint sweet tones of a woman's voice singing the very song which haunted my memory? I started to my feet, and for a moment stood transfixed, paralysed, by a fear such as I had never before experienced. Recovering myself by an effort I took up the night-lamp and left the room.

I noiselessly descended the stairs, crossed the little tiled entrance-hall, and paused outside the door of the closed room. My heart beat fast and thick and a creeping chill stirred the roots of my hair as I stood in the hush of the sleeping house, listening – to what?

The voice of Léonie Lestelle. Faint and aerial as the notes of an Æolean harp; near, yet distant; sweet beyond words, but unutterably sad, it thrilled through the silence, breathing with tender, passionate entreaty: *'Ah, per pietà non dirmi addio!'* I forgot to feel afraid; I forgot even to wonder, as I listened with suspended breath to those entrancing notes, and when they ceased I stood, as if spell-bound, longing to hear more of the sweet, unearthly music.

At length, when the silence had lasted some moments, I ventured to open the door. The room was dark and empty, the piano closed. As I stood on the threshold looking round, I felt a touch on my arm, and turning with a start, found Underwood at my side. He had been watching me unperceived. He beckoned me into the other room and closed the door before he spoke. His face was flushed; his eyes glittering with excitement, and a strange sort of triumph.

'You have heard it last!' he breathed. 'You know now that the sound is no "delusion". It is *her voice* that follows me night and day. Oh, my lady, my queen,' he broke off, 'why do you haunt me? What is it you want of me? If you would but speak instead of mocking me with those sweet piteous songs of yours . . .'

He sank on to a chair near the table, burying his face in his hands.

I set down the lamp and took a seat at his side. 'When did you first hear it?' I asked, involuntarily speaking in a whisper.

He looked up, pushing back the disordered hair from his forehead.

'Last summer. The first time it was but a faint thin sound, like a distant echo, but every day it grew clearer and nearer, seeming to float in the air around me. It is not only in the house that I hear it, but out of doors in broad daylight, as if she were flitting about the garden singing to herself as she used to do. Sometimes she calls me – "Jacques, Jacques!" and her sweet, low laugh sounds so close that I can't help turning, half expecting to see her at my side.'

I shuddered. 'I wonder you have kept your senses!' I exclaimed.

'Do you think I am afraid of it? No – her voice is still to me what it always was, the sweetest sound on this side of heaven. It is only in spring and summer, during the months she lived here, that I hear it,' he continued. 'It ceases at midnight on the first of September; breaking off in the middle of a song – the very song she was singing when – when it happened.'

I glanced at his face, and something I saw there confirmed a suspicion which had already occurred to me.

'Underwood,' I said, suddenly, leaning forward with my arms on the table, 'can you honestly assure me that you do not know or suspect who took her life?'

He looked at me fixedly a moment, then answered, in a tone of curious composure: 'I have known all along.'

I drew back, and stared at him. 'Then, why in heaven's name did you not speak at the time?'

'My lips were sealed by a promise.'

'Given to whom? Who bound you to silence?'

'*She* did, with her last breath, that fatal night, when I found her, lying in the moonlight, with her life ebbing away from the cruel wound. She saw in my face that I guessed who had struck the blow, and with all the strength that was left in her she implored – commanded me never to tell. It was her husband – for she was married, though the world did not know it. I have kept the secret so far, but I feel that if I don't share it with someone I shall go mad in earnest. It is eating my heart away. I dare not break my vow, but you shall know the truth.'

'From whom? How shall I know it – and when?'

He rose and pushed back his chair, pointed over his shoulder, then bent his lips to my ear. 'Watch with me in that room on the night of the first of September, and you shall learn the secret.'

Before I could speak again, he was gone.

III

The last week of August was stormy and wet. Summer took flight hurriedly, scared by the wild gales and heavy rain which stripped the branches and laid the flowers low. The green arcades of the park were dank and dripping; the sunny glades forlorn; the avenues carpeted with fallen leaves, and the little river, transformed from a stream to a torrent, had overflowed its banks, inundating the lower end of The Cedars' lawn, and carrying away the hand-rails and some planks of the bridge.

The tempestuous weather culminated on the first of September. From dawn till dark the wind blew and the rain fell 'as they would never weary'; but in spite of both I was abroad all the afternoon, being in a restless, excited mood which would not allow me to remain between four walls.

The light of a stormy sunset was fading into dusk when I returned through the park, tired and wet, after a long tramp through miry country lanes. As I emerged from the plantation which bordered the stream, I was surprised to see Sir Philip Ranstone, who was standing on the bank, near the bridge. Buttoned up in his ulster he leant against a tree, smoking, in serene indifference to wind and rain, with a large black retriever at his feet.

The dog started up as I approached, barking violently, and Sir Philip turned.

'Ah! good evening, Mr – ah – Wilford,' he said, coming towards me. 'Awful weather, isn't it? But I see you defy the elements, like myself.'

'I was tired of staying indoors,' I explained.

'I should think so. You must be bored to extinction in that dull hole, with no company but your own.'

'I am fond of my own company,' I said, smiling. 'I am never bored when alone.'

He glanced at me with languid curiosity. 'Really. H'm – I can't say as much. I think in your place I should be ready to fraternize with Underwood – bear as he is – in default of other society.'

'Underwood and I are very good friends, Sir Philip. I find he improves on acquaintance.'

'There is room for improvement' was his comment. 'By the way,' he continued, knocking the ash from his cigar, 'I should very much like to know whether he is the author of an absurd report which has only lately reached my ears – that The Cedars is haunted. It struck me that it might be an ingenious device of his to keep tenants away.'

I shook my head. 'I am quite sure that he has never told – I mean that he has never spread such a report.'

He turned and looked at me. 'You seem to think there is some truth in it,' he remarked.

I felt no inclination to take him into my confidence, and stooped to stroke his dog without replying.

'Am I to conclude from your silence that you do?' he persisted, with an ironical smile. 'Come, Mr Wilford, you don't mean to tell me that you, a man of the world, and a lawyer to boot, actually believe in ghosts?'

I hesitated a moment, then looked up. 'I believe in the evidence of my own senses,' I said quietly.

'You excite my curiosity,' he sneered. 'What uncanny thing have you seen, I wonder?'

'I have seen nothing. It is a sound which haunts the house.'

'A sound?' he repeated, with a quick change of tone. 'What sort of sound?'

'A voice,' I said, slowly. 'The voice of the ill-fated girl who met her death beneath its roof.'

The cigar fell from his hand. 'Good heavens!' he breathed. 'What do you mean? It is not . . .'

'Yes, Sir Philip; it is the voice of Léonie Lestelle. I have heard her singing as plainly as I heard you speak just then.'

He looked at me blankly, the colour fading from his face, and his dark eyes dilating till they seemed all pupil. Recovering himself, however, he stooped to pick up his cigar, and burst into a scornful laugh.

'Preposterous! You must have been dreaming, or else it is some trick of Underwood's.'

'Could Underwood imitate such a voice as hers? Besides – he has heard it himself. It has haunted him for the last two years.'

Sir Philip drew in his lips, and was silent a moment. 'That is strange,' he said, at length. 'Why should it haunt him, of all people, unless' – he glanced at me significantly – 'unless there is some foundation for the suspicion which still clings to him.'

'I am quite sure there is none,' I answered, warmly.

'Other people do not share your conviction,' was his reply. 'It is because no one in the neighbourhood would give him the shelter of a roof that I have allowed him to remain at the cottage. However, he will soon have to find fresh quarters, for I am determined to have the house pulled down. Haunted or not, it is a gloomy, ill-omened place.'

And, indeed, it looked so at this moment, with the shadows of the stormy twilight gathering round it, and a white mist rising, wraithlike, from the stream. He stared at it moodily, pulling the long ends of his moustache. 'Where did you hear the – the sound?' he asked, after a pause. 'In what part of the house?'

'In the room where the tragedy occurred.'

He shivered slightly, and threw away his half-smoked cigar.

'The probability is that you had been thinking of that horrible affair, and imagination did the rest. As to Underwood, everyone knows he is half-mad. Anyhow, you will oblige me by keeping the story to yourself. I will wish you good evening now,' he continued, glancing at his watch; 'or, rather, goodbye, for I am going abroad in a few days, and shall probably not see you again.'

He bowed without offering me his hand, whistled to his dog, and walked away.

Dusk deepened into dark, and the wind, instead of subsiding, seemed to increase in violence as the night advanced. The fierce, fitful gusts came sweeping down upon the house, as if bent on unroofing it; now swelling to a roar which made the walls vibrate, then dying away in a long eerie wail. Towards midnight the rain ceased, and the clouds, rent and scattered by the wind, drifted apart like fragments of a torn veil, leaving a space of clear, violet-dark sky, in which the moon rode serenely. Her light touched the brimming stream with silver, and flecked the lawn with fantastic shadows of the tossing trees, giving something of wild poetry to the scene.

Underwood and I were in the second hour of our strange vigil which, so far, had been uninterrupted. I sat near the window; my companion on a low chair at the farther end of the room, his elbows on his knees, his forehead resting on his hands; both of us silent and motionless. The room was unlighted, and both door and window were shut. The atmosphere was close and heavy, and at length, feeling suffocated, I rose and opened the long window, admitting a rush of chill, damp air.

I stood for a moment looking out at the wild night, and, as I glanced towards the bridge, I thought I distinguished a man's figure in the act of crossing it – a figure which, even at that distance, seemed familiar. And yet – what could bring Sir Philip to the place at this untimely hour? I was still straining my eyes through the shadows, when a movement of my companion made me turn hastily from the window. The moonlight showed me that he had risen, and stood grasping the back of his chair, gazing with a look of awe-struck expectation towards the door.

My heart began to throb with the same mysterious dread which I had experienced before. As I held my breath to listen, a faint rustling sound struck my ear, like the soft *'frou-frou'* of a woman's dress. It crossed the room from the door to the piano, passing close to me – so close, that I involuntarily drew back, thrilling in every nerve.

There was a pause, filled by wailing wind and rushing water, then – near to us, yet immeasurably distant, like a divine echo from another world, the solemn, spiritual voice arose.

This time both words and music were English, and there was a ring of passionate pain in its tone which brought the tears to my eyes as I listened.

All the anguish of a breaking heart seemed to find expression in 'The Song of Love and Death':

> Sweet is true love, tho' given in vain, in vain;
> And sweet is death, who puts an end to pain:
> I know not which is sweeter, no, not I.

In the interval after the first verse I caught the sound of footsteps approaching up the gravel walk, and presently a figure appeared at the window, darkly outlined against the moonlit background.

I had not been mistaken; it was Sir Philip. Underwood, whose head was turned towards the piano, did not notice the visitor, nor did the latter appear to perceive that the room was occupied. After a moment's hesitation, he pushed back the lace curtains and noiselessly entered – or was about to enter; but, in the very act of crossing the threshold, he stopped short and recoiled, for at the same moment the song was resumed:

> Love, art thou sweet? then bitter death must be:
> Love, thou art bitter? sweet is death to me.
> Oh Love, if death be sweeter –

There was a sudden break; a quick, short, gasping cry. Involuntarily I glanced towards the watcher at the window. He stood as if turned to stone, and his face, livid in the moonlight, looked like a mask of fear.

There was a silence of several moments – silence within and without, for the fitful wind was hushed. The voice sank to a broken, inarticulate murmur, and died away in a long, shuddering sigh. Then all was still. After a moment, Underwood passed his hand over his eyes, then turned to speak to me. But at the same instant he caught sight of Sir Philip, and, with a hoarse cry of mingled rage and triumph, sprang forwards to the window, and seized him by the throat.

'Villain! traitor! murderer!' he uttered, in a breathless tone of concentrated passion. 'I have spared you too long. By heaven, you shall not escape me now!'

Startled by the unexpected attack, Sir Philip staggered backwards and would have fallen, if he had not caught at one of the rustic pillars of the veranda. Recovering himself, however, he shook off his assailant, and casting a wild, panic-stricken glance around, darted across the lawn. The gardener hurried in pursuit, and I mechanically followed, feeling as if all the events of the night were part of a wild and troubled dream.

In spite of his lameness, Underwood gained on the other, and was close behind him when he reached the gate. Sir Philip quickened his pace and hurried over the bridge. But when half-way across it, his foot caught in one of the loose planks; he stumbled, put out his hand blindly in search of the missing rail, lost his balance, and fell headlong into the deepest part of the stream.

I uttered a cry of dismay, and dashed on to the bridge, where Underwood was standing, his dark hair disordered by the wind, staring blankly down at the spot where the baronet had disappeared.

The latter rose to the surface some yards below the bridge, struggling helplessly against the headstrong current. The moonlight gleamed for a moment on his white face, showing the look of terror and anguish imprinted on it – a look which haunts me still.

'Underwood!' he gasped. 'You can swim – help! save me.'

For all reply, the gardener deliberately folded his arms, looking down at him with a dreadful smile.

'Surely you will not let him drown before your eyes!' I exclaimed. 'Remember, vengeance is not yours. Save him —'

'Not if I could do it by lifting a finger' was his stern reply.

I said no more, perceiving that my words would have no more effect on him than the wind which was raving above our heads. I turned, and was hurrying away, in the faint hope of being able to give aid from the bank, when, without otherwise changing his position, he put out a hand and grasped my wrist, holding it as in a vice.

'Stay where you are,' he said, in a stern imperative undertone. 'It is just that he should perish – a life for a life!'

But even as the words passed his lips, his grasp suddenly relaxed; he dropped my wrist and stepped back a pace from me. Glancing at his face I saw in it a change so extraordinary that it arrested my attention even in the midst of my excitement.

He was gazing intently at something in the space between us; something which was visible to himself alone, for to me there seemed only air and moonlight. What did he see? What was it that brought that look of mingled awe and rapture to his dark face, transfiguring every feature? He gazed steadily for a moment, then bowed his head as if in assent.

'So be it, dear angel,' he whispered. 'I will do your bidding – if it is not too late.'

Without another word he threw off his coat and plunged into the stream. A few vigorous strokes brought him to the spot where the baronet had sunk for a second time. He dived, and presently reappeared supporting him with one muscular arm, while with the other he struck out for the bank. But his movements were impeded by Sir Philip, who clung to him with the convulsive energy of a drowning man.

'If you value your life, loose my arms! How can I swim, hampered like this?' I heard Underwood cry, as the swift current swept them on past a turn of the stream. I hurried along the bank, but it was some moments before I caught sight of them again. The gardener was still struggling in a desperate but ineffectual effort to shake off the frantic clasp which was dragging them both under water.

As I stood watching them with breathless anxiety, a passing cloud veiled the moon, and for a moment blotted out the scene. In that brief interval of darkness a wild despairing cry rose above the rushing of the river and the roaring of the wind. When the moon looked forth again they had sunk to rise no more.

The bodies of the two men, still closely locked together, were found, entangled in water-weeds, some yards lower down the stream. The account I gave of the accident was confirmed by the condition of the bridge, and my statement that Underwood had perished in endeavouring to save his master, caused a complete reversal of feeling towards the gardener, who having been shunned as a criminal during his life-time, was honoured as a hero after his death.

What brought Sir Philip to the cottage that night remained a mystery to all but myself. Immediately after the inquest I returned to town, feeling no inclination to remain in a place haunted by such terrible associations. I have never revisited Ranstone, nor until now have I ever disclosed what I know concerning the beautiful but ill-fated tenant of The Cedars.

Louisa Baldwin

SIR NIGEL OTTERBURNE'S CASE

Like Mary Penn, the work of Louisa Baldwin (1845–1925) – who usually wrote under the name Mrs Alfred Baldwin but was known to everyone as Louie – has for the most part been forgotten, and again it was the work of Richard Dalby who brought back the best of her weird tales in The Shadow on the Blind and Other Ghost Stories *in 2001. However, unlike Mary Penn, we know a considerable amount about Louisa Baldwin, because she was part of a remarkable family. Her maiden name was Louisa Macdonald. Her eldest sister Alice became the mother of Rudyard Kipling. Another sister, Georgiana, married the artist Edward Burne-Jones, whilst her elder sister Agnes, married another artist, Edward Poynter. Louisa herself became the mother of the future British Prime Minister Stanley Baldwin. These sisters became so closely associated with the Pre-Raphaelite painters and featured in so many of their works that they became known as the Pre-Raphaelite Sisterhood. There is a painting of Louisa by Edward Poynter dating from 1868 which shows a rather introspective, almost melancholy individual. This may be because for much of her young life she was a bedridden invalid enduring an unhappy marriage. Yet she survived and lived on until she was nearly eighty, outliving all but two of her brothers and sisters. Though she wrote several books, only one collection of her ghost stories appeared during her lifetime, the original edition of* The Shadow on the Blind, *published in 1895. The following, one of the best in the collection, shows the influence of the dead over the living.*

Sir Nigel Otterburne's Case

IT IS THIRTY years since I completed my career at the Eastminster Hospital. I had passed all my examinations successfully, and taken more than my share of medical honours, when one of our most celebrated physicians, Dr Grindrod, asked me to watch an important case for him, the study of which I should find of the deepest professional interest.

Dr Grindrod's patient was suffering from an obscure form of malaria, contracted abroad, which had developed into an extremely rare form of intermittent fever, with really beautiful complications, such as he had never met with before in all his wide practice. But Sir Nigel Otterburne lived a three hours' journey from town in Hampshire, and when the doctor went to see him it practically took a whole day of his valuable time, which was more than he could afford to devote to any one case. Dr Grindrod therefore proposed that he should see the patient himself once a week, and send down one of the most promising of the hospital students to watch the case under him, and to take minute medical notes of its progress.

I was the fortunate man selected for the work, and was to go into the country with Dr Grindrod, taking with us a couple of our most trustworthy nurses. I can never again feel as important as I did on that first day of August when I entered upon my onerous duty. The doctor and I were met at the station, and driven through lovely country to the Hammel, which was the name of Sir Nigel Otterburne's house. It was a fine specimen of Jacobean architecture, and, externally at least, had undergone but little change for a couple of centuries past. It was a three-storeyed building, with tall fluted chimneys, and dormer windows in its high-pitched roof. The front of the house was nine windows wide – narrow sash windows with a great deal of framework in proportion to the glass. The front of the house, with its wings to right and left, made three sides of a quadrangle, the fourth side of which was formed by wrought-iron railings, with great gates in the centre.

Leaving the carriage outside for fear of disturbing the patient by the sound of our arrival, we crossed the wide courtyard on foot. The front door was approached by shallow steps, and sheltered by a richly carved penthouse of black oak. Upon the wall between the second and third storeys was a sundial, and the bright August sunshine threw the sharply defined shadow of the gilded gnomon on the figure denoting the hour of four o'clock in the afternoon.

Above the dial a small turret rose from the centre of the roof surmounted by an elaborate piece of ironwork, with quaintly twisted letters N. S. E. and W., and a glittering arrow for a weather-vane.

I was struck by the appearance of the house, at once stately and homely. But I received from it an impression of melancholy which was not lessened when the door was opened by a grey-headed servant, who led us across the panelled hall into a vast and dreary dining-room. It contained nothing in the way of furniture except a long table with a row of high-backed chairs pushed close against it on either side, and a sideboard of carved oak, on which stood a row of silver flagons. A china bowl on the middle of the table, filled with roses and white lilies, made the atmosphere of the room heavy with their perfume. A few gloomy old portraits looked down from their tarnished frames, some with faces austere and rigid as though they had been painted after death.

Dr Grindrod had acquainted me with the details of Sir Nigel Otterburne's case on our journey, and, having nothing further to say till we had seen the patient, he stood with his hands behind his back, looking at the portrait of a lady over the mantelpiece, so lavish of her charms that I assigned her at a glance to Charles II's period.

'That is what I call a magnificent woman,' said the doctor, waving his hand sumptuously towards the expanse of bare neck and bosom depicted on the canvas. But I should have rather applied the words to the lady who entered the room while he was speaking and whom he introduced to me as Miss Otterburne. The doctor had told me that Sir Nigel Otterburne was a widower with an only daughter, but he had said nothing to prepare me for the appearance of so amazingly handsome a creature.

I have never met a woman who so completely fascinated and interested me at first sight. Miss Otterburne was not a girl. She was in the ripe beauty of womanhood, and with a most dignified and haughty carriage. She covered me with a glance of her beautiful dark eyes, and curtsied so low that it was almost a sarcasm to a young man like myself. She was tall and slender, of an ivory pallor of complexion, with fine sensitive features, and a mass of dark hair worn high on her head. She was dressed in some soft, cream-coloured fabric, and her sleeves came only to the elbow, displaying to the utmost advantage her beautifully formed hands and arms.

'I promised you, Miss Otterburne, that I would bring one of our hospital students to watch Sir Nigel's case for me,' said Dr Grindrod. 'You must not mistrust Mr Caxton because he is young. He has had experience in the hospital which many older men might envy. He will post to me daily notes of the patient's condition. I shall be down myself once a week, and you would telegraph for me in any emergency. Indeed, my dear young lady, I can assure you that Sir Nigel is in good hands,' and Dr Grindrod smiled, and attempted a light and easy manner.

But Miss Otterburne was entirely irresponsive. 'Heaven grant that you may be right,' she said in chilling tones, and she led us upstairs to the patient's room. As she walked erect before us, there was that in her bearing and appearance which reminded me of some distinguished Frenchwoman at the time of the Revolution, and I thought how many a proud head like hers had fallen from its white shoulders under the guillotine.

Sir Nigel's room was dark and dreary, and he lay in a funereal bed with heavy hangings, and I mentally vowed to have him out of it and in a more cheerful room within four-and-twenty hours. If the house did not contain some light, undraped bedstead, I would send to the hospital for one such as we use for our patients.

Sir Nigel Otterburne was in a half-comatose state when I first saw him, and I judged him to be about sixty-two or -three years of age. He was tall and thin, and looking at his face I saw at a glance whence Miss Otterburne derived her fine features. His hair and moustache were thick and grey, and he looked what he was, a soldier. In his lucid intervals there was a dignity and self-restraint in his manner which again reminded me of his daughter. The local practitioner, Mr Walton, was present in the room, a good-humoured, rustic-looking man, more like a farmer than a doctor, but who, if he was unprofessional in appearance, luckily for me had less than the usual amount of professional jealousy. So far from being annoyed at seeing me installed in the house to watch the case of his distinguished patient for Dr Grindrod, he expressed his approval of an arrangement that relieved him of so much responsibility. But he said nothing before Miss Otterburne, and I saw that she exercised the same repressive influence over him that I felt so strongly myself.

But when we were in the dining-room again, and I was receiving my final instructions from Dr Grindrod, Mr Walton said, as he poured himself out a glass of sherry: 'I don't profess that single-handed I could pull Sir Nigel round. I've not had the opportunity of studying malarious fevers. But if you gentlemen succeed in curing the patient, I share the glory of it, and if he slips through your fingers Miss Otterburne cannot reproach me, for nothing could be expected of me where Dr Grindrod failed.'

'Is Miss Otterburne likely to reproach you, if the case ends fatally?' I asked.

Mr Walton looked round to see if the door was shut, emptied another glass of wine before he spoke, and said in a low voice: 'Miss Otterburne is Miss Otterburne, and it would be unprofessional to gossip about any member of my patient's family. Eyes and ears open and mouth shut at the Hammel is my advice.'

After Dr Grindrod's departure I went upstairs to make arrangements for my first night in charge of Sir Nigel. A small room leading out of the patient's had been assigned to my use, and I went to the window to look at the view. My eyes never rested on a more peaceful scene. Immediately in front of the house, bounded on either side by its projecting wings, was the great courtyard, with its wide grass borders bathed in sunshine, and beyond the iron palisades and the high gates stretched an expanse of undulating country thickly wooded with trees in their heaviest summer foliage. On the brow of a gentle ascent, some quarter of a mile distant, stood a grey church with an ivy-grown tower, and the evening sunshine was glittering on the weather-vane.

When I had seen the night nurse enter upon her duties, I went for a stroll in the open air, leaving the house by a door at the back of the hall. I found myself in an old-fashioned garden with grass terraces and clipped yew hedges. I thought that I was alone in the garden, when suddenly I caught sight of Miss Otterburne's light dress, white and ghostly in the gathering gloom, and in a moment we were face to face in the path. I raised my hat and stood aside for her to pass, and I felt the blood mount to my cheeks. She might think that I was intruding on her privacy, and following her on her evening walk. Miss Otterburne did not quicken her pace as she passed me. She regarded me with grave intensity. But her eyes were void of speculation, like those of one who was walking in her sleep. I watched her stately figure recede amongst the darkening alleys, and heard the door close as she entered the house. I felt chilled and disconcerted, why I could not tell; but I would run no second risk of appearing to intrude upon Miss Otterburne.

At eleven o'clock Miss Otterburne entered her father's room to bid him goodnight. He scarcely knew her, yet I fancied that he smiled faintly as she pressed his hand, or it may have been the flickering of the lamplight on his face that I mistook for a smile.

'I trust Sir Nigel will have a tranquil night,' I said.

'His nights are always tranquil,' she replied in measured tones.

'And yet he has gained no strength the five weeks he has lain here.'

'He never will,' she said in the same passionless voice.

'You speak more positively, Miss Otterburne, than any doctor would dare to do. Such an illness as Sir Nigel's is not necessarily fatal. We do not know . . .'

'But I know,' and her voice sank to a whisper. 'It is useless your staying here. My father will never leave this house alive.'

'It is wrong to speak so,' I said firmly. 'And if Sir Nigel understands what you say, it must cause him the most exquisite pain.'

Not a line in her white handsome face softened or changed.

'My father knows it already,' she said, and swept from the room, leaving me bewildered by her manner.

I slept but little during my first night at the Hammel. My mind was so much occupied with Sir Nigel's case that I went frequently to see my patient and to note any change in his condition, however slight. My obstinacy, too, was roused by Miss Otterburne's assertion that her father would die, by the way in which she ignored anything that medical skill could do for him. Her manner was that of a person expressing a profoundly melancholy conclusion forced upon her against her will, and yet that she believed to be irrevocably true.

'If that man's sentence has not gone forth from heaven, he shall live,' I exclaimed, 'and that handsome, obstinate creature shall be taught that she is not infallible!'

My resolution being made, I tried to sleep, but tried in vain. The profound silence of the country after the roar of London had the same effect upon me that noise has upon those who are accustomed to quiet, and kept me wide awake. And from time to time I was startled by the screeching of owls, sounding like the cries of terrified children lost in the dark.

At length the dawn came, and I rose to go into Sir Nigel's room. This time he was conscious, and as I felt his pulse he whispered, 'Are they come?'

'Yes,' I replied, supposing that he alluded to me and the nurses. 'We came yesterday, and we shall try to relieve you as much as we can.'

But he sighed impatiently, closed his eyes, and turned his head from me. It was useless to lie down again, so I dressed myself, and the clock was striking four as I opened the window and leant out to enjoy the freshness of the morning air. To my great surprise, Miss

Otterburne also was looking out of her window in the centre of the right wing of the house. I drew back at once, but she had not heard me throw up the sash, and she was not looking in my direction. Her dark eyes were fixed in a trance-like gaze on the entrance to the courtyard, or on the church crowning the grassy slope. She certainly was not looking at any part of the house. She was ghastly pale, and her eyes wore the same unseeing expression that I had noticed in them on the previous evening.

For more than a quarter of an hour Miss Otterburne remained immovable, and how long she may have been at her casement before I saw her I cannot tell. She was wrapped in a white robe, and her dark hair lay in waves on her shoulders, but her face was not like that of a living woman. It seemed probable that I might have two patients in the house to look after. And I felt a distinct sense of relief when at length she withdrew from the window and I lost sight of her.

That day I carried out my intention with regard to Sir Nigel. We moved him into a small bed and carried him to a bright, cheerful sitting-room on the same floor – a room suggesting pleasant, sunny life as clearly as the gloomy bedroom had suggested death. I felt sure that the patient would appreciate the change, that it would prove beneficial to him. But to my disappointment, he did not appear to notice it, and it produced no effect on his physical condition. I heard him murmuring to himself as he lay, 'It will make no difference; it will make no difference.'

It was singular, too, that Miss Otterburne seemed to take no interest in her father's removal to more cheerful quarters. However, I had Dr Grindrod's approval of what I had done, and I was content.

'How do you get on with Miss Otterburne?' the doctor asked me abruptly on one of his visits, when I had been more than a week in the house.

'You might as well ask me how I get on with that picture on the wall,' I replied. 'But I think she is the handsomest woman I ever saw in my life.'

'You do, do you? H'm! Not my style; I prefer flesh and blood', and Dr Grindrod shot a glance in the direction of the Charles II lady, and fell to talking of purely medical matters.

When I had been in hourly attendance on Sir Nigel for a fortnight, I began to realize not only that my patient was making no progress but that I was making no progress with my patient. I expected no lively gratitude from him. But it would have been pleasant if there had been any token of recognition, either on his part or his daughter's, that I was doing my utmost for him. I imagine that he regarded me as a servant whose attentions were indispensable to his comfort but with whom he could not be familiar. It did not annoy me, sometimes it even amused me, for I never count a sick man in the category of sane persons, and should no more think myself insulted by an invalid than by a madman. This excuse, however, did not apply to Miss Otterburne, and I was puzzled more and more by her conduct.

Every morning at earliest dawn, if I looked out, she was leaning on her window-sill, gazing with a tragic melancholy, not I am sure at any tangible object, but on something that presented itself to her mental vision.

Not only did I gain no ground with Sir Nigel and his daughter, but the old housekeeper and butler, though perfectly civil to me, were both exceedingly reserved. Sometimes the housekeeper would have a short confab with me on her master's state, consisting on her part chiefly of sighs and head-shakings, and once the butler went so far as to observe, 'Master Raymond will wish that he'd parted friends with his father when he went to India!' So then Sir Nigel had a son, a fact of which I was not aware, and furthermore it would seem that father and son had had some quarrel or misunderstanding.

Meanwhile there was no disguising the unwelcome fact that my patient was steadily sinking. Dr Grindrod approved of all that I did in carrying out his instructions to the letter, but nothing we could do availed to check the downward course, and we racked our brains for treatment and remedies which should keep the enemy at bay. The disease was not running a normal course. Unexpected complications arose at an unusual period in its progress, and how interesting the battle between the force of disease and the power of science became to me none but an enthusiast in the medical profession can tell. I seldom quitted the patient's room. Only when he was sleeping did I venture to leave him for an hour in charge of a nurse while I went for a stroll in the fresh air.

It was just before sunset one evening, when I had been nearly a month at the Hammel, that I closed the front door gently behind me, and, crossing the courtyard, let myself out into the park and made my way towards the church on the grassy slope. I was exhausted and excited, and I walked bareheaded that the cool breeze might blow about my heated temples. I hated to be baffled. I had been so sure of victory, and now defeat stared me in the face. Miss Otterburne would have a melancholy triumph. She would be right after all, and I should be wrong. I went over every event of the previous weeks in detail. I was satisfied that all that medical science could do for Sir Nigel, at the point to which it had then attained, had been done and was still being done for him. But I reflected with a crushing sense of impotence on the irresistible power of the force with which I was contending. I, a finite being, was measuring my strength against death, the conqueror of man. The contest was hideously unequal. I was sure to be worsted. Even if the patient recovered, it would be at best but a reprieve, and sooner or later he must retrace his anguished steps towards that bourne from whence I was striving with all my strength to turn him back.

I entered the churchyard in the deepest depression of spirit. It was not merely the anticipated loss of my patient that weighed on me; that was but one item in the incalculable total of human misery. In his death I saw the doom of every son of Adam – the death of the whole human race. I was ready to wish that I had died myself before I had embraced a profession which constantly brought me face to face with a terrible elementary fact in nature, with which the utmost skill of man is powerless to cope.

The church door stood hospitably open, and I entered the cool twilight within. Here were tombs of the Otterburnes, from the time when intra-mural burial was a universal custom to the present period, when a memorial tablet or monument is all that is permitted within the church itself. I thought how soon Sir Nigel would be numbered amongst his ancestors, and be as remote from us who still lived as his own earliest forebears were from him now. Suddenly I heard a deep sigh, and, starting, I turned and saw Miss Otterburne close to me but almost hidden by a great pillar against which she leant. Her dark eyes were fixed with the wide unseeing gaze which I had noticed in them each early morning as she looked from her window. I spoke to her, and when she heard my voice the pupils of her eyes dilated as though the twilight had deepened round her.

'Miss Otterburne, if there is anything that you wish to say to Sir Nigel, I should advise you to take the opportunity of his next interval of consciousness. It grieves me to be obliged to say this, but I have no choice in the matter. I must tell you the truth.'

'Yes, they will soon come. I know it,' she said with a slight shudder.

I thought that she was wandering in her mind, and, taking no notice of her incoherent reply, I continued. 'I would give my life, Miss Otterburne, if I could prolong the life of one so dear to you.'

But she looked past and through me, as though she were piercing into futurity, and I heard her say: 'When they come you will know that I was right.'

And she glided like a ghost out of the dim church into the amber light of evening. Her manner disquieted me profoundly, and I wished that Miss Otterburne was not so lonely; that her brother in India was at home to take his share of the trouble, and to comfort his sister.

I hastened back to my patient's bedside, and, knowing that it would be impossible to leave him that night, I sat down to copy my notes of the case for my own private use.

About eleven o'clock Sir Nigel rallied slightly. I administered a powerful restorative, and sent the nurse to fetch Miss Otterburne at once. As she entered the room, I said: 'If you would like to be alone with your father, I will remain within call outside the door.'

She bowed her head in assent, and I left them together. I remained waiting in my own room, listening to Miss Otterburne's voice distinctly audible in low urgent tones. Then, as Sir Nigel again lapsed into unconsciousness, she spoke a little louder, and I heard her say: 'Father, will you not forgive Raymond?' and then all was silent. I re-entered the room, and Miss Otterburne was kneeling by her father's bedside. She had been weeping, and I saw that beneath the armour of pride and reserve there was a woman's tender heart. But my return was the signal for her to depart, and she left the room hastily, as though displeased that I had witnessed her emotion.

I looked at my dying patient with more regret than I should have thought possible to feel for a man who, in his short intervals of consciousness, had always treated me as a stranger. Certainly I had no affection for Sir Nigel, but I was struck by the pathos of the situation. There he lay, needing, like each one of us, both divine and human forgiveness, but unable to ask it for himself or to grant it to another, even when it was his daughter who knelt weeping by his side, imploring pardon for her brother.

Slowly the night passed, and slowly the patient died. I noted the decreasing temperature, the failing pulse, and I applied restoratives which formerly had power to rally him, though now they had lost their virtue. But the heart still beat, and now and then a sighing breath escaped his lips.

There was nothing more that I could do. But that I might leave no expedient untried, I sent the nurse into my room for an air cushion, which I told her to inflate and bring to me. If I raised the patient's head by means of it, it was possible that he might feel a momentary ease, though he would be unconscious of its cause.

I looked at my watch. It was four o'clock, and the grey light of dawn glimmered through the curtains. I wondered whether Miss Otterburne was at her window, according to her strange custom, when the door opened swiftly and silently, and she entered the room as I had often seen her at that hour, clad in a loose white robe, and her dark hair hanging about her shoulders. There was mortal pallor on her face. She did not cast a glance in the direction of her dying father, but, exclaiming in tones that chilled my blood, 'They have come, they have come!' She went to the window, drew back the curtains, let in the cold light of dawn, and stood with clasped hands gazing into the courtyard below. I was by her side in an instant.

'They have come, they have come. I knew they would come!' And I heard the effort she made to speak with a tongue that was dry with terror. In the courtyard beneath, directly opposite to the window, was a strange, silent crowd of men, women, and children, looking up at us in the faint morning light with faces of the dead. And though they pressed and thronged each other on the gravel path, not a sound was heard.

I am not a superstitious man, and in those days my nerves were of iron. But I reeled as I stood, and the blood rushed to my head with a singing sound. I saw the dead of centuries ago, and the dead of yesterday, grey-bearded men who fought in the civil wars, young men and maidens who never were contemporaries in this life, and little children, all gazing at us with upturned faces. Miss Otterburne spoke again as one speaks in nightmare, with deadly effort and oppression.

'I know them. I saw them when they came to fetch my grandfather, and when they fetched my mother. Oh, Mother! Mother! You are there!' And she leant forward in an agony, and gazed with set and rigid face at a slim form that drifted through the ghostly throng and lifted its sad eyes to hers. By her side stood a tall man in uniform, whose white face I shall never forget, and he solemnly waved his hand towards us. 'Oh Heaven! my brother Raymond is with them!' shrieked Miss Otterburne, and sank on the floor insensible, at the moment that Sir Nigel gave his last groan. I hastily fetched a cushion and placed it under her head, and then turned once more to the window. But the courtyard was absolutely empty, nor was there a trace of its recent occupation. I could not have been absent from the window a couple of minutes, and the instantaneous disappearance of the ghastly throng shook my nerves fully as much as the sight of it had done. There was not a mark on the untrodden dewy grass. Not a pebble displaced on the broad gravel path that had been so crowded a moment before. On the spot where the tall figure had stood and waved its hand to us a cat was seated, licking her paws, and I heard the fitful chirp of the first awakened birds.

I felt physically ill, and turning from the window I poured out and drank a powerful cordial that restored an artificial calmness to my nerves. Just then the nurse returned. She had not been absent from the room more than five minutes.

'The patient is dead, and Miss Otterburne has fainted,' I said. 'Help me to lay her on the couch.'

I have never in all my experience seen any one in so deep a swoon. The nurse and I were unspeakably relieved when at length she showed signs of returning consciousness, though I dreaded what she might say when she recovered. I gave her a composing draught which would secure her some hours' rest, and committed her to the care of her maid.

I sent at once for the family doctor, who had seen Sir Nigel on the previous night, to acquaint him with the death of the patient. He was exceedingly inquisitive about every possible detail, and appeared to long for information concerning something he dared not enquire about directly.

'Were there any circumstances of an unusual character attending the death?' he asked anxiously.

'It was the ordinary termination of such an illness as Sir Nigel's,' I replied guardedly.

'And Miss Otterburne, how did she bear the shock?'

'She had a severe fainting fit, and remained insensible for fully half an hour. She appears to feel her loss acutely.'

Mr Walton agreed with me that I had better remain in the house till the following day, to make the necessary arrangements for the funeral, and to write to Miss Otterburne's relations, with whose names and addresses the butler supplied me, to prevent his mistress from being disturbed. The old man became almost talkative for so taciturn a person.

'The family has died and died till yonder churchyard is full of them,' he said. 'The very soil of it was once Otterburne flesh and blood, and there's no one left of this branch but Miss Otterburne and the Major in India, that's now Sir Raymond. There's a few cousins up in the north, and a widowed sister of the master's, and they'll like to come for the funeral, if it's only to see where they'll be laid themselves when their time comes, for all the Otterburnes are brought here to be buried.'

'Will one of the ladies of the family stay with Miss Otterburne till her brother returns from India?' I said, and as it was the first question I had asked the old man cast a suspicious glance at me, resumed his uncommunicative manner, and changed the subject of conversation. By noon I had sent the nurses back to London. Then there remained the long afternoon and evening in which to collect my distracted thoughts and to get my nerves into something like order for a return to the active duties of life. I could not for an instant forget the horror of that early dawn. I saw, as clearly as I now see the pen with which I am writing this narrative, the ghostly throng with upturned, dead faces gazing at us, and Miss Otterburne's words and cry still rang in my ears. Whatever the ghostly vision was, we had both of us seen it. If only one person had seen it, and that one myself, I should not have been convinced of its reality. I should have believed that I was subjected to some terrible hallucination. But we both saw it at the same moment. And Miss Otterburne had seen it twice before, and each time under the same ghastly circumstances. There was no doubt that it had been as visible to us as natural objects are. It was no picture conjured up separately in our brains.

I confess that I was so unnerved I could not look out of that window again, nor could I spend my last night at the Hammel in any room at the front of the house. I asked the housekeeper to give me a bed in one of the back rooms. She cast a peculiar glance at me and said: 'You don't care for a room that looks out into the court-yard, and I don't blame you for it. But you need not mind it now, sir; they won't come again till – till they are sent.'

I made frequent enquiries during the day about Miss Otterburne. But I did not ask to see her, so fearful was I of the effect my presence might have in recalling the horror we had witnessed together. The last thing at night I sent a message to her saying that I should return to town in the morning, and I hoped that she would send for me if I could be of the slightest service to her. But she did not require me, and I retired for the night to a small back room on the second floor. Sleep was out of the question. I did not undress, but sat smoking pipe after pipe and trying to read, till when the grey dawn came a great terror took possession of me, and I shook like a man in a fit of ague. I scorned myself for my weakness. But the feeling was beyond my own control.

At length, when daylight flooded the room, I threw myself across the bed and fell into a deep sleep which must have lasted for hours, and from which I was awakened by loud knocking at the door. 'Who is there?' I said, starting to my feet, and the knock was again repeated. I ran to the door and opened it.

The old butler stood before me pale and trembling. 'Miss Otterburne wishes to see you, sir, in her sitting-room.'

'Tell her I will be with her directly,' and I hastened to make myself fit to enter the presence of a lady, and went downstairs to Miss Otterburne's room, where her maid stood waiting for me with a scared face. She said nothing, but opened the door of her mistress's room. I entered, and she closed it after me.

Miss Otterburne was standing by the table with an open letter in her hand. I should not have known her. Her hair had turned white in the last twenty-four hours, and there was a strange glitter in her eye. She handed me the letter, saying: 'It was Raymond that we saw with them. I knew it.'

I read the letter. It was very short. A few lines written in haste by a friend of the Major's to Sir Nigel, telling him of the death of his son, of cholera at Meerut a month ago, and promising all particulars by the next mail. As my mind took in the meaning of it I grew giddy. The room became suddenly dark to me, and I groped for a chair like a blind man. Miss Otterburne laughed, the cackling laugh of insanity, and it recalled me to myself in an instant through extremity of compassion for her.

'Why do you pretend to be surprised? You knew that Raymond was dead as well as I; we both saw him. Oh, he was merry! They were all a merry company; why should we be sad?' and the poor lady laughed in such an awful fashion I could have shed tears of blood to listen to her.

It was the last time that I saw Miss Otterburne. Twenty long years she continued to live at the Hammel in a state of hopeless insanity, dangerous neither to herself nor to others while she was allowed to remain there. But if any attempt was made to take her elsewhere, her frenzy became ungovernable. 'They would not know where to find me,' she would say. 'They can only fetch me from here, and I want the merry, white-faced folk to come for me', and her anger would subside into dreadful laughter.

Every day in the early dawn she rose to look out of her window into the courtyard. But one morning she failed to do so, and her attendant was thankful to find Miss Otterburne lying peacefully dead, on the twentieth anniversary of her father's death.

Mary Wilkins Freeman
LUELLA MILLER

Mary Eleanor Wilkins (1852–1930), who became Mary Wilkins Freeman after her marriage in 1902, is regarded as one of the best of the American writers of regional fiction and arguably the best of the New England writers (of which there were a remarkable number) of ghost stories. She was for many years private secretary to the physician, poet and writer Oliver Wendell Holmes. Her regional stories include several that hint at witchcraft, but the majority of her genuinely supernatural stories were written during the 1890s and early 1900s. Some are scattered through several books, but only one volume was entirely devoted to the ghost story, The Wind in the Rose Bush *(1903). Her* Collected Ghost Stories *was published in 1974, but a complete volume has yet to be assembled.*

Luella Miller

CLOSE TO THE village street stood the one-storey house in which Luella Miller, who had an evil name in the village, had dwelt. She had been dead for years, yet there were those in the village who, in spite of the clearer light which comes on a vantage-point from a long-past danger, half believed in the tale which they had heard from their childhood. In their hearts, though they scarcely would have owned it, was a survival of the wild horror and frenzied fear of their ancestors who had dwelt in the same age with Luella Miller. Young people even would stare with a shudder at the old house as they passed, and children never played around it as was their wont around an untenanted building. Not a window in the old Miller house was broken: the panes reflected the morning sunlight in patches of emerald and blue, and the latch of the sagging front door was never lifted, though no bolt secured it. Since Luella Miller had been carried out of it, the house had had no tenant except one friendless old soul who had no choice between that and the far-off shelter of the open sky. This old woman, who had survived her kindred and friends, lived in the house one week, then one morning no smoke came out of the chimney, and a body of neighbours, a score strong, entered and found her dead in her bed. There were dark whispers as to the cause of her death, and there were those who testified to an expression of fear so exalted that it showed forth the state of the departing soul upon the dead face. The old woman had been hale and hearty when she entered the house, and in seven days she was dead; it seemed that she had fallen a victim to some uncanny power. The minister talked in the pulpit with covert severity against the sin of superstition; still the belief prevailed. Not a soul in the village but would have chosen the almshouse rather than that dwelling. No vagrant, if he heard the tale, would seek shelter beneath that old roof, unhallowed by nearly half a century of superstitious fear.

There was only one person in the village who had actually known Luella Miller. That person was a woman well over eighty, but a marvel of vitality and unextinct youth. Straight as an arrow, with the spring of one recently let loose from the bow of life, she moved about the streets, and she always went to church, rain or shine. She had never married, and had lived alone for years in a house across the road from Luella Miller's.

This woman had none of the garrulousness of age, but never in all her life had she ever held her tongue for any will save her own, and she never spared the truth when she essayed to present it. She it was who bore testimony to the life, evil, though possibly wittingly or designedly so, of Luella Miller, and to her personal appearance. When this old woman spoke – and she had the gift of description, though her thoughts were clothed in the rude vernacular of her native village – one could seem to see Luella Miller as she had really looked. According to this woman, Lydia Anderson by name, Luella Miller had been a beauty of a type rather unusual in New England. She had been a slight, pliant sort of creature, as ready with a strong yielding to fate and as unbreakable as a willow. She had glimmering lengths of straight, fair hair, which she wore softly looped round a long, lovely face. She had blue eyes full of soft pleading, little slender, clinging hands, and a wonderful grace of motion and attitude.

'Luella Miller used to sit in a way nobody else could if they sat up and studied a week of Sundays,' said Lydia Anderson, 'and it was a sight to see her walk. If one of them willows over there on the edge of the brook could start up and get its roots free of the ground, and move off, it would go just the way Luella Miller used to. She had a green shot silk she used to wear, too, and a hat with green ribbon streamers, and a lace veil blowing across her face and out sideways, and a green ribbon flyin' from her waist. That was what she came out bride in when she married Erastus Miller. Her name before she was married was Hill. There was always a sight of "l"s' in her name, married or single. Erastus Miller was good-lookin', too, better lookin' than Luella. Sometimes I used to think that Luella wa'n't so handsome after all. Erastus just about worshipped her. I used to know him pretty well. He lived next door to me, and we went to school together. Folks used to say he was waitin' on me, but he wa'n't. I never thought he was except once or twice when he said things that some girls might have suspected meant somethin'. That was before Luella came here to teach the district school. It was funny how she came to get it, for folks said she hadn't any edu-cation, and that one of the big girls, Lottie Henderson, used to do all the teachin' for her, while she sat back and did embroidery work on a cambric pocket-handkerchief. Lottie Henderson was a real smart girl, a splendid scholar, and she just set her eyes by Luella, as all the girls did. Lottie would have made a real smart woman, but she died when Luella had been here about a year – just faded away and died: nobody knew what ailed her. She dragged herself to that schoolhouse and helped Luella teach till the very last minute. The committee all knew how Luella didn't do much of the work herself, but they winked at it. It wa'n't long after Lottie died that Erastus married her. I always thought he hurried it up because she wa'n't fit to teach. One of the big boys used to help her after Lottie died, but he hadn't much government, and the school didn't do very well, and Luella might have had to give it up, for the committee couldn't have shut their eyes to things much longer. The boy that helped her was a real honest, innocent sort of fellow, and he was a good scholar, too. Folks said he overstudied, and that was the reason he took crazy the year after Luella married, but I don't know. And I don't know what made Erastus Miller go into consumption of the blood the year after he was married: consumption wa'n't in his family. He just grew weaker and weaker, and went almost bent double when he tried to wait on Luella, and he spoke feeble, like an old man. He worked terrible hard till the last trying to save up a little to leave Luella. I've seen him out in the worst storms on a wood-sled – he used to cut and sell wood – and he was hunched up on top lookin' more dead than alive. Once I couldn't stand it: I went over and helped him pitch some wood on the cart – I was always strong in my arms. I wouldn't stop for all he told me to, and I guess he was glad enough for the help. That was only a week before he died. He fell on the kitchen floor while he was gettin' breakfast. He always got the breakfast and let Luella lay abed. He did all the sweepin' and the washin' and the ironin' and most of the cookin'. He couldn't bear to have Luella lift her finger, and she let him do for her. She lived like a queen for all the work she did. She didn't even do her sewin'. She said it made her shoulder ache to sew, and poor Erastus's sister Lily used to do all her sewin'. She wa'n't able to, either; she was never strong in her back, but she did it beautifully. She had to, to suit Luella, she was so dreadful particular. I never saw anythin' like the fagottin' and hem-stitchin' that Lily Miller did for Luella. She made all Luella's weddin' outfit, and that green silk dress, after Maria Babbit cut it. Maria she cut it for nothin', and she did a lot more cuttin' and fittin' for nothin' for Luella, too. Lily Miller went to live with Luella after Erastus died. She gave up her home, though she was real attached to it and wa'n't a mite afraid to stay alone. She rented it and she went to live with Luella right away after the funeral.'

Then this old woman, Lydia Anderson, who remembered Luella Miller, would go on to relate the story of Lily Miller. It seemed that on the removal of Lily Miller to the house of her dead brother, to live with his widow, the village people first began to talk. This Lily Miller had been hardly past her first youth, and a most robust and blooming woman, rosy-cheeked, with curls of strong, black hair overshadowing round, candid temples and bright dark eyes. It was not six months after she had taken up her residence with her sister-in-law that her rosy colour faded and her pretty curves became wan hollows. White shadows began to show in the black rings of her hair, and the light died out of her eyes, her features sharpened, and there were pathetic lines at her mouth, which yet wore always an expression of utter sweetness and even happiness. She was devoted to her sister; there was no doubt that she loved her with her whole heart, and was perfectly content in her service. It was her sole anxiety lest she should die and leave her alone.

'The way Lily Miller used to talk about Luella was enough to make you mad and enough to make you cry,' said Lydia Anderson. 'I've been in there sometimes toward the last when she was too feeble to cook and carried her some blanc-mange or custard – somethin' I thought she might relish, and she'd thank me, and when I asked her how she was, say she felt better than she did yesterday, and asked me if I didn't think she looked better, dreadful pitiful, and say poor Luella had an awful time takin' care of her and doin' the work – she wa'n't strong enough to do anythin' – when all the time Luella wa'n't liftin' her finger and poor Lily didn't get any care except what the neighbours gave her, and Luella eat up everythin' that was carried in for Lily. I had it real straight that she did. Luella used to just sit and cry and do nothin'. She did act real fond of Lily, and she pined away considerable, too. There was those that thought she'd go into a decline herself. But after Lily died, her Aunt, Abby Mixter came, and then Luella picked up and grew as fat and rosy as ever. But poor Aunt Abby begun to droop just the way Lily had, and I guess somebody wrote to her married daughter, Mrs Sam Abbot, who lived in Barre, for she wrote her mother that she must leave right away and come and make her a visit, but Aunt Abby wouldn't go. I can see her now. She was a real good-lookin' woman, tall and large, with a big, square face and a high forehead that looked of itself kind of benevolent and good. She just tended out on Luella as if she had been a baby, and when her married daughter sent for her she wouldn't stir one inch. She'd always thought a lot of her daughter, too, but she said Luella needed her and her married daughter didn't. Her daughter kept writin' and writin', but it didn't do any good. Finally she came, and when she saw how bad her mother looked, she broke down and cried and all but went on her knees to have her come away. She spoke her mind out to Luella, too. She told her that she'd killed her husband and everybody that had anythin' to do with her, and she'd thank her to leave her mother alone. Luella went into hysterics, and Aunt Abby was so frightened that she called me after her daughter went. Mrs Sam Abbot she went away fairly cryin' out loud in the buggy, the neighbours heard her, and well she might, for she never saw her mother again alive. I went in that night when Aunt Abby called for me, standin' in the door with her little green-checked shawl over her head. I can see her now. 'Do come over here, Miss Anderson,' she sung out, kind of gaspin' for breath. I didn't stop for anythin'. I put over as fast as I could, and when I got there, there was Luella laughin' and cryin' all together, and Aunt Abby trying to hush her, and all the time she herself was white as a sheet and shakin' so she could hardly stand. "For the land sakes, Mrs Mixter," says I, "you look worse than she does. You ain't fit to be up out of your bed."

' "Oh, there ain't anythin' the matter with me," says she. Then she went on talkin' to Luella. "There, there, don't, don't, poor little lamb," says she. "Aunt Abby is here. She ain't goin' away and leave you. Don't, poor little lamb."

' "Do leave her with me, Mrs Mixter, and you get back to bed," says I, for Aunt Abby had been layin' down considerable lately, though somehow she contrived to do the work.

' "I'm well enough," says she. "Don't you think she had better have the doctor, Miss Anderson?"

' "The doctor," says I. "I think _you_ had better have the doctor. I think you need him much worse than some folks I could mention." And I looked right straight at Luella Miller laughin' and cryin' and goin' on as if she was the centre of all creation. All the time she was actin' so – seemed as if she was too sick to sense anythin' – she was keepin' a sharp lookout as to how we took it out of the corner of one eye. I see her. You could never cheat me about Luella Miller. Finally I got real mad and I run home and I got a bottle of valerian I had, and I poured some boilin' hot water on a handful of catnip, and I mixed up that catnip tea with most half a wineglass of valerian, and I went with it over to Luella's. I marched right up to Luella, a-holdin' out of that cup, all smokin'. "Now," says I, "Luella Miller, _you swaller this!_"

' "What is – what is it, oh, what is it?" she sort, of screeches out. Then she goes off a-laughin' enough to kill.

' "Poor lamb, poor little lamb," says Aunt Abby, standin' over her, all kind of tottery, and tryin' to bathe her head with camphor.

' "*You swaller this right down*," says I. And I didn't waste any cere-mony. I just took hold of Luella Miller's chin and I tipped her head back, and I caught her mouth open with laughin', and I clapped that cup to her lips, and I fairly hollered at her: "Swaller, swaller, swaller!" and she gulped it right down. She had to, and I guess it did her good. Anyhow, she stopped cryin' and laughin' and let me put her to bed, and she went to sleep like a baby inside of half an hour. That was more than poor Aunt Abby did. She lay awake all that night and I stayed with her, though she tried not to have me; said she wa'n't sick enough for watchers. But I stayed, and I made some good cornmeal gruel and I fed her a teaspoon every little while all night long. It seemed to me as if she was jest dyin' from bein' all wore out. In the mornin' as soon as it was light I run over to the Bisbees and sent Johnny Bisbee for the doctor. I told him to tell the doctor to hurry, and he come pretty quick. Poor Aunt Abby didn't seem to know much of anythin' when he got there. You couldn't hardly tell she breathed, she was so used up. When the doctor had gone, Luella came into the room lookin' like a baby in her ruffled nightgown. I can see her now. Her eyes were as blue and her face all pink and white like a blossom, and she looked at Aunt Abby in the bed sort of innocent and surprised. "Why," says she, "Aunt Abby"ain't got up yet?'

' "No, she ain't," says I, pretty short.

' "I thought I didn't smell the coffee," says Luella.

' "Coffee," says I. "I guess if you have coffee this mornin' you'll make it yourself."

' "I never made the coffee in all my life," says she, dreadful aston-ished. "Erastus always made the coffee as long as he lived, and then Lily she made it, and then Aunt Abby made it. I don't believe I can make the coffee, Miss Anderson."

' "You can make it or go without, jest as you please," says I.

' "Ain't Aunt Abby goin' to get up?" says she.

' "I guess she won't get up," says I, "sick as she is." I was gettin' madder and madder. There was somethin' about that little pink-and-white thing standin' there and talkin' about coffee, when she had killed so many better folks than she was, and had jest killed another, that made me feel 'most as if I wished somebody would up and kill her before she had a chance to do any more harm.

' "Is Aunt Abby sick?" says Luella, as if she was sort of aggrieved and injured.

' "Yes," says I, "she's sick, and she's goin' to die, and then you'll be left alone, and you'll have to do for yourself and wait on yourself, or do without things." I don't know but I was sort of hard, but it was the truth, and if I was any harder than Luella Miller had been I'll give up. I ain't never been sorry that I said it. Well, Luella, she up and had hysterics again at that, and I jest let her have 'em. All I did was to bundle her into the room on the other side of the entry where Aunt Abby couldn't hear her, if she wa'n't past it – I don't know but she was – and set her down hard in a chair and told her not to come back into the other room, and she minded. She had her hysterics in there till she got tired. When she found out that nobody was comin' to coddle her and do for her she stopped. At least I suppose she did. I had all I could do with poor Aunt Abby tryin' to keep the breath of life in her. The doctor had told me that she was dreadful low, and give me some very strong medicine to give to her in drops real often, and told me real particular about the nourishment. Well, I did as he told me real faithful till she wa'n't able to swaller any longer. Then I had her daughter sent for. I had begun to realize that she wouldn't last any time at all. I hadn't realized it before, though I spoke to Luella the way I did. The doctor he came, and Mrs Sam Abbot, but when she got there it was too late; her mother was dead. Aunt Abby's daughter just give one look at her mother layin' there, then she turned sort of sharp and sudden and looked at me.

' "Where is she?" says she, and I knew she meant Luella.

' "She's out in the kitchen," says I. "She's too nervous to see folks die. She's afraid it will make her sick."

'The Doctor he speaks up then. He was a young man. Old Doctor Park had died the year before, and this was a young fellow just out of college. "Mrs Miller is not strong," says he, kind of severe, "and she is quite right in not agitating herself."

'You are another, young man; she's got her pretty claw on you, thinks I, but I didn't say anythin' to him. I just said over to Mrs Sam Abbot that Luella was in the kitchen, and Mrs Sam Abbot she went out there, and I went, too, and I never heard anythin' like the way she talked to Luella Miller. I felt pretty hard to Luella myself, but this was more than I ever would have dared to say. Luella she was too scared to go into hysterics. She jest flopped. She seemed to jest shrink away to nothin' in that kitchen chair, with Mrs Sam Abbot standin' over her and talkin' and tellin' her the truth. I guess the truth was most too much for her and no mistake, because Luella presently actually did faint away, and there wa'n't any sham about it, the way I always suspected there was about them hysterics. She fainted dead away and we had to lay her flat on the floor, and the Doctor he came runnin' out and he said somethin' about a weak heart dreadful fierce to Mrs Sam Abbot, but she wa'n't a mite scared. She faced him jest as white as even Luella was layin' there lookin' like death and the Doctor feelin' of her pulse.

"Weak heart," says she, "weak heart; weak fiddlesticks! There ain't nothin' weak about that woman. She's got strength enough to hang on to other folks till she kills 'em. Weak? It was my poor mother that was weak: this woman killed her as sure as if she had taken a knife to her."

'But the Doctor he didn't pay much attention. He was bendin' over Luella layin' there with her yellow hair all streamin' and her pretty pink-and-white face all pale, and her blue eyes like stars gone out, and he was holdin' on to her hand and smoothin' her forehead, and tellin' me to get the brandy in Aunt Abby's room, and I was sure as I wanted to be that Luella had got somebody else to hang on to, now Aunt Abby was gone, and I thought of poor Erastus Miller, and I sort of pitied the poor young Doctor, led away by a pretty face, and I made up my mind I'd see what I could do.

'I waited till Aunt Abby had been dead and buried about a month, and the Doctor was goin' to see Luella steady and folks were beginnin' to talk; then one evenin', when I knew the Doctor had been called out of town and wouldn't be round, I went over to Luella's. I found her all dressed up in a blue muslin with white polka dots on it, and her hair curled jest as pretty, and there wa'n't a young girl in the place could compare with her. There was somethin' about Luella Miller seemed to draw the heart right out of you, but she didn't draw it out of *me*. She was settin' rocking in the chair by her sittin'-room window, and Maria Brown had gone home. Maria Brown had been in to help her, or rather to do the work, for Luella wa'n't helped when she didn't do anythin'. Maria Brown was real capable and she didn't have any ties; she wa'n't married, and lived alone, so she'd offered. I couldn't see why she should do the work any more than Luella; she wa'n't any too strong; but she seemed to think she could and Luella seemed to think so, too, so she went over and did all the work – washed, and ironed, and baked, while Luella sat and rocked. Maria didn't live long afterward. She began to fade away just the same fashion the others had. Well, she was warned, but she acted real mad when folks said anythin': said Luella was a poor, abused woman, too delicate to help herself, and they'd ought to be ashamed, and if she died helpin' them that couldn't help themselves she would – and she did.

'"I s'pose Maria has gone home," says I to Luella, when I had gone in and sat down opposite her.

'"Yes, Maria went half an hour ago, after she had got supper and washed the dishes," says Luella, in her pretty way.

'"I suppose she has got a lot of work to do in her own house to-night," says I, kind of bitter, but that was all thrown away on Luella Miller. It seemed to her right that other folks that wa'n't any better able than she was herself should wait on her, and she couldn't get it through her head that anybody should think it *wa'n't* right.

'"Yes," says Luella, real sweet and pretty, "yes, she said she had to do her washin' to-night. She has let it go for a fortnight along of comin' over here."

' "Why don't she stay home and do her washin' instead of comin' over here and doin' *your* work, when you are just as well able, and enough sight more so, than she is to do it?" says I.

'Then Luella she looked at me like a baby who has a rattle shook at it. She sort of laughed as innocent as you please. "Oh, I can't do the work myself, Miss Anderson," says she. "I never did. Maria *has* to do it."

'Then I spoke out: "Has to do it!" says I. "Has to do it! She don't have to do it, either. Maria Brown has her own home and enough to live on. She ain't beholden to you to come over here and slave for you and kill herself."

'Luella she jest set and stared at me for all the world like a doll-baby that was so abused that it was comin' to life.

' "Yes," says I, "she's killin' herself. She's goin' to die just the way Erastus did, and Lily, and your Aunt Abby. You're killin' her jest as you did them. I don't know what there is about you, but you seem to bring a curse," says I. "You kill everybody that is fool enough to care anythin' about you and do for you."

'She stared at me and she was pretty pale.

' "And Maria ain't the only one you're goin' to kill," says I. "You're goin' to kill Doctor Malcom before you're done with him."

'Then a red colour came flamin' all over her face. "I ain't goin' to kill him, either," says she, and she begun to cry.

' "Yes, you *be!*" says I. Then I spoke as I had never spoke before. You see, I felt it on account of Erastus. I told her that she hadn't any business to think of another man after she'd been married to one that had died for her: that she was a dreadful woman; and she was, that's true enough, but sometimes I have wondered lately if she knew it – if she wa'n't like a baby with scissors in its hand cuttin' everybody without knowin' what it was doin'.

'Luella she kept gettin' paler and paler, and she never took her eyes off my face. There was somethin' awful about the way she looked at me and never spoke one word. After a while I quit talkin' and I went home. I watched that night, but her lamp went out before nine o'clock, and when Doctor Malcom came drivin' past and sort of slowed up he see there wa'n't any light and he drove along. I saw her sort of shy out of meetin' the next Sunday, too, so he shouldn't go home with her, and I begun to think mebbe she did have some conscience after all. It was only a week after that that Maria Brown died – sort of sudden at the last, though everybody had seen it was comin'. Well, then there was a good deal of feelin' and pretty dark whispers. Folks said the days of witchcraft had come again, and they were pretty shy of Luella. She acted sort of offish to the Doctor and he didn't go there, and there wa'n't anybody to do anythin' for her. I don't know how she *did* get along. I wouldn't go in there and offer to help her – not because I was afraid of dyin' like the rest, but I thought she was just as well able to do her own work as I was to do it for her, and I thought it was about time that she did it and stopped killin' other folks. But it wa'n't very long before folks began to say that Luella herself was goin' into a decline jest the way her husband, and Lily, and Aunt Abby and the others had, and I saw myself that she looked pretty bad. I used to see her goin' past from the store with a bundle as if she could hardly crawl, but I remembered how Erastus used to wait and 'tend when he couldn't hardly put one foot before the other, and I didn't go out to help her. But at last one afternoon I saw the Doctor come drivin' up like mad with his medicine chest, and Mrs Babbit came in after supper and said that Luella was real sick.

' "I'd offer to go in and nurse her," says she, "but I've got my children to consider and mebbe it ain't true what, they say, but it's queer how many folks that have done for her have died."

'I didn't say anythin', but I considered how she had been Erastus's wife and how he had set his eyes by her, and I made up my mind to go in the next mornin', unless she was better, and see what I could do; but the next mornin' I see her at the window, and pretty soon she came steppin' out as spry as you please, and a little while afterward Mrs Babbit came in and told me that the Doctor had got a girl from out of town, a Sarah Jones, to come there, and she said she was pretty sure that the Doctor was goin' to marry Luella.

'I saw him kiss her in the door that night myself, and I knew it was true. The woman came that afternoon, and the way she flew around was a caution. I don't believe Luella had swept since Maria died. She swept and dusted, and washed and ironed; wet clothes and dusters and carpets were flyin' over there all day, and every time Luella set her foot out when the Doctor wa'n't there, there was that Sarah Jones helpin' of her up and down the steps, as if she hadn't learnt to walk.

'Well, everybody knew that Luella and the Doctor were goin' to be married, but it wa'n't long before they began to talk about his lookin' so poorly, jest as they had about the others; and they talked about Sarah Jones, too.

'Well, the Doctor did die, and he wanted to be married first, so as to leave what little he had to Luella, but he died before the minister could get there, and Sarah Jones died a week afterward.

'Well, that wound up everything for Luella Miller. Not another soul in the whole town would lift a finger for her. There got to be a sort of panic. Then she began to droop in good earnest. She used to have to go to the store herself, for Mrs Babbit was afraid to let Tommy go for her, and I've seen her goin' past and stoppin' every two or three steps to rest. Well, I stood it as long as I could, but one day I see her comin' with her arms full and stoppin' to lean against the Babbit fence, and I run out and took her bundles and carried them to her house. Then I went home and never spoke one word to her though she called after me dreadful kind of pitiful. Well, that night I was taken sick with a chill, and I was sick as I wanted to be for two weeks. Mrs Babbit had seen me run out to help Luella and she came in and told me I was goin' to die on account of it. I didn't know whether I was or not, but I considered I had done right by Erastus's wife.

'That last two weeks Luella she had a dreadful hard time, I guess. She was pretty sick, and as near as I could make out nobody dared go near her. I don't know as she was really needin' anythin' very much, for there was enough to eat in her house and it was warm weather, and she made out to cook a little flour gruel every day, I know, but I guess she had a hard time, she that had been so petted and done for all her life.

'When I got so I could go out, I went over there one morning. Mrs Babbit had just come in to say she hadn't seen any smoke and she didn't know but it was somebody's duty to go in, but she couldn't help thinkin' of her children, and I got right up, though I hadn't been out of the house for two weeks, and I went in there, and Luella she was layin' on the bed, and she was dyin'.

'She lasted all that day and into the night. But I sat there after the new doctor had gone away. Nobody else dared to go there. It was about midnight that I left her for a minute to run home and get some medicine I had been takin', for I begun to feel rather bad.

'It was a full moon that night, and just as I started out of my door to cross the street back to Luella's, I stopped short, for I saw something.'

Lydia Anderson at this juncture always said with a certain defiance that she did not expect to be believed, and then proceeded in a hushed voice:

'I saw what I saw, and I know I saw it, and I will swear on my death bed that. I saw it. I saw Luella Miller and Erastus Miller, and Lily, and Aunt Abby, and Maria, and the Doctor, and Sarah, all goin' out of her door, and all but Luella shone white in the moonlight, and they were all helpin' her along till she seemed to fairly fly in the midst of them. Then it all disappeared. I stood a minute with my heart poundin', then I went over there. I thought of goin' for Mrs Babbit, but I thought she'd be afraid. So I went alone, though I knew what had happened. Luella was layin' real peaceful, dead on her bed.'

This was the story that the old woman, Lydia Anderson, told, but the sequel was told by the people who survived her, and this is the tale which has become folklore in the village.

Lydia Anderson died when she was eighty-seven. She had continued wonderfully hale and hearty for one of her years until about two weeks before her death.

One bright moonlight evening she was sitting beside a window in her parlour when she made a sudden exclamation, and was out of the house and across the street before the neighbour who was taking care of her could stop her. She followed as fast as possible and found Lydia Anderson stretched on the ground before the door of Luella Miller's deserted house, and she was quite dead.

The next night there was a red gleam of fire athwart the moon-light and the old house of Luella Miller was burned to the ground.

Nothing is now left of it except a few old cellar stones and a lilac bush, and in summer a helpless trail of morning glories amongst the weeds, which might be considered emblematic of Luella herself.

Violet Quirk

THE THREE KISSES

Little is known about Violet Quirk. She was a frequent contributor to the popular fiction magazines during the first few decades of the twentieth century, and, though most of her stories were romances, several featured elements of the supernatural. There has been no collection of her ghost stories and the following story has never been reprinted since it first appeared as part of the regular 'uncanny tale' feature in the February 1920 issue of The Novel Magazine. *This and the next story in this volume dwell on the significance of the number three. We frequently recognize how things come in threes – the number is symbolic of completeness and closure. For example, in fairy tales the number often occurs, such as* Goldilocks and the Three Bears, The Three Little Piggies *or* The Three Wishes. *In the next two stories it is the third occurrence of the event that seals fate.*

The Three Kisses

OLD ANNA WAS busy in the kitchen when she heard her daughter scream. She rushed up into the bedroom. Antonia was sitting up, both arms around her new-born baby. Her face was chalky white and her eyes stared in terror.

'What is the matter?' asked her mother.

'A woman came in,' said Antonia, trembling.

'A woman? What woman?'

'I don't know. I have never seen her before. Oh, my child, my baby!' She bent over the baby, covering its face with hers.

'There has been nobody,' said Anna. 'Wouldn't I hear footsteps pass the door?'

'I was asleep,' said Antonia, 'and the woman came in and kissed the baby. I thought I was dreaming, but when I opened my eyes I saw her go out by the door.'

'You must have been dreaming, child!'

'No, no, Mother.'

'Such fancies! A woman, indeed! And in any case, what does a kiss matter?'

'My child! My baby!' wailed Antonia, remembering the kiss.

Anna shook the pillows and arranged the coverlet with deft, efficient fingers. She picked up the baby, passing her hands over his body.

'Sound as a bell,' she said. 'The little pretty one. What is his mother talking about? Such fancies.'

Antonia lay back on the pillow, exhausted. Her lips were parted as though she found it difficult to breathe. Faint perspiration covered her face.

'Now you go to sleep, both of you,' said Anna, pretending to scold. 'In the morning you will forget all about it. Everything seems strange when you wake suddenly from sleep.' She bustled out of the room, shaking her head. 'A woman, indeed!'

But she went into the outhouse and brought four sticks. Two she placed in the form of a cross on the ground underneath the bedroom window. The other two she placed outside the door, also in the form of a cross.

Afterwards, when she went to bed, Antonia and her child were sound asleep.

The next evening she was startled again by hearing her daughter scream. She ran up to the bedroom in a fright. 'What is it?' she cried.

'She came again,' said Antonia in terror.

'Now, now,' replied her mother. 'What is the matter with you? Who came?'

'The woman,' said Antonia forcefully, trembling visibly. 'She kissed him again. When I opened my eyes she was walking round the bottom of the bed. Oh, my child, my baby.'

She bent over him, her face on his, both her arms round him, as though she wished her body to surround him again. Her hair was damp, and her eyes were wild and distraught.

'It was a dream,' said Anna, in her tenderest mother voice. 'Didn't I dream such things when I was your age? My darling, don't look like that. Your cheeks are like paper. A glass of wine will put you right. It will calm him, too. He has been fretful.'

'Since yesterday,' said Antonia, slowly. She raised her face from the baby's to look at him. He opened his eyes and looked back at her in a steady, earnest way. 'Oh, Mother, Mother, look at him. Look! His eyes have changed!'

'Changed? What do you mean?'

Anna bent down and looked into the baby's eyes. They had turned from grey to a peculiar, misty blue, making his face look almost unfamiliar.

'What of that?' she said staunchly. 'That is nothing. Babies' eyes often change. Now, go to sleep and rest. I'll bring you up a glass of Malaga. It will put you right.'

Antonia still stared at the baby's eyes.

'It is nothing, nothing at all,' said Anna reassuringly. 'Say your prayers and forget it.'

Anna went down and brought her the wine. When she came to bed afterwards, both were asleep. She took off her daughter's wedding ring and with it made the sign of the cross on the baby's face. She looked out of the window and saw the two sticks gleam in the moonlight. The mighty silence of the place was like a sound. The little wood looked black against the sky. The crooked mountain, crouched above it, looked blacker still. She blew out the candle and got into bed.

The next day the baby was very fretful, allowing Antonia no rest. Anna prepared supper for Philip, her daughter's husband, and when he came in she said to him: 'Everything is ready. You can have supper by yourself tonight, can't you. I want to go to bed now. Antonia is not so well.'

'What is the matter with her?' This was the first Philip had heard of the problem.

'She has been seeing a woman come into the bedroom. She kissed the baby twice, apparently.'

Philip, dismissing his wife's fancies, laughed good-naturedly. 'Little Antonia! Yes, I can look after myself.'

'Good night. Don't go in to see her. She might be asleep.'

'Good night.'

He finished his supper and was turning the lamp down when a woman came through the open door.

'Catherine!' he cried, startled. 'What are you doing here? What do you want?'

She looked at him without answering, and he felt the old hatred sweep over him. He had felt attracted to her at first, but that was all. He had never loved her. He had tried to tell her so often, but she had always hushed his words with her clinging, terrible embraces. She had sickened him. She was too fierce, too wild. Women should be like Antonia: passive and responsive, like a fire whose brightness depends on the amount of fuel cast upon it. Catherine was like a flame which burnt of itself, unceasingly, unwaveringly. He had left her without saying a word, fearing she might utterly consume him, and had turned to Antonia. Now Catherine stood close to him again.

'What do you want?' he said roughly. 'How have you come all this way?'

'To us,' she said, 'distance is nothing.'

How he remembered her husky, quiet voice. How he had writhed under her yearning love words and her possessive hungry eyes, mistily blue. He had thought many a time he could never escape her, and when he did at last it was stealthily, at dead of night, leaving a good wage for a poorer one.

'Get out of my house,' he said. 'Why have you come here? Get out!'

'Yes – when I have given my third kiss and can claim what should have been mine.'

'He stretched out to push her away, but his hands touched nothingness. He started back, catching his breath. He turned to light the lamp and when he turned back, she was gone. But he heard the sound of secret, smothered laughter beyond the door.

He felt no incredulity. He accepted her visit with the fateful resignation of a man whose ancestors have always lived in remote and lonely places. In his mind were no arguments, no questionings, no wondering whether he had dreamt. He knew what she was. But his brain was not calm enough to consider the significance of what she had said.

He sat down heavily by the table. Then he heard a scream upstairs. He ran into the bedroom. Antonia was sitting up, her face dead white, her eyes looking blind. Her arms were tight around her baby, as she moaned, 'Oh, my child, my baby!'

Anna had also run into the room. 'What is it?'

'He is dead,' said Antonia, rocking to and fro.

'Dead?' echoed Anna. 'What are you talking about?'

'She came again,' said Antonia, her voice suddenly hushed and calm. 'I meant to keep awake all night, but I fell asleep. She brushed my face aside to kiss him. Her lips were cold. When I opened my eyes she was gone, but I knew my baby was dead.'

'He can't be,' said Anna. 'Let me look at him.'

She moved her daughter's arm away to look at the child, but when she saw him she knew, too. She wanted to lift him away, but Antonia held him fast.

'He is mine,' she said.

Philip, with tears welling in his eyes and a numbness seething through his mind, bent over his little son, whose eyes were open. He started when he saw their familiar misty blue. They seemed to look back at him in recognition, dead as they were.

Edith Nesbit

THE THIRD DRUG

*Many people are surprised when they learn that Edith Nesbit
(1858–1924) wrote horror and ghost stories. She is, of course, best
known for her children's stories, most notably* The Railway Children
(1906) and Five Children and It *(1902). But long before she established that reputation she had contributed many macabre tales to the
magazines and several were collected as* Grim Tales *(1893) and*
Something Wrong *(1893), with a later compendium* Fear *(1910).
Though Hugh Lamb assembled a volume of her best weird stories,* In
the Dark *(2000), a complete volume of all of her macabre fiction has
yet to be compiled. Edith Nesbit, or Mrs Hubert Bland as she became
after her marriage in 1880, was a remarkable woman. She seemed to
accept her husband's philandering and even raised one of his illegitimate
children as her own. She also had her own affairs. Along with Hubert she
founded the Fabian Society, which was in many ways the forerunner of
the Labour Party, and through that became acquainted with the literary
establishment of the day. Among her friends was H.G. Wells, and there
may well have been some Wellsian influence in the following story,
which dates from 1908. It may be regarded as early science fiction in
its exploration of a drug to create a superman.*

The Third Drug

I

ROGER WROXHAM LOOKED round his studio before he blew out the candle, and wondered whether, perhaps, he looked for the last time. It was large and empty, yet his trouble had filled it, and, pressing against him in the prison of those four walls, forced him out into the world, where lights and voices and the presence of other men should give him room to draw back, to set a space between it and him, to decide whether he would ever face it again – he and it alone together. The nature of his trouble is not germane to this story. There was a woman in it, of course, and money, and a friend, and regrets and embarrassments – and all of those reached out tendrils that wove and interwove till they made a puzzle-problem of which heart and brain were now weary. It was as though his life depended on his deciphering the straggling characters traced by some spider who, having fallen into the ink-well, had dragged clogged legs in a black zig-zag across his map of the world.

He blew out the candle and went quietly downstairs. It was nine at night, a soft night of May in Paris. Where should he go? He thought of the Seine, and took – an omnibus. The chestnut trees of the boulevards brushed against the sides of the one that he boarded blindly in the first light street. He did not know where the omnibus was going. It did not matter. When at last it stopped he got off, and so strange was the place to him that for an instant it almost seemed as though the trouble itself had been left behind. He did not feel it in the length of three or four streets that he traversed slowly. But in the open space, very light and lively, where he recognized the Taverne de Paris and knew himself in Montmartre, the trouble set its teeth in his heart again, and he broke away from the lamps and the talk to struggle with it in the dark quiet streets beyond.

A man braced for such a fight has little thought to spare for the detail of his surroundings. The next thing that Wroxham knew of the outside world was the fact that he had known for some time that he was not alone in the street. There was someone on the other side of the road keeping pace with him – yes, certainly keeping pace, for, as he slackened his own, the feet on the other pavement also went more slowly. And now they were four feet, not two. Where had the other man sprung from? He had not been there a moment ago. And now, from an archway a little ahead of him, a third man came.

Wroxham stopped. Then three men converged upon him, and, like a sudden magic-lantern picture on a sheet prepared, there came to him all that he had heard and read of Montmartre – dark archways, knives, Apaches, and men who went away from homes where they were beloved and never again returned. He, too – well, if he never returned again, it would be quicker than the Seine and, in the event of ultramundane possibilities, safer.

He stood still and laughed in the face of the man who first reached him.

'Well, my friend?' said he, and at that the other two drew close.

'Monsieur walks late,' said the first, a little confused, as it seemed, by that laugh.

'And will walk still later, if it pleases him,' said Roger. 'Good night, my friends.'

'Ah!' said the second, 'friends do not say adieu so quickly. Monsieur will tell us the hour.'

'I have not a watch,' said Roger, quite truthfully.

'I will assist you to search for it,' said the third man, and laid a hand on his arm.

Roger threw it off. That was instinctive. One may be resigned to a man's knife between one's ribs, but not to his hands pawing one's shoulders. The man with the hand staggered back.

'The knife searches more surely,' said the second.

'No, no,' said the third quickly, 'he is too heavy. I for one will not carry him afterwards.'

They closed round him, hustling him between them. Their pale, degenerate faces spun and swung round him in the struggle. For there was a struggle. He had not meant that there should be a struggle. Someone would hear – someone would come.

But if any heard, none came. The street retained its empty silence, the houses, masked in close shutters, kept their reserve. The four were wrestling, all pressed close together in a writhing bunch, drawing breath hardly through set teeth, their feet slipping, and not slipping, on the rounded cobble-stones.

The contact with these creatures, the smell of them, the warm, greasy texture of their flesh as, in the conflict, his face or neck met neck or face of theirs – Roger felt a cold rage possess him. He wrung two clammy hands apart and threw something off – something that staggered back clattering, fell in the gutter, and lay there.

It was then that Roger felt the knife. Its point glanced off the cigarette-case in his breast pocket and bit sharply at his inner arm. And at the sting of it Roger knew that he did not desire to die. He feigned a reeling weakness, relaxed his grip, swayed sideways, and then suddenly caught the other two in a new grip, crushed their faces together, flung them off, and ran. It was but for an instant that his feet were the only ones that echoed in the street. Then he knew that the others, too, were running.

It was like one of those nightmares wherein one runs for ever, leaden-footed, through a city of the dead. Roger turned sharply to the right. The sound of the other footsteps told that the pursuers also had turned that corner. Here was another street – a steep ascent. He ran more swiftly – he was running now for his life – the life that he held so cheap three minutes before. And all the streets were empty – empty like dream-streets, with all their windows dark and unhelpful, their doors fast closed against his need.

Far away down the street and across steep roofs lay Paris, poured out like a pool of light in the mist of the valley. But Roger was running with his head down – he saw nothing but the round heads of the cobble stones. Only now and again he glanced to right or left, if perchance some window might show light to justify a cry for help, some door advance the welcome of an open inch.

There was at last such a door. He did not see it till it was almost behind him. Then there was the drag of the sudden stop – the eternal instant of indecision. Was there time? There must be. He dashed his fingers through the inch crack, grazing the backs of them, leapt within, drew the door after him, felt madly for a lock or bolt, found a key, and, hanging his whole weight on it, strove to get the door home. The key turned. His left hand, by which he braced himself against the door-jamb, found a hook and pulled on it. Door and door-post met – the latch clicked – with a spring as it seemed. He turned the key, leaning against the door, which shook to the deep sobbing breaths that shook him, and to the panting bodies that pressed a moment without. Then someone cursed breathlessly outside; there was the sound of feet that went away.

Roger was alone in the strange darkness of an arched carriage-way, through the far end of which showed the fainter darkness of a courtyard, with black shapes of little formal rubbed orange trees. There was no sound at all there but the sound of his own desperate breathing; and, as he stood, the slow, warm blood crept down his wrist, to make a little pool in the hollow of his hanging, half-clenched hand. Suddenly he felt sick.

This house, of which he knew nothing, held for him no terrors. To him at that moment there were but three murderers in all the world, and where they were not, there safety was. But the spacious silence that soothed at first, presently clawed at the set, vibrating nerves already overstrained. He found himself listening, listening, and there was nothing to hear but the silence, and once, before he thought to twist his handkerchief round it, the drip of blood from his hand.

By and by, he knew that he was not alone in this house, for from far away there came the faint sound of a footstep, and, quite near, the faint answering echo of it. And at a window, high up on the other side of the courtyard, a light showed. Light and sound and echo intensified, the light passing window after window, till at last it moved across the courtyard, and the little trees threw back shifting shadows as it came towards him – a lamp in the hand of a man.

It was a short, bald man, with pointed beard and bright, friendly eyes. He held the lamp high as he came, and when he saw Roger, he drew his breath in an inspiration that spoke of surprise, sympathy, and pity.

'Hold! hold!' he said, in a singularly pleasant voice, 'there has been a misfortune? You are wounded, monsieur?'

'Apaches,' said Roger, and was surprised at the weakness of his own voice.

'Your hand?'

'My arm,' said Roger.

'Fortunately,' said the other, 'I am a surgeon. Allow me.'

He set the lamp on the step of a closed door, took off Roger's coat, and quickly tied his own handkerchief round the wounded arm.

'Now,' he said, 'courage! I am alone in the house. No one comes here but me. If you can walk up to my rooms, you will save us both much trouble. If you cannot, sit here and I will fetch you a cordial. But I advise you to try and walk. That *porte cochère* is, unfortunately, not very strong, and the lock is a common spring lock, and your friends may return with *their* friends; whereas the door across the courtyard is heavy and the bolts are new.'

Roger moved towards the heavy door whose bolts were new. The stairs seemed to go on for ever. The doctor lent his arm, but the carved bannisters and their lively shadows whirled before Roger's eyes. Also, he seemed to be shod with lead, and to have in his leg bones that were red-hot. Then the stairs ceased, and there was light, and cessation of the dragging of those leaden feet. He was on a couch, and his eyes might close. There was no need to move any more, nor to look, nor to listen.

When next he saw and heard, he was lying at ease, the close intimacy of a bandage clasping his arm, and in his mouth the vivid taste of some cordial.

The doctor was sitting in an armchair near a table, looking benevolent through gold-rimmed pince-nez.

'Better?' he said. 'No, lie still, you'll be a new man soon.'

'I am desolated,' said Roger, 'to have occasioned you all this trouble.'

'Not at all,' said the doctor. 'We live to heal, and it is a nasty cut, that in your arm. If you are wise, you will rest at present. I shall be honoured if you will be my guest for the night.'

Roger again murmured something about trouble.

'In a big house like this,' said the doctor, as it seemed a little sadly, 'there are many empty rooms, and some rooms which are not empty. There is a bed altogether at your service, monsieur, and I counsel you not to delay in seeking it. You can walk?'

Wroxham stood up. 'Why, yes,' he said, stretching himself. 'I feel, as you say, a new man.'

A narrow bed and rush-bottomed chair showed like dolls'-house furniture in the large, high, gaunt room to which the doctor led him.

'You are too tired to undress yourself,' said the doctor. 'Rest – only rest', and covered him with a rug, roundly tucked him up, and left him.

'I leave the door open,' he said, 'in case you have any fever. Good night. Do not torment yourself. All goes well.'

Then he took away the lamp, and Wroxham lay on his back and saw the shadows of the window-frames cast on the wall by the moon now risen. His eyes, growing accustomed to the darkness, perceived the carving of the white panelled walls and mantelpiece. There was a door in the room, another door from the one which the doctor had left open. Roger did not like open doors. The other door, however, was closed. He wondered where it led, and whether it were locked. Presently he got up to see. It was locked. He lay down again.

His arm gave him no pain, and the night's adventure did not seem to have overset his nerves. He felt, on the contrary, calm, confident, extraordinarily at ease and master of himself. The trouble – how could that ever have seemed important? This calmness – it felt like the calmness that precedes sleep. Yet sleep was far from him. What was it that kept sleep away? The bed was comfortable – the pillows soft. What was it? It came to him presently that it was the scent which distracted him, worrying him with a memory that he could not define. A faint scent of – what was it? perfumery? Yes – and camphor – and something else – something vaguely disquieting. He had not noticed it before he had risen and tried the handle of that other door. But now He covered his face with the sheet, but through the sheet he smelt it still. He rose and threw back one of the long french windows. It opened with a click and a jar, and he looked across the dark well of the courtyard. He leant out, breathing the chill, pure air of the May night, but when he withdrew his head, the scent was there again. Camphor – perfume – and something else. What was it that it reminded him of? He had his knee on the bed-edge when the answer came to that question. It was the scent that had struck at him from a darkened room when, a child, clutching at a grown-up hand, he had been led to the bed where, amid flowers, something white lay under a sheet – his mother they had told him. It was the scent of death, disguised with drugs and perfumes.

He stood up and went, with carefully controlled swiftness, towards the open door. He wanted light and a human voice. The doctor was in the room upstairs; he —

The doctor was face to face with him on the landing, not a yard away, moving towards him quietly in shoeless feet.

'I can't sleep,' said Wroxham, a little wildly, 'it's too dark —'

'Come upstairs,' said the doctor, and Wroxham went.

There was comfort in the large, lighted room, with its shelves and shelves full of well-bound books, its tables heaped with papers and pamphlets – its air of natural everyday work. There was a warmth of red curtain at the windows. On the window ledge a plant in a pot, its leaves like red misshapen hearts. A green-shaded lamp stood on the table. A peaceful, pleasant interior.

'What's behind that door,' said Wroxham, abruptly – 'that door downstairs?'

'Specimens,' the doctor answered, 'preserved specimens. My line is physiological research. You understand?'

So that was it.

'I feel quite well, you know,' said Wroxham, laboriously explaining – 'fit as any man – only I can't sleep.'

'I see,' said the doctor.

'It's the scent from your specimens, I think,' Wroxham went on. 'There's something about that scent —'

'Yes,' said the doctor.

'It's very odd.' Wroxham was leaning his elbow on his knee and his chin on his hand. 'I feel so frightfully well – and yet – there's a strange feeling —'

'Yes,' said the doctor. 'Yes, tell me exactly what you feel.'

'I feel,' said Wroxham, slowly, 'like a man on the crest of a wave.'

The doctor stood up. 'You feel well, happy, full of life and energy – as though you could walk to the world's end, and yet —'

'And yet,' said Roger, 'as though my next step might be my last – as though I might step into my grave.' He shuddered.

'Do you,' asked the doctor, anxiously – 'do you feel thrills of pleasure – something like the first waves of chloroform – thrills running from your hair to your feet?'

'I felt all that,' said Roger, slowly, 'downstairs before I opened the window.'

The doctor looked at his watch, frowned, and got up quickly. 'There is very little time,' he said.s

Suddenly Roger felt an unexplained opposition stiffen his mind.

The doctor went to a long laboratory bench with bottle-filled shelves above it, and on it crucibles and retorts, test tubes, beakers – all a chemist's apparatus – reached a bottle from a shelf, and measured out certain drops into a graduated glass, added water, and stirred it with a glass rod.

'Drink that,' he said.

'No,' said Roger, and as he spoke a thrill like the first thrill of the first chloroform wave swept through him, and it was a thrill not of pleasure but of pain. 'No,' he said, and 'Ah!' for the pain was sharp.

'If you don't drink,' said the doctor, carefully, 'you are a dead man.'

'You may be giving me poison,' Roger gasped, his hands at his heart.

'I may,' said the doctor. 'What do you suppose poison makes you feel like? What do you feel like now?'

'I feel,' said Roger, 'like death.'

Every nerve, every muscle thrilled to a pain not too intense to be underlined by a shuddering nausea.

'Then drink,' cried the doctor, in tones of such cordial entreaty, such evident anxiety, that Wroxham half held his hand out for the glass. 'Drink! Believe me, it is your only chance.'

Again the pain swept through him like an electric current. The beads of sweat sprang out on his forehead.

'That wound,' the doctor pleaded, standing over him with the glass held out. 'For God's sake, drink! Don't you understand, man? You *are* poisoned. Your wound – '

'The knife?' Wroxham murmured, and as he spoke, his eyes seemed to swell in his head, and his head itself to grow enormous. 'Do you know the poison – and its antidote?'

'I know all.' The doctor soothed him. 'Drink, then, my friend.'

As the pain caught him again in a clasp more close than any lover's he clutched at the glass and drank. The drug met the pain and mastered it. Roger, in the ecstasy of pain's cessation, saw the world fade and go out in a haze of vivid violet.

II

Faint films of lassitude, shot with contentment, wrapped him round. He lay passive as a man lies in the convalescence that follows a long fight with Death. Fold on fold of white peace lay all about him.

'I'm better now,' he said, in a voice that was a whisper – tried to raise his hand from where it lay helpless in his sight, failed, and lay looking at it in confident repose – 'much better.'

'Yes,' said the doctor, and his pleasant, soft voice had grown softer, pleasanter. 'You are now in the second stage. An interval is necessary before you can pass to the third. I will enliven the interval by conversation. Is there anything you would like to know?'

'Nothing,' said Roger; 'I am quite contented.'

'This is very interesting,' said the doctor. 'Tell me exactly how you feel.'

Roger faintly and slowly told him.

'Ah!' the doctor said, 'I have not before heard this. You are the only one of them all who ever passed the first stage. The others —'

'The others?' said Roger, but he did not care much about the others.

'The others,' said the doctor frowning, 'were unsound. Decadent students, degenerate, Apaches. You are highly trained – in fine physical condition. And your brain! God be good to the Apaches, who so delicately excited it to just the degree of activity needed for my purpose.'

'The others?' Wroxham insisted.

'The others? They are in the room whose door was locked. Look – you should be able to see them. The second drug should lay your consciousness before me, like a sheet of white paper on which I can write what I choose. If I choose that you should see my specimens – *Allons donc.* I have no secrets from you now. Look – look – strain your eyes. In theory, I know all that you can do and feel and see in this second stage. But practically – enlighten me – look – shut your eyes and look!'

Roger closed his eyes and looked. He saw the gaunt, uncarpeted staircase, the open doors of the big rooms, passed to the locked door, and it opened at his touch. The room inside was like the others, spacious and panelled. A lighted lamp with a blue shade hung from the ceiling, and below it an effect of spread whiteness. Roger looked. There *were* things to be seen.

With a shudder he opened his eyes on the doctor's delightful room, the doctor's intent face.

'What did you see?' the doctor asked. 'Tell me!'

'Did you kill them all?' Roger asked back.

'They died – of their own inherent weakness,' the doctor said. 'And you saw them?'

'I saw,' said Roger, 'the quiet people lying all along the floor in their death clothes – the people who have come in at that door of yours that is a trap – for robbery, or curiosity, or shelter, and never gone out any more.'

'Right,' said the doctor. 'Right. My theory is proved at every point. You can see what I choose you to see. Yes, decadents all. It was in embalming that I was a specialist before I began these other investigations.'

'What,' Roger whispered, 'what is it all for?'

'To make the superman,' said the doctor. 'I will tell you.'

He told. It was a long story – the story of a man's life, a man's work, a man's dreams, hopes, ambitions.

'The secret of life,' the doctor ended. 'That is what all the alchemists sought. They sought it where Fate pleased. I sought it where I have found it – in death.'

Roger thought of the room behind the locked door. 'And the secret is?' he asked.

'I have told you,' said the doctor impatiently; 'it is in the third drug that life – splendid, superhuman life – is found. I have tried it on animals. Always they became perfect, all that an animal should be. And more, too – much more. They were too perfect, too near humanity. They looked at me with human eyes. I could not let them live. Such animals it is not necessary to embalm. I had a laboratory in those days – and assistants. They called me the Prince of Vivisectors.'

The man on the sofa shuddered.

'I am naturally,' the doctor went, 'a tender-hearted man. You see it in my face; my voice proclaims it. Think what I have suffered in the sufferings of these poor beasts who never injured me. My God! Bear witness that I have not buried my talent. I have been faithful. I have laid down all – love, and joy, and pity, and the little beautiful things of life – all, all, on the altar of science, and seen them consume away. I deserved my heaven, if ever man did. And now by all the saints in heaven I am near it!'

'What is the third drug?' Roger asked, lying limp and flat on his couch.

'It is the Elixir of Life,' said the doctor. 'I am not its discoverer;

the old alchemists knew it well, but they failed because they sought to apply the elixir to a normal – that is, a diseased and faulty – body. I knew better. One must have first a body abnormally healthy, abnormally strong. Then, not the elixir, but the two drugs that prepare. The first excites prematurely the natural conflict between the principles of life and death, and then, just at the point where Death is about to win his victory, the second drug intensifies life so that it conquers – intensifies, and yet chastens. Then the whole life of the subject, risen to an ecstasy, falls prone in an almost voluntary submission to the coming super-life. Submission – submission! The garrison must surrender before the splendid conqueror can enter and make the citadel his own. Do you understand? Do you submit?'

'I submit,' said Roger, for, indeed, he did. 'But – soon – quite soon – I will not submit.'

He was too weak to be wise, or those words had remained unspoken.

The doctor sprang to his feet.

'It works too quickly!' he cried. 'Everything works too quickly with you. Your condition is too perfect. So now I bind you.'

From a drawer beneath the bench where the bottles gleamed, the doctor drew rolls of bandages – violet, like the haze that had drowned, at the urgency of the second drug, the consciousness of Roger. He moved, faintly resistant, on his couch. The doctor's hands, most gently, most irresistibly, controlled his movement.

'Lie still,' said the gentle, charming voice. 'Lie still; all is well.' The clever, soft hands were unrolling the bandages – passing them round arms and throat – under and over the soft narrow couch. 'I cannot risk your life, my poor boy. The least movement of yours might ruin everything. The third drug, like the first, must be offered directly to the blood which absorbs it. I bound the first drug as an unguent upon your knife-wound.'

The swift hands, the soft bandages, passed back and forth, over and under – flashes of violet passed to and fro in the air, like the shuttle of a weaver through his warp. As the bandage clasped his knees, Roger moved.

'For God's sake, no!' the doctor cried. 'The time is so near. If you cease to submit it is death.'

With an incredible, accelerated swiftness he swept the bandages round and round knees and ankles, drew a deep breath – stood upright.

'I must make an incision,' he said – 'in the head this time. It will not hurt. See! I spray it with the Constantia Nepenthe; that also I discovered. My boy, in a moment you know all things – you are as God. For God's sake, be patient. Preserve your submission.'

And Roger, with life and will resurgent hammering at his heart, preserved it.

He did not feel the knife that made the cross-cut on his temple, but he felt the hot spurt of blood that followed the cut; he felt the cool flap of a plaster, spread with some sweet, clean-smelling unguent that met the blood and stanched it. There was a moment – or was it hours? – of nothingness. Then from that cut on his forehead there seemed to radiate threads of infinite length, and of a strength that one could trust to – threads that linked one to all knowledge past and present. He felt that he controlled all wisdom, as a driver controls his four-in-hand. Knowledge, he perceived, belonged to him, as the air belongs to the eagle. He swam in it, as a great fish in a limitless ocean.

He opened his eyes and met those of the doctor, who sighed as one to whom breath has grown difficult.

'Ah, all goes well. Oh, my boy, was it not worth it? What do you feel?'

'I. Know. Everything,' said Roger, with full stops between the words.

'Everything? The future?'

'No. I know all that man has ever known.'

'Look back – into the past. See someone. See Pharaoh. You see him – on his throne?'

'Not on his throne. He is whispering in a corner of his great gardens to a girl, who is the daughter of a water-carrier.'

'Bah! Any poet of my dozen decadents who lie so still could have told me that. Tell me secrets – the *Masque de Fer.*'

The other told a tale, wild and incredible, but it satisfied the teller.

'That, too – it might be imagination. Tell me the name of the woman I loved and —'

The echo of the name of the anaesthetic came to Roger. 'Constantia,' said he, in an even voice.

'Ah,' the doctor cried, 'now I see you know all things. It was not murder. I hoped to dower her with all the splendours of the super-life.'

'Her bones lie under the lilacs, where you used to kiss her in the spring,' said Roger, quite without knowing what it was that he was going to say.

'It is enough,' the doctor cried. He sprang up, ranged certain bottles and glasses on a table convenient to his chair. 'You know all things. It was not a dream, this, the dream of my life. It is true. It is a fact accomplished. Now I, too, will know all things. I will be as the gods.'

He sought amongst leather cases on a far table, and came back swiftly into the circle of light that lay below the green-shaded lamp.

Roger, floating contentedly on the new sea of knowledge that seemed to support him, turned eyes on the trouble that had driven him out of that large, empty studio so long ago, so far away. His new-found wisdom laughed at that problem, laughed and solved it. 'To end that trouble I must do so-and-so, say such-and-such,' Roger told himself again and again.

And now the doctor, standing by the table, laid on it his pale, plump hand outspread. He drew a knife from a case – a long, shiny knife – and scored his hand across and across its back, as a cook scores pork for cooking. The slow blood followed the cuts in beads and lines.

Into the cuts he dropped a green liquid from a little bottle, replaced its stopper, bound up his hand, and sat down.

'The beginning of the first stage,' he said, 'almost at once I shall begin to be a new man. It will work quickly. My body, like yours, is sane and healthy.'

There was a long silence.

'Oh, but this is good,' the doctor broke it to say. 'I feel the hand of Life sweeping my nerves like harp-strings.'

Roger had been thinking, the old common sense that guides an ordinary man breaking through this consciousness of illimitable wisdom. 'You had better,' he said, 'unbind me. When the hand of Death sweeps your nerves, you may need help.'

'No,' the doctor said, 'and no, and no, and no many times. I am afraid of you. You know all things, and even in your body you are stronger than I. When I, too, am a god, and filled with the wine of knowledge, I will loose you, and together we will drink of the fourth drug – the mordant that shall fix the others and set us eternally on a level with the immortals.'

'Just as you like, of course,' said Roger, with a conscious effort after commonplace. Then suddenly, not commonplace any more: 'Loose me!' he cried; 'loose me, I tell you! I am wiser than you.'

'You are also stronger,' said the doctor, and then suddenly and irresistibly the pain caught him. Roger saw his face contorted with agony, his hands clench on the arm of his chair; and it seemed that, either this man was less able to bear pain than he, or that the pain was much more violent than had been his own. Between the grippings of the anguish the doctor dragged on his watch-chain; the watch leapt from his pocket, and rattled as his trembling hand laid it on the table.

'Not yet,' he said, when he had looked at its face, 'not yet, not yet, not yet.' It seemed to Roger, lying there bound, that the other man repeated those words for long days and weeks. And the plump, pale hand, writhing and distorted by anguish, again and again drew near to take the glass that stood ready on the table, and with convulsive self-restraint again and again drew back without it.

The short May night was waning – the shiver of dawn rustled the leaves of the plant whose leaves were like red misshaped hearts.

'Now!' The doctor screamed the word, grasped the glass, drained it, and sank back in his chair. His hand struck the table beside him. Looking at his limp body and head thrown back, one could almost see the cessation of pain, the coming of kind oblivion.

III

The dawn had grown to daylight, a poor, grey, rain-stained daylight, not strong enough to pierce the curtains and persiennes; and yet not so weak but that it could mock the lamp, now burnt low and smelling vilely.

Roger lay very still on his couch, a man wounded, anxious and extravagantly tired. In those hours of long, slow dawning, face to face with the unconscious figure in the chair, he had felt, slowly and little by little, the recession of that sea of knowledge on which he had felt himself float in such content. The sea had withdrawn itself, leaving him high and dry on the shore of the normal. The only relic that he had clung to and that he still grasped was the answer to the problem of the trouble – the only wisdom that he had put into words. These words remained to him, and he knew that they held wisdom – very simple wisdom, too.

'To end the trouble, I must do so-and-so and say such-and-such.'

But of all that had seemed to set him on a pinnacle, had evened him with the immortals, nothing else was left. He was just Roger Wroxham – wounded, and bound, in a locked house, one of whose rooms was full of very quiet people, and in another room himself and a dead man. For now it was so long since the doctor had moved that it seemed he must be dead. He had got to know every line of that room, every fold of drapery, every flower on the wall-paper, the number of the books, the shapes and sizes of things. Now he could no longer look at these. He looked at the other man.

Slowly a dampness spread itself over Wroxham's forehead and tingled amongst the roots of his hair. He writhed in his bonds. They held fast. He could not move hand or foot. Only his head could turn a little, so that he could at will see the doctor or not see him. A shaft of desolate light pierced the persienne at its hinge and rested on the table, where an overturned glass lay.

Wroxham thrilled from head to foot.

The body in the chair stirred – hardly stirred – shivered rather – and a very faint, far-away voice said: 'Now the third – give me the third.'

'What?' said Roger, stupidly; and he had to clear his throat twice before he could say even that.

'The moment is now,' said the doctor. 'I remember all. I made you a god. Give me the third drug.'

'Where is it?' Roger asked.

'It is at my elbow,' the doctor murmured. 'I submit – I submit. Give me the third drug, and let me be as you are.'

'As *I* am?' said Roger. 'You forget. *I* am bound.'

'Break your bonds,' the doctor urged, in a quick, small voice. 'I trust you now. You are stronger than all men, as you are wiser. Stretch your muscles, and the bandages will fall asunder like snow-wreaths.'

'It is too late,' Wroxham said, and laughed; 'all that is over. I am not wise any more, and I have only the strength of a man. I am tired and wounded. I cannot break your bonds – I cannot help you!'

'But if you cannot help me – it is death,' said the doctor.

'It is death,' said Roger. 'Do you feel it coming on you?'

'I feel life returning,' said the doctor; 'it is now the moment – the one possible moment. And I cannot reach it. Oh, give it me – give it me!'

Then Roger cried out suddenly, in a loud voice: 'Now, by God in heaven, you damned decadent, I am *glad* that I cannot give it. Yes if it costs me my life, it's worth it, you madman, so that your life ends too. Now be silent, and die like a man, if you have it in you.'

Only one word seemed to reach the man in the chair.

'A decadent!' he repeated. 'I? But no, I am like you – I see what I will. I close my eyes, and I see – no – not that – ah! – not that!' He writhed faintly in his chair, and to Roger it seemed that for that writhing figure there would be no return of power and life and will.

'Not that,' he moaned. 'Not that,' and writhed in a gasping anguish that bore no more words.

Roger lay and watched him, and presently he writhed from the chair to the floor, tearing feebly at it with his fingers, moaned, shuddered, and lay very still.

Of all that befell Roger in that house, the worst was now. For now he knew that he was alone with the dead, and between him and death stretched certain hours and days. For the *porte cochère* was locked; the doors of the house itself were locked – heavy doors and the locks new.

'I am alone in the house,' the doctor had said. 'No one comes here but me.'

No one would come. He would die there – he, Roger Wroxham – 'poor old Roger Wroxham, who was no one's enemy but his own.' Tears pricked his eyes. He shook his head impatiently and they fell from his lashes.

'You fool,' he said, 'can't *you* die like a man either?'

Then he set his teeth and made himself lie still. It seemed to him that now Despair laid her hand on his heart. But, to speak truth, it was Hope whose hand lay there. This was so much more than a man should be called on to bear – it could not be true. It was an evil dream. He would wake presently. Or if it were, indeed, real – then someone would come, someone must come. God could not let nobody come to save him.

And late at night, when heart and brain had been stretched to the point where both break and let in the sea of madness, someone came.

The interminable day had worn itself out. Roger had screamed, yelled, shouted till his throat was dried up, his lips baked and cracked. No one heard. How should they? The twilight had thickened and thickened, till at last it made a shroud for the dead man on the floor by the chair. And there were other dead men in that house; and as Roger ceased to see the one he saw the others – the quiet, awful faces, the lean hands, the straight, stiff limbs laid out one beyond another in the room of death. They at least were not bound. If they should rise in their white wrappings and, crossing that empty sleeping chamber very softly, come slowly up the stairs . . .

A stair creaked.

His ears, strained with hours of listening, thought themselves befooled. But his cowering heart knew better.

Again a stair creaked. There was a hand on the door.

'Then it is all over,' said Roger in the darkness, 'and I *am* mad.'

The door opened very slowly, very cautiously. There was no light. Only the sound of soft feet and draperies that rustled.

Then suddenly a match spurted – light struck at his eyes; a flicker of lit candle-wick steadying to flame. And the things that had come were not those quiet people creeping up to match their death with his death in life, but human creatures, alive, breathing, with eyes that moved and glittered, lips that breathed and spoke.

'He must be here,' one said. 'Lisette watched all day; he never came out. He must be here – there is nowhere else.'

Then they set up the candle-end on the table, and he saw their faces. They were the Apaches who had set on him in that lonely street, and who had sought him here – to set on him again.

He sucked his dry tongue, licked his dry lips, and cried aloud: 'Here I am! Oh, kill me! For the love of God, brothers, kill me *now!*'

And even before he spoke, they had seen him, and seen what lay on the floor.

'He died this morning. I am bound. Kill me, brothers. I cannot die slowly here alone. Oh, kill me, for Christ's sake!'

But already the three were pressing on each other at a doorway suddenly grown too narrow. They could kill a living man, but they could not face death, quiet, enthroned.

'For the love of Christ,' Roger screamed, 'have pity! Kill me outright! Come back – come back!'

And then, since even Apaches are human, one of them did come back. It was the one he had flung into the gutter. The feet of the others sounded on the stairs as he caught up the candle and bent over Roger, knife in hand.

'Make sure,' said Roger, through set teeth.

'*Nom d'un nom,*' said the Apache, with worse words, and cut the bandages here, and here, and here again, and there, and lower, to the very feet.

Then this good Samaritan helped Roger to rise, and when he could not stand, the Samaritan half pulled, half carried him down those many steps, till they came upon the others putting on their boots at the stair-foot.

Then between them the three men who could walk carried the other out and slammed the outer door, and presently set him against a gate-post in another street, and went their wicked ways.

And after a time, a girl with furtive eyes brought brandy and hoarse, muttered kindnesses, and slid away in the shadows.

Against that gate-post the police came upon him. They took him to the address they found on him. When they came to question him he said, 'Apaches', and his late variations on that theme were deemed sufficient, though not one of them touched truth or spoke of the third drug.

There has never been anything in the papers about that house. I think it is still closed, and inside it still lie in the locked room the very quiet people; and above, there is the room with the narrow couch and the scattered, cut, violet bandages, and the thing on the floor by the chair, under the lamp that burned itself out in that May dawning.

George Eliot

THE LIFTED VEIL

George Eliot was the male pseudonym adopted by Mary Anne Evans (1819–80), or Marian Evans as she later preferred to be known. Like Mary Braddon, and to some extent Edith Nesbit (who lived a generation later), Mary Evans was a freethinker who lived outside the moral code of her day. In 1855 she moved in with the journalist and philosopher George Henry Lewes and called herself his wife, even though he had not divorced his real wife who was then living with fellow journalist, Thornton Hunt. She also accepted the mothering role for Lewes's existing children. Though Evans hid her sex and identity from her reading public under the male alias George Eliot, she rode the scandal over her unorthodox life and her home became an open salon to the literary giants of the day. Her novels, notably Adam Bede *(1859),* Silas Marner *(1861) and* Middlemarch *(1872), were highly regarded and have remained classics of their day. She was one of the highest paid writers of her time. 'The Lifted Veil', first published in* Blackwood's Magazine *for July 1859, is her one and only trip into the occult or at least into the world of precognition and predestiny. It also includes a remarkable scene, reminiscent of* Frankenstein, *in which the protagonists seek to revive a dead body. This story serves as a counterbalance to Emily Brontë's 'The Palace of Death' in its study of the attempts by the living to overpower death.*

The Lifted Veil

Give me no light, great Heaven, but such as turns
To energy of human fellowship;
No powers beyond the growing heritage
That makes completer manhood.

I

THE TIME OF my end approaches. I have lately been subject to attacks of *angina pectoris*; and in the ordinary course of things, my physician tells me, I may fairly hope that my life will not be protracted many months. Unless, then, I am cursed with an exceptional physical constitution, as I am cursed with an exceptional mental character, I shall not much longer groan under the wearisome burthen of this earthly existence. If it were to be otherwise – if I were to live on to the age most men desire and provide for – I should for once have known whether the miseries of delusive expectation can outweigh the miseries of true provision. For I foresee when I shall die, and everything that will happen in my last moments.

Just a month from this day, on September 20, 1850, I shall be sitting in this chair, in this study, at ten o'clock at night, longing to die, weary of incessant insight and foresight, without delusions and without hope. Just as I am watching a tongue of blue flame rising in the fire, and my lamp is burning low, the horrible contraction will begin at my chest. I shall only have time to reach the bell, and pull it violently, before the sense of suffocation will come. No one will answer my bell. I know why. My two servants are lovers, and will have quarrelled. My housekeeper will have rushed out of the house in a fury, two hours before, hoping that Perry will believe she has gone to drown herself. Perry is alarmed at last, and is gone out after her. The little scullery-maid is asleep on a bench: she never answers the bell; it does not wake her. The sense of suffocation increases: my lamp goes out with a horrible stench: I make a great effort, and snatch at the bell again. I long for life, and there is no help. I thirsted for the unknown: the thirst is gone. O God, let me stay with the known, and be weary of it: I am content. Agony of pain and suffocation – and all the while the earth, the fields, the pebbly brook at the bottom of the rookery, the fresh scent after the rain, the light of the morning through my chamber-window, the warmth of the hearth after the frosty air – will darkness close over them for ever?

Darkness – darkness – no pain – nothing but darkness: but I am passing on and on through the darkness: my thought stays in the darkness, but always with a sense of moving onward . . .

Before that time comes, I wish to use my last hours of ease and strength in telling the strange story of my experience. I have never fully unbosomed myself to any human being; I have never been encouraged to trust much in the sympathy of my fellow-men. But we have all a chance of meeting with some pity, some tenderness, some charity, when we are dead: it is the living only who cannot be forgiven – the living only from whom men's indulgence and reverence are held off, like the rain by the hard east wind. While the heart beats, bruise it – it is your only opportunity; while the eye can still turn towards you with moist, timid entreaty, freeze it with an icy unanswering gaze; while the ear, that delicate messenger to the inmost sanctuary of the soul, can still take in the tones of kindness, put it off with hard civility, or sneering compliment, or envious affectation of indifference; while the creative brain can still throb with the sense of injustice, with the yearning for brotherly recognition – make haste – oppress it with your ill-considered judgements, your trivial comparisons, your careless misrepresentations. The heart will by and by be still – '*ubi saeva indignatio ulterius cor lacerare nequit*'; the eye will cease to entreat; the ear will be deaf; the brain will have ceased from all wants as well as from all work. Then your charitable speeches may find vent; then you may remember and pity the toil and the struggle and the failure; then you may give due honour to the work achieved; then you may find extenuation for errors, and may consent to bury them.

That is a trivial schoolboy text; why do I dwell on it? It has little reference to me, for I shall leave no works behind me for men to honour. I have no near relatives who will make up, by weeping over my grave, for the wounds they inflicted on me when I was among them. It is only the story of my life that will perhaps win a little more sympathy from strangers when I am dead, than I ever believed it would obtain from my friends while I was living.

My childhood perhaps seems happier to me than it really was, by contrast with all the after-years. For then the curtain of the future was as impenetrable to me as to other children: I had all their delight in the present hour, their sweet indefinite hopes for the morrow; and I had a tender mother: even now, after the dreary lapse of long years, a slight trace of sensation accompanies the remembrance of her caress as she held me on her knee – her arms round my little body, her cheek pressed on mine. I had a complaint of the eyes that made me blind for a little while, and she kept me on her knee from morning till night. That unequalled love soon vanished out of my life, and even to my childish consciousness it was as if that life had become more chill I rode my little white pony with the groom by my side as before, but there were no loving eyes looking at me as I mounted, no glad arms opened to me when I came back. Perhaps I missed my mother's love more than most children of seven or eight would have done, to whom the other pleasures of life remained as before; for I was certainly a very sensitive child. I remember still the mingled trepidation and delicious excitement with which I was affected by the tramping of the horses on the pavement in the echo-ing stables, by the loud resonance of the groom's voices, by the booming bark of the dogs as my father's carriage thundered under the archway of the courtyard, by the din of the gong as it gave notice of luncheon and dinner. The measured tramp of soldiery which I sometimes heard – for my father's house lay near a county town where there were large barracks – made me sob and tremble; and yet when they were gone past, I longed for them to come back again.

I fancy my father thought me an odd child, and had little fond-ness for me; though he was very careful in fulfilling what he regarded as a parent's duties. But he was already past the middle of life, and I was not his only son. My mother had been his second wife, and he was five-and-forty when he married her. He was a firm, unbending, intensely orderly man, in root and stem a banker, but with a flourishing graft of the active landholder, aspiring to county influence: one of those people who are always like themselves from day to day, who are uninfluenced by the weather, and neither know melancholy nor high spirits. I held him in great awe, and appeared more timid and sensitive in his presence than at other times; a circumstance which, perhaps, helped to confirm him in the intention to educate me on a different plan from the prescriptive one with which he had complied in the case of my elder brother, already a tall youth at Eton. My brother was to be his representative and successor; he must go to Eton and Oxford, for the sake of making connexions, of course: my father was not a man to underrate the bearing of Latin satirists or Greek dramatists on the attainment of an aristocratic position. But, intrinsically, he had slight esteem for 'those dead but sceptred spirits'; having qualified himself for forming an independent opinion by reading Potter's *Æschylus*, and dipping into Francis's *Horace*. To this negative view he added a positive one, derived from a recent connection with mining speculations; namely, that a scientific education was the really useful training for a younger son. Moreover, it was clear that a shy, sensitive boy like me was not fit to encounter the rough experience of a public school. Mr Letherall had said so very decidedly. Mr Letherall was a large man in spectacles, who one day took my small head between his large hands, and pressed it here and there in an exploratory, auspicious manner – then placed each of his great thumbs on my temples, and pushed me a little way from him, and stared at me with glittering spectacles. The contemplation appeared to displease him, for he frowned sternly, and said to my father, drawing his thumbs across my eyebrows –

'The deficiency is there, sir – there; and here,' he added, touching the upper sides of my head, 'here is the excess. That must be brought out, sir, and this must be laid to sleep.'

I was in a state of tremor, partly at the vague idea that I was the object of reprobation, partly in the agitation of my first hatred –

hatred of this big, spectacled man, who pulled my head about as if he wanted to buy and cheapen it.

I am not aware how much Mr Letherall had to do with the system afterwards adopted towards me, but it was presently clear that private tutors, natural history, science, and the modern languages, were the appliances by which the defects of my organization were to be remedied. I was very stupid about machines, so I was to be greatly occupied with them; I had no memory for classification, so it was particularly necessary that I should study systematic zoology and botany; I was hungry for human deeds and humane motions, so I was to be plentifully crammed with the mechanical powers, the elementary bodies, and the phenomena of electricity and magnetism. A better-constituted boy would certainly have profited under my intelligent tutors, with their scientific apparatus; and would, doubtless, have found the phenomena of electricity and magnetism as fascinating as I was, every Thursday, assured they were. As it was, I could have paired off, for ignorance of whatever was taught me, with the worst Latin scholar that was ever turned out of a classical academy. I read Plutarch, and Shakespeare, and Don Quixote by the sly, and supplied myself in that way with wandering thoughts, while my tutor was assuring me that 'an improved man, as distinguished from an ignorant one, was a man who knew the reason why water ran downhill'. I had no desire to be this improved man; I was glad of the running water; I could watch it and listen to it gurgling among the pebbles, and bathing the bright green water-plants, by the hour together. I did not want to know *why* it ran; I had perfect confidence that there were good reasons for what was so very beautiful.

There is no need to dwell on this part of my life. I have said enough to indicate that my nature was of the sensitive, unpractical order, and that it grew up in an uncongenial medium, which could never foster it into happy, healthy development. When I was sixteen I was sent to Geneva to complete my course of education; and the change was a very happy one to me, for the first sight of the Alps, with the setting sun on them, as we descended the Jura, seemed to me like an entrance into heaven; and the three years of my life there were spent in a perpetual sense of exaltation, as if from a draught of delicious wine, at the presence of Nature in all her awful loveliness. You will think, perhaps, that I must have been a poet, from this early sensibility to Nature. But my lot was not so happy as that. A poet pours forth his song and *believes* in the listening ear and answering soul, to which his song will be floated sooner or later. But the poet's sensibility without his voice – the poet's sensibility that finds no vent but in silent tears on the sunny bank, when the noonday light sparkles on the water, or in an inward shudder at the sound of harsh human tones, the sight of a cold human eye – this dumb passion brings with it a fatal solitude of soul in the society of one's fellow-men. My least solitary moments were those in which I pushed off in my boat, at evening, towards the centre of the lake; it seemed to me that the sky, and the glowing mountain-tops, and the wide blue water, surrounded me with a cherishing love such as no human face had shed on me since my mother's love had vanished out of my life. I used to do as Jean Jacques did – lie down in my boat and let it glide where it would, while I looked up at the departing glow leaving one mountain-top after the other, as if the prophet's chariot of fire were passing over them on its way to the home of light. Then, when the white summits were all sad and corpse-like, I had to push homeward, for I was under careful surveillance, and was allowed no late wanderings. This disposition of mine was not favourable to the formation of intimate friendships among the numerous youths of my own age who are always to be found studying at Geneva. Yet I made *one* such friendship; and, singularly enough, it was with a youth whose intellectual tendencies were the very reverse of my own. I shall call him Charles Meunier; his real surname – an English one, for he was of English extraction – having since become celebrated. He was an orphan, who lived on a miserable pittance while he pursued the medical studies for which he had a special genius. Strange! that with my vague mind, susceptible and unobservant, hating enquiry and given up to contemplation, I should have been drawn towards a youth whose strongest passion was science. But the bond was not an intellectual one; it came from a source that can happily blend the stupid with the brilliant, the dreamy with the practical: it came from community of feeling. Charles was poor and ugly, derided by Genevese *gamins*, and not acceptable in drawing-rooms. I saw that he was isolated, as I was, though from a different cause, and, stimulated by a sympathetic resentment, I made timid advances towards him. It is enough to say that there sprang up as much comradeship between us as our different habits would allow; and in Charles's rare holidays we went up the Salève together, or took the boat to Vevay, while I listened dreamily to the monologues in which he unfolded his bold conceptions of future experiment and discovery. I mingled them confusedly in my thought with glimpses of blue water and delicate floating cloud, with the notes of birds and the distant glitter of the glacier. He knew quite well that my mind was half absent, yet he liked to talk to me in this way; for don't we talk of our hopes and our projects even to dogs and birds, when they love us? I have mentioned this one friendship because of its connection with a strange and terrible scene which I shall have to narrate in my subsequent life.

This happier life at Geneva was put an end to by a severe illness, which is partly a blank to me, partly a time of dimly remembered suffering, with the presence of my father by my bed from time to time. Then came the languid monotony of convalescence, the days gradually breaking into variety and distinctness as my strength enabled me to take longer and longer drives.

On one of these more vividly remembered days, my father said to me, as he sat beside my sofa, 'When you are quite well enough to travel, Latimer, I shall take you home with me. The journey will amuse you and do you good, for I shall go through the Tyrol and Austria, and you will see many new places. Our neighbours, the Filmores, are come; Alfred will join us at Basle, and we shall all go together to Vienna, and back by Prague . . .'

My father was called away before he had finished his sentence, and he left my mind resting on the word *Prague*, with a strange sense that a new and wondrous scene was breaking upon me: a city under the broad sunshine, that seemed to me as if it were the summer sunshine of a long-past century arrested in its course – unrefreshed for ages by dews of night, or the rushing rain-cloud; scorching the dusty, weary, time-eaten grandeur of a people doomed to live on in the stale repetition of memories, like deposed and superannuated kings in their regal gold-inwoven tatters. The city looked so thirsty that the broad river seemed to me a sheet of metal; and the blackened statues, as I passed under their blank gaze, along the unending bridge, with their ancient garments and their saintly crowns, seemed to me the real inhabitants and owners of this place, while the busy, trivial men and women, hurrying to and fro, were a swarm of ephemeral visitants infesting it for a day. It is such grim, stony beings as these, I thought, who are the fathers of ancient faded children, in those tanned time-fretted dwellings that crowd the steep before me; who pay their court in the worn and crumbling pomp of the palace which stretches its monotonous length on the height; who worship wearily in the stifling air of the churches, urged by no fear or hope, but compelled by their doom to be ever old and undying, to live on in the rigidity of habit, as they live on in perpetual midday, without the repose of night or the new birth of morning.

A stunning clang of metal suddenly thrilled through me, and I became conscious of the objects in my room again: one of the fire-irons had fallen as Pierre opened the door to bring me my draught. My heart was palpitating violently, and I begged Pierre to leave my draught beside me; I would take it presently.

As soon as I was alone again, I began to ask myself whether I had been sleeping. Was this a dream – this wonderfully distinct vision – minute in its distinctness down to a patch of rainbow light on the pavement, transmitted through a coloured lamp in the shape of a star – of a strange city, quite unfamiliar to my imagination? I had seen no picture of Prague: it lay in my mind as a mere name, with vaguely remembered historical associations – ill-defined memories of imperial grandeur and religious wars.

Nothing of this sort had ever occurred in my dreaming experience before, for I had often been humiliated because my dreams were only saved from being utterly disjointed and commonplace by the frequent terrors of nightmare. But I could not believe that I had been asleep, for I remembered distinctly the gradual breaking-in of the vision upon me, like the new images in a dissolving view, or the growing distinctness of the landscape as the sun lifts up the veil of the morning mist. And while I was conscious of this incipient vision, I was also conscious that Pierre came to tell my father Mr Filmore was waiting for him, and that my father hurried out of the room. No, it was not a dream; was it – the thought was full of tremulous exultation – was it the poet's nature in me, hitherto only a troubled yearning sensibility, now manifesting itself suddenly as spontaneous creation? Surely it was in this way that Homer saw the plain of Troy, that Dante saw the abodes of the departed, that Milton saw the earthward flight of the Tempter. Was it that my illness had wrought some happy change in my organization – given a firmer tension to my nerves – carried off some dull obstruction? I had often read of such effects – in works of fiction at least. Nay; in genuine biographies I had read of the subtilizing or exalting influence of some diseases on the mental powers. Did not Novalis feel his inspiration intensified under the progress of consumption?

When my mind had dwelt for some time on this blissful idea, it seemed to me that I might perhaps test it by an exertion of my will. The vision had begun when my father was speaking of our going to Prague. I did not for a moment believe it was really a representation of that city; I believed – I hoped it was a picture that my newly liberated genius had painted in fiery haste, with the colours snatched from lazy memory. Suppose I were to fix my mind on some other place – Venice, for example, which was far more familiar to my imagination than Prague: perhaps the same sort of result would follow. I concentrated my thoughts on Venice; I stimulated my imagination with poetic memories, and strove to feel myself present in Venice, as I had felt myself present in Prague. But in vain. I was only colouring the Canaletto engravings that hung in my old bedroom at home; the picture was a shifting one, my mind wandering uncertainly in search of more vivid images; I could see no accident of form or shadow without conscious labour after the necessary conditions. It was all prosaic effort, not rapt passivity, such as I had experienced half an hour before. I was discouraged; but I remembered that inspiration was fitful.

For several days I was in a state of excited expectation, watching for a recurrence of my new gift. I sent my thoughts ranging over my world of knowledge, in the hope that they would find some object which would send a reawakening vibration through my slumbering genius. But no; my world remained as dim as ever, and that flash of strange light refused to come again, though I watched for it with palpitating eagerness.

My father accompanied me every day in a drive, and a gradually lengthening walk as my powers of walking increased; and one evening he had agreed to come and fetch me at twelve the next day, that we might go together to select a musical box, and other purchases rigorously demanded of a rich Englishman visiting Geneva. He was one of the most punctual of men and bankers, and I was always nervously anxious to be quite ready for him at the appointed time. But, to my surprise, at a quarter past twelve he had not appeared. I felt all the impatience of a convalescent who has nothing particular to do, and who has just taken a tonic in the prospect of immediate exercise that would carry off the stimulus.

Unable to sit still and reserve my strength, I walked up and down the room, looking out on the current of the Rhone, just where it leaves the dark-blue lake; but thinking all the while of the possible causes that could detain my father.

Suddenly I was conscious that my father was in the room, but not alone: there were two persons with him. Strange! I had heard no footstep, I had not seen the door open; but I saw my father, and at his right hand our neighbour Mrs Filmore, whom I remembered very well, though I had not seen her for five years. She was a commonplace middle-aged woman, in silk and cashmere; but the lady on the left of my father was not more than twenty, a tall, slim, willowy figure, with luxuriant blonde hair, arranged in cunning braids and folds that looked almost too massive for the slight figure and the small-featured, thin-lipped face they crowned. But the face had not a girlish expression: the features were sharp, the pale grey eyes at once acute, restless, and sarcastic. They were fixed on me in half-smiling curiosity, and I felt a painful sensation as if a sharp wind were cutting me. The pale-green dress, and the green leaves that seemed to form a border about her pale blonde hair, made me think of a Water-Nixie – for my mind was full of German lyrics, and this pale, fatal-eyed woman, with the green weeds, looked like a birth from some cold sedgy stream, the daughter of an aged river.

'Well, Latimer, you thought me long,' my father said . . .

But while the last word was in my ears, the whole group vanished, and there was nothing between me and the Chinese printed folding-screen that stood before the door. I was cold and trembling; I could only totter forward and throw myself on the sofa. This strange new power had manifested itself again . . . But *was* it a power? Might it not rather be a disease – a sort of intermittent delirium, concentrating my energy of brain into moments of unhealthy activity, and leaving my saner hours all the more barren? I felt a dizzy sense of unreality in what my eye rested on; I grasped the bell convulsively, like one trying to free himself from nightmare, and rang it twice. Pierre came with a look of alarm in his face.

'Monsieur ne se trouve pas bien?' he said anxiously.

'I'm tired of waiting, Pierre,' I said, as distinctly and emphatically as I could, like a man determined to be sober in spite of wine; 'I'm afraid something has happened to my father – he's usually so punctual. Run to the Hôtel des Bergues and see if he is there.'

Pierre left the room at once, with a soothing 'Bien, monsieur'; and I felt the better for this scene of simple, waking prose. Seeking to calm myself still further, I went into my bedroom, adjoining the *salon*, and opened a case of eau-de-Cologne; took out a bottle; went through the process of taking out the cork very neatly, and then rubbed the reviving spirit over my hands and forehead, and under my nostrils, drawing a new delight from the scent because I had pro-cured it by slow details of labour, and by no strange sudden madness. Already I had begun to taste something of the horror that belongs to the lot of a human being whose nature is not adjusted to simple human conditions.

Still enjoying the scent, I returned to the salon, but it was not unoccupied, as it had been before I left it. In front of the Chinese folding-screen there was my father, with Mrs Filmore on his right hand, and on his left – the slim, blonde-haired girl, with the keen face and the keen eyes fixed on me in half-smiling curiosity.

'Well, Latimer, you thought me long,' my father said . . .

I heard no more, felt no more, till I became conscious that I was lying with my head low on the sofa, Pierre, and my father by my side.

As soon as I was thoroughly revived, my father left the room, and presently returned, saying, 'I've been to tell the ladies how you are, Latimer. They were waiting in the next room. We shall put off our shopping expedition to-day.' Presently he said, 'That young lady is Bertha Grant, Mrs Filmore's orphan niece. Filmore has adopted her, and she lives with them, so you will have her for a neighbour when we go home – perhaps for a near relation; for there is a tenderness between her and Alfred, I suspect, and I should be gratified by the match, since Filmore means to provide for her in every way as if she were his daughter. It had not occurred to me that you knew nothing about her living with the Filmores.'

He made no further allusion to the fact of my having fainted at the moment of seeing her, and I would not for the world have told him the reason: I shrank from the idea of disclosing to anyone what might be regarded as a pitiable peculiarity, most of all from betraying it to my father, who would have suspected my sanity ever after.

I do not mean to dwell with particularity on the details of my experience. I have described these two cases at length, because they had definite, clearly traceable results in my after-lot.

Shortly after this last occurrence – I think the very next day – I began to be aware of a phase in my abnormal sensibility, to which, from the languid and slight nature of my intercourse with others since my illness, I had not been alive before. This was the obtrusion on my mind of the mental process going forward in first one person, and then another, with whom I happened to be in contact: the vagrant, frivolous ideas and emotions of some uninteresting acquaintance – Mrs Filmore, for example – would force themselves on my consciousness like an importunate, ill-played musical instrument, or the loud activity of an imprisoned insect. But this unpleasant sensibility was fitful, and left me moments of rest, when the souls of my companions were once more shut out from me, and I felt a relief such as silence brings to wearied nerves. I might have believed this importunate insight to be merely a diseased activity of the imagination, but that my prevision of incalculable words and actions proved it to have a fixed relation to the mental process in other minds. But this superadded consciousness, wearying and annoying enough when it urged on me the trivial experience of indifferent people, became an intense pain and grief when it seemed to be opening to me the souls of those who were in a close relation to me – when the rational talk, the graceful attentions, the wittily-turned phrases, and the kindly deeds, which used to make the web of their characters, were seen as if thrust asunder by a microscopic vision, that showed all the intermediate frivolities, all the suppressed egoism, all the struggling chaos of puerilities, meanness, vague capricious memories, and indolent makeshift thoughts, from which human words and deeds emerge like leaflets covering a fermenting heap.

At Basle we were joined by my brother Alfred, now a handsome, self-confident man of six-and-twenty – a thorough contrast to my fragile, nervous, ineffectual self. I believe I was held to have a sort of half-womanish, half-ghostly beauty; for the portrait-painters, who are thick as weeds at Geneva, had often asked me to sit to them, and I had been the model of a dying minstrel in a fancy picture. But I thoroughly disliked my own physique and nothing but the belief that it was a condition of poetic genius would have reconciled me to it. That brief hope was quite fled, and I saw in my face now nothing but the stamp of a morbid organization, framed for passive suffering – too feeble for the sublime resistance of poetic production. Alfred, from whom I had been almost constantly separated, and who, in his present stage of character and appearance, came before me as a perfect stranger, was bent on being extremely friendly and brother-like to me. He had the superficial kindness of a good-humoured, self-satisfied nature, that fears no rivalry, and has encountered no contrarieties. I am not sure that my disposition was good enough for me to have been quite free from envy towards him, even if our desires had not clashed, and if I had been in the healthy human condition which admits of generous confidence and charitable construction. There must always have been an antipathy between our natures. As it was, he became in a few weeks an object of intense hatred to me; and when he entered the room, still more when he spoke, it was as if a sensation of grating metal had set my teeth on edge. My diseased consciousness was more intensely and continually occupied with his thoughts and emotions, than with those of any other person who came in my way. I was perpetually exasperated with the petty promptings of his conceit and his love of patronage, with his self-complacent belief in Bertha Grant's passion for him, with his half-pitying contempt for me – seen not in the ordinary indications of intonation and phrase and slight action, which an acute and suspicious mind is on the watch for, but in all their naked skinless complication.

For we were rivals, and our desires clashed, though he was not aware of it. I have said nothing yet of the effect Bertha Grant produced in me on a nearer acquaintance. That effect was chiefly determined by the fact that she made the only exception, amongst all the human beings about me, to my unhappy gift of insight. About Bertha I was always in a state of uncertainty: I could watch the expression of her face, and speculate on its meaning; I could ask for her opinion with the real interest of ignorance; I could listen for her words and watch for her smile with hope and fear: she had for me the fascination of an unravelled destiny. I say it was this fact that chiefly determined the strong effect she produced on me: for, in the abstract, no womanly character could seem to have less affinity for that of a shrinking, romantic, passionate youth than Bertha's. She was keen, sarcastic, unimaginative, prematurely cynical, remaining critical and unmoved in the most impressive scenes, inclined to dissect all my favourite poems, and especially contemptuous towards the German lyrics which were my pet literature at that time. To this moment I am unable to define my feeling towards her: it was not ordinary boyish admiration, for she was the very opposite, even to the colour of her hair, of the ideal woman who still remained to me the type of loveliness; and she was without that enthusiasm for the great and good, which, even at the moment of her strongest dominion over me, I should have declared to be the highest element of character. But there is no tyranny more complete than that which a self-centred negative nature exercises over a morbidly sensitive nature perpetually craving sympathy and support. The most independent people feel the effect of a man's silence in heightening their value for his opinion – feel an additional triumph in conquering the reverence of a critic habitually captious and satirical: no wonder, then, that an enthusiastic self-distrusting youth should watch and wait before the closed secret of a sarcastic woman's face, as if it were the shrine of the doubtfully benignant deity who ruled his destiny. For a young enthusiast is unable to imagine the total negation in another mind of the emotions which are stirring his own: they may be feeble, latent, inactive, he thinks, but they are there – they may be called forth; sometimes, in moments of happy hallucination, he believes they may be there in all the greater strength because he sees no outward sign of them. And this effect, as I have intimated, was heightened to its utmost intensity in me, because Bertha was the only being who remained for me in the mysterious seclusion of soul that renders such youthful delusion possible. Doubtless there was another sort of fascination at work – that subtle physical attraction which delights in cheating our psychological predictions, and in compelling the men who paint sylphs, to fall in love with some *bonne et brave femme*, heavy-heeled and freckled.

Bertha's behaviour towards me was such as to encourage all my illusions, to heighten my boyish passion, and make me more and more dependent on her smiles. Looking back with my present wretched knowledge, I conclude that her vanity and love of power were intensely gratified by the belief that I had fainted on first seeing

her purely from the strong impression her person had produced on
me. The most prosaic woman likes to believe herself the object of a
violent, a poetic passion; and without a grain of romance in her,
Bertha had that spirit of intrigue which gave piquancy to the idea
that the brother of the man she meant to marry was dying with love
and jealousy for her sake. That she meant to marry my brother, was
what at that time I did not believe; for though he was assiduous in
his attentions to her, and I knew well enough that both he and my
father had made up their minds to this result, there was not yet an
understood engagement – there had been no explicit declaration; and
Bertha habitually, while she flirted with my brother, and accepted
his homage in a way that implied to him a thorough recognition of
its intention, made me believe, by the subtlest looks and phrases –
feminine nothings which could never be quoted against her – that
he was really the object of her secret ridicule; that she thought him,
as I did, a coxcomb, whom she would have pleasure in disappoint-
ing. Me she openly petted in my brother's presence, as if I were too
young and sickly ever to be thought of as a lover; and that was the
view he took of me. But I believe she must inwardly have delighted
in the tremors into which she threw me by the coaxing way in which
she patted my curls, while she laughed at my quotations. Such
caresses were always given in the presence of our friends; for when
we were alone together, she affected a much greater distance
towards me, and now and then took the opportunity, by words or
slight actions, to stimulate my foolish timid hope that she really preferred me. And why should she not follow her inclination? I was not
in so advantageous a position as my brother, but I had fortune, I was
not a year younger than she was, and she was an heiress, who would
soon be of age to decide for herself.

The fluctuations of hope and fear, confined to this one channel,
made each day in her presence a delicious torment. There was one
deliberate act of hers which especially helped to intoxicate me.
When we were at Vienna her twentieth birthday occurred, and as
she was very fond of ornaments, we all took the opportunity of the
splendid jewellers' shops in that Teutonic Paris to purchase her a

birthday present of jewellery. Mine, naturally, was the least expensive; it was an opal ring – the opal was my favourite stone, because it seems to blush and turn pale as if it had a soul. I told Bertha so when I gave it her, and said that it was an emblem of the poetic nature, changing with the changing light of heaven and of woman's eyes. In the evening she appeared elegantly dressed, and wearing conspicuously all the birthday presents except mine. I looked eagerly at her fingers, but saw no opal. I had no opportunity of noticing this to her during the evening; but the next day, when I found her seated near the window alone, after breakfast, I said, 'You scorn to wear my poor opal. I should have remembered that you despised poetic natures, and should have given you coral, or turquoise, or some other opaque unresponsive stone.' 'Do I despise it?' she answered, taking hold of a delicate gold chain which she always wore round her neck and drawing out the end from her bosom with my ring hanging to it; 'it hurts me a little, I can tell you,' she said, with her usual dubious smile, 'to wear it in that secret place; and since your poetical nature is so stupid as to prefer a more public position, I shall not endure the pain any longer.'

She took off the ring from the chain and put it on her finger, smiling still, while the blood rushed to my cheeks, and I could not trust myself to say a word of entreaty that she would keep the ring where it was before.

I was completely fooled by this, and for two days shut myself up in my own room whenever Bertha was absent, that I might intoxicate myself afresh with the thought of this scene and all it implied.

I should mention that during these two months – which seemed a long life to me from the novelty and intensity of the pleasures and pains I underwent – my diseased anticipation in other people's consciousness continued to torment me; now it was my father, and now my brother, now Mrs Filmore or her husband, and now our German courier, whose stream of thought rushed upon me like a ringing in the ears not to be got rid of, though it allowed my own impulses and ideas to continue their uninterrupted course. It was like a preternaturally heightened sense of hearing, making audible to one a roar of sound where others find perfect stillness. The weariness and disgust of this involuntary intrusion into other souls was counteracted only by my ignorance of Bertha, and my growing passion for her; a passion enormously stimulated, if not produced, by that ignorance. She was my oasis of mystery in the dreary desert of knowledge. I had never allowed my diseased condition to betray itself, or to drive me into any unusual speech or action, except once, when, in a moment of peculiar bitterness against my brother, I had forestalled some words which I knew he was going to utter – a clever observation, which he had prepared beforehand. He had occasionally a slightly affected hesitation in his speech, and when he paused an instant after the second word, my impatience and jealousy impelled me to continue the speech for him, as if it were something we had both learnt by rote. He coloured and looked astonished, as well as annoyed; and the words had no sooner escaped my lips than I felt a shock of alarm lest such an anticipation of words – very far from being words of course, easy to divine – should have betrayed me as an exceptional being, a sort of quiet energumen, whom every one, Bertha above all, would shudder at and avoid. But I magnified, as usual, the impression any word or deed of mine could produce on others; for no one gave any sign of having noticed my interruption as more than a rudeness, to be forgiven me on the score of my feeble nervous condition.

While this superadded consciousness of the actual was almost constant with me, I had never had a recurrence of that distinct prevision which I have described in relation to my first interview with Bertha; and I was waiting with eager curiosity to know whether or not my vision of Prague would prove to have been an instance of the same kind. A few days after the incident of the opal ring, we were paying one of our frequent visits to the Lichtenberg Palace. I could never look at many pictures in succession; for pictures, when they are at all powerful, affect me so strongly that one or two exhaust all my capability of contemplation. This morning I had been looking at Giorgione's picture of the cruel-eyed woman, said to be a likeness of Lucrezia Borgia. I had stood long alone before it, fascinated by the terrible reality of that cunning, relentless face, till I felt a strange poisoned sensation, as if I had long been inhaling a fatal odour, and was just beginning to be conscious of its effects. Perhaps even then I should not have moved away, if the rest of the party had not returned to this room, and announced that they were going to the Belvedere Gallery to settle a bet which had arisen between my brother and Mr Filmore about a portrait. I followed them dreamily, and was hardly alive to what occurred till they had all gone up to the gallery, leaving me below; for I refused to come within sight of another picture that day. I made my way to the Grand Terrace, since it was agreed that we should saunter in the gardens when the dispute had been decided. I had been sitting here a short space, vaguely conscious of trim gardens, with a city and green hills in the distance, when, wishing to avoid the proximity of the sentinel, I rose and walked down the broad stone steps, intending to seat myself farther on in the gardens. Just as I reached the gravel-walk, I felt an arm slipped within mine, and a light hand gently pressing my wrist. In the same instant a strange intoxicating numbness passed over me, like the continuance or climax of the sensation I was still feeling from the gaze of Lucrezia Borgia. The gardens, the summer sky, the consciousness of Bertha's arm being within mine, all vanished, and I seemed to be suddenly in darkness, out of which there gradually broke a dim firelight, and I felt myself sitting in my father's leather chair in the library at home. I knew the fireplace – the dogs for the wood-fire – the black marble chimney-piece with the white marble medallion of the dying Cleopatra in the centre. Intense and hopeless misery was pressing on my soul; the light became stronger, for Bertha was entering with a candle in her hand – Bertha, my wife – with cruel eyes, with green jewels and green leaves on her white ball-dress; every hateful thought within her present to me . . . 'Madman, idiot! Why don't you kill yourself, then?' It was a moment of hell. I saw into her pitiless soul – saw its barren worldli-ness, its scorching hate – and felt it clothe me round like an air I was obliged to breathe. She came with her candle and stood over me with a bitter smile of contempt; I saw the great emerald brooch on her bosom, a studded serpent with diamond eyes. I shuddered – I despised this woman with the barren soul and mean thoughts; but I felt helpless before her, as if she clutched my bleeding heart, and would clutch it till the last drop of life-blood ebbed away. She was my wife, and we hated each other. Gradually the hearth, the dim library, the candle-light disappeared – seemed to melt away into a background of light, the green serpent with the diamond eyes remaining a dark image on the retina. Then I had a sense of my eyelids quivering, and the living daylight broke in upon me; I saw gardens, and heard voices; I was seated on the steps of the Belvedere Terrace, and my friends were round me.

The tumult of mind into which I was thrown by this hideous vision made me ill for several days, and prolonged our stay at Vienna. I shuddered with horror as the scene recurred to me; and it recurred constantly, with all its minutiæ, as if they had been burnt into my memory; and yet, such is the madness of the human heart under the influence of its immediate desires, I felt a wild hell-braving joy that Bertha was to be mine; for the fulfilment of my former prevision concerning her first appearance before me, left me little hope that this last hideous glimpse of the future was the mere diseased play of my own mind, and had no relation to external realities. One thing alone I looked towards as a possible means of casting doubt on my terrible conviction – the discovery that my vision of Prague had been false – and Prague was the next city on our route.

Meanwhile, I was no sooner in Bertha's society again than I was as completely under her sway as before. What if I saw into the heart of Bertha, the matured woman – Bertha, my wife? Bertha, the *girl*, was a fascinating secret to me still: I trembled under her touch; I felt the witchery of her presence; I yearned to be assured of her love. The fear of poison is feeble against the sense of thirst. Nay, I was just as jealous of my brother as before – just as much irritated by his small patronizing ways; for my pride, my diseased sensibility, were there as they had always been, and winced as inevitably under every offence as my eye winced from an intruding mote. The future, even when brought within the compass of feeling by a vision that made me shudder, had still no more than the force of an idea, compared with the force of present emotion – of my love for Bertha, of my dislike and jealousy towards my brother.

It is an old story, that men sell themselves to the tempter, and sign a bond with their blood, because it is only to take effect at a distant day; then rush on to snatch the cup their souls thirst after with an impulse not the less savage because there is a dark shadow beside them for evermore. There is no short cut, no patent tram-road, to wisdom: after all the centuries of invention, the soul's path lies through the thorny wilderness which must be still trodden in solitude, with bleeding feet, with sobs for help, as it was trodden by them of old time.

My mind speculated eagerly on the means by which I should become my brother's successful rival, for I was still too timid, in my ignorance of Bertha's actual feeling, to venture on any step that would urge from her an avowal of it. I thought I should gain confidence even for this, if my vision of Prague proved to have been veracious; and yet, the horror of that certitude! Behind the slim girl Bertha, whose words and looks I watched for, whose touch was bliss, there stood continually that Bertha with the fuller form, the harder eyes, the more rigid mouth – with the barren, selfish soul laid bare; no longer a fascinating secret, but a measured fact, urging itself perpetually on my unwilling sight. Are you unable to give me your sympathy – you who react this? Are you unable to imagine this double consciousness at work within me, flowing on like two parallel streams which never mingle their waters and blend into a common hue? Yet you must have known something of the presentiments that spring from an insight at war with passion; and my visions were only like presentiments intensified to horror. You have known the powerlessness of ideas before the might of impulse; and my visions, when once they had passed into memory, were mere ideas – pale shadows that beckoned in vain, while my hand was grasped by the living and the loved.

In after-days I thought with bitter regret that if I had foreseen something more or something different – if instead of that hideous vision which poisoned the passion it could not destroy, or if even along with it I could have had a foreshadowing of that moment when I looked on my brother's face for the last time, some softening influence would have been shed over my feeling towards him: pride and hatred would surely have been subdued into pity, and the record of those hidden sins would have been shortened. But this is one of the vain thoughts with which we men flatter ourselves. We try to believe that the egoism within us would have easily been melted, and that it was only the narrowness of our knowledge which hemmed in our generosity, our awe, our human piety, and hindered them from submerging our hard indifference to the sensations and emotions of our fellows. Our tenderness and self-renunciation seem strong when our egoism has had its day – when, after our mean striving for a triumph that is to be another's loss, the triumph comes suddenly, and we shudder at it, because it is held out by the chill hand of death.

Our arrival in Prague happened at night, and I was glad of this, for it seemed like a deferring of a terribly decisive moment, to be in the city for hours without seeing it. As we were not to remain long in Prague, but to go on speedily to Dresden, it was proposed that we should drive out the next morning and take a general view of the place, as well as visit some of its specially interesting spots, before the heat became oppressive – for we were in August, and the season was hot and dry. But it happened that the ladies were rather late at their morning toilet, and to my father's politely repressed but perceptible annoyance, we were not in the carriage till the morning was far advanced. I thought with a sense of relief, as we entered the Jews' quarter, where we were to visit the old synagogue, that we should be kept in this flat, shut-up part of the city, until we should all be too tired and too warm to go farther, and so we should return without seeing more than the streets through which we had already passed. That would give me another day's suspense – suspense, the only form in which a fearful spirit knows the solace of hope. But, as I stood under the blackened, groined arches of that old synagogue, made dimly visible by the seven thin candles in the sacred lamp, while our Jewish cicerone reached down the Book of the Law, and read to us in its ancient tongue – I felt a shuddering impression that this strange building, with its shrunken lights, this surviving withered remnant of medieval Judaism, was of a piece with my vision. Those darkened dusty Christian saints, with their loftier arches and their larger candles, needed the consolatory scorn with which they might point to a more shrivelled death-in-life than their own.

As I expected, when we left the Jews' quarter the elders of our party wished to return to the hotel. But now, instead of rejoicing in this, as I had done beforehand, I felt a sudden overpowering impulse to go on at once to the bridge, and put an end to the suspense I had been wishing to protract. I declared, with unusual decision, that I would get out of the carriage and walk on alone; they might return without me. My father, thinking this merely a sample of my usual 'poetic nonsense', objected that I should only do myself harm by walking in the heat; but when I persisted, he said angrily that I might follow my own absurd devices, but that Schmidt (our courier) must go with me. I assented to this, and set off with Schmidt towards the bridge. I had no sooner passed from under the archway of the grand old gate leading on to the bridge, than a trembling seized me, and I turned cold under the midday sun; yet I went on; I was in search of something – a small detail which I remembered with special intensity as part of my vision. There it was – the patch of rainbow light on the pavement transmitted through a lamp in the shape of a star.

II

Before the autumn was at an end, and while the brown leaves still stood thick on the beeches in our park, my brother and Bertha were engaged to each other, and it was understood that their marriage was to take place early in the next spring. In spite of the certainty I had felt from that moment on the bridge at Prague that Bertha would one day be my wife, my constitutional timidity and distrust had continued to benumb me, and the words in which I had some-times premeditated a confession of my love, had died away unuttered. The same conflict had gone on within me as before – the longing for an assurance of love from Bertha's lips, the dread lest a word of contempt and denial should fall upon me like a corrosive acid. What was the conviction of a distant necessity to me? I trembled under a present glance, I hungered after a present joy, I was clogged and chilled by a present fear. And so the days passed on: I witnessed Bertha's engagement and heard her marriage discussed as if I were under a conscious nightmare – knowing it was a dream that would vanish, but feeling stifled under the grasp of hard-clutching fingers.

When I was not in Bertha's presence – and I was with her very often, for she continued to treat me with a playful patronage that wakened no jealousy in my brother – I spent my time chiefly in wandering, in strolling, or taking long rides while the daylight lasted, and then shutting myself up with my unread books; for books had lost the power of chaining my attention. My self-consciousness was heightened to that pitch of intensity in which our own emotions take the form of a drama which urges itself imperatively on our contemplation, and we begin to weep, less under the sense of our suffering than at the thought of it. I felt a sort of pitying anguish over the pathos of my own lot: the lot of a being finely organized for pain but with hardly any fibres that responded to pleasure – to whom the idea of future evil robbed the present of its joy, and for whom the idea of future good did not still the uneasiness of a present yearning or a present dread. I went dumbly through that stage of the poet's suffering, in which he feels the delicious pang of utterance, and makes an image of his sorrows.

I was left entirely without remonstrance concerning this dreamy wayward life: I knew my father's thought about me: 'That lad will never be good for anything in life: he may waste his years in an insignificant way on the income that falls to him: I shall not trouble myself about a career for him.'

One mild morning in the beginning of November, it happened

that I was standing outside the portico patting lazy old Cæsar, a Newfoundland almost blind with age, the only dog that ever took any notice of me – for the very dogs shunned me, and fawned on the happier people about me – when the groom brought up my brother's horse which was to carry him to the hunt, and my brother himself appeared at the door, florid, broad-chested, and self-complacent, feeling what a good-natured fellow he was not to behave insolently to us all on the strength of his great advantages.

'Latimer, old boy,' he said to me in a tone of compassionate cordiality, 'what a pity it is you don't have a run with the hounds now and then! The finest thing in the world for low spirits!'

'Low spirits!' I thought bitterly, as he rode away; 'that is the sort of phrase with which coarse, narrow natures like yours think to describe experience of which you can know no more than your horse knows. It is to such as you that the good of this world falls: ready dullness, healthy selfishness, good-tempered conceit – these are the keys to happiness.'

The quick thought came, that my selfishness was even stronger than his – it was only a suffering selfishness instead of an enjoying one. But then, again, my exasperating insight into Alfred's self-complacent soul, his freedom from all the doubts and fears, the unsatisfied yearnings, the exquisite tortures of sensitiveness, that had made the web of my life, seemed to absolve me from all bonds towards him. This man needed no pity, no love; those fine influences would have been as little felt by him as the delicate white mist is felt by the rock it caresses. There was no evil in store for *him*: if he was not to marry Bertha, it would be because he had found a lot pleasanter to himself.

Mr Filmore's house lay not more than half a mile beyond our own gates, and whenever I knew my brother was gone in another direction, I went there for the chance of finding Bertha at home. Later on in the day I walked thither. By a rare accident she was alone, and we walked out in the grounds together, for she seldom went on foot beyond the trimly swept gravel-walks. I remember what a beautiful sylph she looked to me as the low November sun shone on her blonde hair, and she tripped along teasing me with her usual light banter, to which I listened half fondly, half moodily; it was all the sign Bertha's mysterious inner self ever made to me. To-day perhaps, the moodiness predominated, for I had not yet shaken off the access of jealous hate which my brother had raised in me by his parting patronage. Suddenly I interrupted and startled her by saying, almost fiercely, 'Bertha, how can you love Alfred?'

She looked at me with surprise for a moment, but soon her light smile came again, and she answered sarcastically, 'Why do you suppose I love him?'

'How can you ask that, Bertha?'

'What! your wisdom thinks I must love the man I'm going to marry? The most unpleasant thing in the world. I should quarrel with him; I should be jealous of him; our *ménage* would be conducted in a very ill-bred manner. A little quiet contempt contributes greatly to the elegance of life.'

'Bertha, that is not your real feeling. Why do you delight in trying to deceive me by inventing such cynical speeches?'

'I need never take the trouble of invention in order to deceive you, my small Tasso' (that was the mocking name she usually gave me). 'The easiest way to deceive a poet is to tell him the truth.'

She was testing the validity of her epigram in a daring way, and for a moment the shadow of my vision – the Bertha whose soul was no secret to me – passed between me and the radiant girl, the playful sylph whose feelings were a fascinating mystery. I suppose I must have shuddered, or betrayed in some other way my momentary chill of horror.

'Tasso!' she said, seizing my wrist, and peeping round into my face, 'are you really beginning to discern what a heartless girl I am? Why, you are not half the poet I thought you were; you are actually capable of believing the truth about me.'

The shadow passed from between us, and was no longer the object nearest to me. The girl whose light fingers grasped me, whose elfish charming face looked into mine – who, I thought, was betraying an interest in my feelings that she would not have directly avowed, – this warm, breathing presence again possessed my senses and imagination like a returning siren melody which had been overpowered for an instant by the roar of threatening waves. It was a moment as delicious to me as the waking up to a consciousness of youth after a dream of middle age. I forgot everything but my passion, and said with swimming eyes, 'Bertha, shall you love me when we are first married? I wouldn't mind if you really loved me only for a little while.'

Her look of astonishment, as she loosed my hand and started away from me, recalled me to a sense of my strange, my criminal indiscretion.

'Forgive me,' I said, hurriedly, as soon as I could speak again. 'I did not know what I was saying.'

'Ah, Tasso's mad fit has come on, I see,' she answered quietly, for she had recovered herself sooner than I had. 'Let him go home and keep his head cool. I must go in, for the sun is setting.'

I left her – full of indignation against myself. I had let slip words which, if she reflected on them, might rouse in her a suspicion of my abnormal mental condition – a suspicion which of all things I dreaded. And besides that, I was ashamed of the apparent baseness I had committed in uttering them to my brother's betrothed wife. I wandered home slowly, entering our park through a private gate instead of by the lodges. As I approached the house, I saw a man dashing off at full speed from the stable-yard across the park. Had any accident happened at home? No; perhaps it was only one of my father's peremptory business errands that required this headlong haste.

Nevertheless I quickened my pace without any distinct motive, and was soon at the house. I will not dwell on the scene I found there. My brother was dead – had been pitched from his horse, and killed on the spot by a concussion of the brain.

I went up to the room where he lay, and where my father was seated beside him with a look of rigid despair. I had shunned my father more than any one since our return home, for the radical antipathy between our natures made my insight into his inner self a constant affliction to me. But now, as I went up to him, and stood beside him in sad silence, I felt the presence of a new element that blended us as we had never been blent before. My father had been one of the most successful men in the money-getting world: he had had no sentimental sufferings, no illness. The heaviest trouble that had befallen him was the death of his first wife. But he married my mother soon after; and I remember he seemed exactly the same, to my keen childish observation, the week after her death as before. But now, at last, a sorrow had come – the sorrow of old age, which suffers the more from the crushing of its pride and its hopes, in proportion as the pride and hope are narrow and prosaic. His son was to have been married soon – would probably have stood for the borough at the next election. That son's existence was the best motive that could be alleged for making new purchases of land every year to round off the estate. It is a dreary thing on to live on doing the same things year after year, without knowing why we do them. Perhaps the tragedy of disappointed youth and passion is less piteous than the tragedy of disappointed age and worldliness.

As I saw into the desolation of my father's heart, I felt a movement of deep pity towards him, which was the beginning of a new affection – an affection that grew and strengthened in spite of the strange bitterness with which he regarded me in the first month or two after my brother's death. If it had not been for the softening influence of my compassion for him – the first deep compassion I had ever felt – I should have been stung by the perception that my father transferred the inheritance of an eldest son to me with a mortified sense that fate had compelled him to the unwelcome course of caring for me as an important being. It was only in spite of himself that he began to think of me with anxious regard. There is hardly any neglected child for whom death has made vacant a more favoured place, who will not understand what I mean.

Gradually, however, my new deference to his wishes, the effect of that patience which was born of my pity for him, won upon his affection, and he began to please himself with the endeavour to make me fill my brother's place as fully as my feebler personality would admit. I saw that the prospect which by and by presented itself of my becoming Bertha's husband was welcome to him, and he even contemplated in my case what he had not intended in my brother's – that his son and daughter-in-law should make one household with him. My softened feelings towards my father made this the happiest time I had known since childhood; – these last months in which I retained the delicious illusion of loving Bertha, of longing and doubting and hoping that she might love me. She behaved with a certain new consciousness and distance towards me after my brother's death; and I too was under a double constraint – that of delicacy towards my brother's memory and of anxiety as to the impression my abrupt words had left on her mind. But the additional screen this mutual reserve erected between us only brought me more completely under her power: no matter how empty the adytum, so that the veil be thick enough. So absolute is our soul's need of something hidden and uncertain for the maintenance of that doubt and hope and effort which are the breath of its life, that if the whole future were laid bare to us beyond to-day, the interest of all mankind would be bent on the hours that lie between; we should pant after the uncertainties of our one morning and our one afternoon; we should rush fiercely to the Exchange for our last possibility of speculation, of success, of disappointment: we should have a glut of political prophets foretelling a crisis or a no-crisis within the only twenty-four hours left open to prophecy. Conceive the condition of the human mind if all propositions whatsoever were self-evident except one, which was to become self-evident at the close of a summer's day, but in the meantime might be the subject of question, of hypothesis, of debate. Art and philosophy, literature and science, would fasten like bees on that one proposition which had the honey of probability in it, and be the more eager because their enjoyment would end with sunset. Our impulses, our spiritual activities, no more adjust themselves to the idea of their future nullity, than the beating of our heart, or the irritability of our muscles.

Bertha, the slim, fair-haired girl, whose present thoughts and emotions were an enigma to me amidst the fatiguing obviousness of the other minds around me, was as absorbing to me as a single unknown to-day – as a single hypothetic proposition to remain problematic till sunset; and all the cramped, hemmed-in belief and disbelief, trust and distrust, of my nature, welled out in this one narrow channel.

And she made me believe that she loved me. Without ever quitting her tone of *badinage* and playful superiority, she intoxicated me with the sense that I was necessary to her, that she was never at ease, unless I was near her, submitting to her playful tyranny. It costs a woman so little effort to beset us in this way! A half-repressed word, a moment's unexpected silence, even an easy fit of petulance on our account, will serve us as *hashish* for a long while. Out of the subtlest web of scarcely perceptible signs, she set me weaving the fancy that she had always unconsciously loved me better than Alfred, but that, with the ignorant fluttered sensibility of a young girl, she had been imposed on by the charm that lay for her in the distinction of being admired and chosen by a man who made so brilliant a figure in the world as my brother. She satirized herself in a very graceful way for her vanity and ambition. What was it to me that I had the light of my wretched provision on the fact that now it was I who possessed at least all but the personal part of my brother's advantages? Our sweet illusions are half of them conscious illusions, like effects of colour that we know to be made up of tinsel, broken glass, and rags.

We were married eighteen months after Alfred's death, one cold, clear morning in April, when there came hail and sunshine both together; and Bertha, in her white silk and pale-green leaves, and the pale hues of her hair and face, looked like the spirit of the morning. My father was happier than he had thought of being again: my marriage, he felt sure, would complete the desirable modification of my character, and make me practical and worldly enough to take my place in society among sane men. For he delighted in Bertha's tact and acuteness, and felt sure she would be mistress of me, and make me what she chose: I was only twenty-one, and madly in love with her. Poor father! He kept that hope a little while after our first year of marriage, and it was not quite extinct when paralysis came and saved him from utter disappointment.

I shall hurry through the rest of my story, not dwelling so much as I have hitherto done on my inward experience. When people are well known to each other, they talk rather of what befalls them externally, leaving their feelings and sentiments to be inferred.

We lived in a round of visits for some time after our return home, giving splendid dinner-parties, and making a sensation in our neighbourhood by the new lustre of our equipage, for my father had reserved this display of his increased wealth for the period of his son's marriage; and we gave our acquaintances liberal opportunity for remarking that it was a pity I made so poor a figure as an heir and a bridegroom. The nervous fatigue of this existence, the insincerities and platitudes which I had to live through twice over – through my inner and outward sense – would have been maddening to me, if I had not had that sort of intoxicated callousness which came from the delights of a first passion. A bride and bridegroom, surrounded by all the appliances of wealth, hurried through the day by the whirl of society, filling their solitary moments with hastily snatched caresses, are prepared for their future life together as the novice is prepared for the cloister – by experiencing its utmost contrast.

Through all these crowded excited months, Bertha's inward self remained shrouded from me, and I still read her thoughts only through the language of her lips and demeanour: I had still the human interest of wondering whether what I did and said pleased her, of longing to hear a word of affection, of giving a delicious exaggeration of meaning to her smile. But I was conscious of a growing difference in her manner towards me; sometimes strong enough to be called haughty coldness, cutting and chilling me as the hail had done that came across the sunshine on our marriage morning; sometimes only perceptible in the dexterous avoidance of a *tête-à-tête* walk or dinner to which I had been looking forward. I had been deeply pained by this – had even felt a sort of crushing of the heart, from the sense that my brief day of happiness was near its setting; but still

I remained dependent on Bertha, eager for the last rays of a bliss that would soon be gone for ever, hoping and watching for some after-glow more beautiful from the impending night.

I remember – how should I not remember? – the time when that dependence and hope utterly left me, when the sadness I had felt in Bertha's growing estrangement became a joy that I looked back upon with longing as a man might look back on the last pains in a paralysed limb. It was just after the close of my father's last illness, which had necessarily withdrawn us from society and thrown us more on each other. It was the evening of father's death. On that evening the veil which had shrouded Bertha's soul from me – had made me find in her alone among my fellow-beings the blessed possibility of mystery, and doubt, and expectation – was first withdrawn. Perhaps it was the first day since the beginning of my passion for her, in which that passion was completely neutralized by the presence of an absorbing feeling of another kind. I had been watching by my father's deathbed: I had been witnessing the last fitful yearning glance his soul had cast back on the spent inheritance of life – the last faint consciousness of love he had gathered from the pressure of my hand. What are all our personal loves when we have been sharing in that supreme agony? In the first moments when we come away from the presence of death, every other relation to the living is merged, to our feeling, in the great relation of a common nature and a common destiny.

In that state of mind I joined Bertha in her private sitting-room. She was seated in a leaning posture on a settee, with her back towards the door; the great rich coils of her pale blonde hair surmounting her small neck, visible above the back of the settee. I remember, as I closed the door behind me, a cold tremulousness seizing me, and a vague sense of being hated and lonely – vague and strong, like a presentiment. I know how I looked at that moment, for I saw myself in Bertha's thought as she lifted her cutting grey eyes, and looked at me: a miserable ghost-seer, surrounded by phantoms in the noonday, trembling under a breeze when the leaves were still, without appetite for the common objects of human desires, but pining after the moon-beams. We were front to front with each other, and judged each other. The terrible moment of complete illumination had come to me, and I saw that the darkness had hidden no landscape from me, but only a blank prosaic wall: from that evening forth, through the sickening years which followed, I saw all round the narrow room of this woman's soul – saw petty artifice and mere negation where I had delighted to believe in coy sensibilities and in wit at war with latent feeling – saw the light floating vanities of the girl defining themselves into the systematic coquetry, the scheming selfishness, of the woman – saw repulsion and antipathy harden into cruel hatred, giving pain only for the sake of wreaking itself.

For Bertha too, after her kind, felt the bitterness of disillusion. She had believed that my wild poet's passion for her would make me her slave; and that, being her slave, I should execute her will in all things. With the essential shallowness of a negative, unimaginative nature, she was unable to conceive the fact that sensibilities were anything else than weaknesses. She had thought my weaknesses would put me in her power, and she found them unmanageable forces. Our positions were reversed. Before marriage she had completely mastered my imagination, for she was a secret to me; and I created the unknown thought before which I trembled as if it were hers. But now that her soul was laid open to me, now that I was compelled to share the privacy of her motives, to follow all the petty devices that preceded her words and acts, she found herself powerless with me, except to produce in me the chill shudder of repulsion – powerless, because I could be acted on by no lever within her reach. I was dead to worldly ambitions, to social vanities, to all the incentives within the compass of her narrow imagination, and I lived under influences utterly invisible to her.

She was really pitiable to have such a husband, and so all the world thought. A graceful, brilliant woman, like Bertha, who smiled on morning callers, made a figure in ball-rooms, and was capable of that light repartee which, from such a woman, is accepted as wit, was secure of carrying off all sympathy from a husband who was sickly, abstracted, and, as some suspected, crack-brained. Even the servants in our house gave her the balance of their regard and pity. For there were no audible quarrels between us; our alienation, our repulsion from each other, lay within the silence of our own hearts; and if the mistress went out a great deal, and seemed to dislike the master's society, was it not natural, poor thing? The master was odd. I was kind and just to my dependants, but I excited in them a shrinking, half-contemptuous pity; for this class of men and women are but slightly determined in their estimate of others by general considerations, or even experience, of character. They judge of persons as they judge of coins, and value those who pass current at a high rate.

After a time I interfered so little with Bertha's habits that it might seem wonderful how her hatred towards me could grow so intense and active as it did. But she had begun to suspect, by some involuntary betrayal of mine, that there was an abnormal power of penetration in me – that fitfully, at least, I was strangely cognizant of her thoughts and intentions, and she began to be haunted by a terror of me, which alternated every now and then with defiance. She meditated continually how the incubus could be shaken off her life – how she could be freed from this hateful bond to a being whom she at once despised as an imbecile, and dreaded as an inquisitor. For a long while she lived in the hope that my evident wretchedness would drive me to the commission of suicide; but suicide was not in my nature. I was too completely swayed by the sense that I was in the grasp of unknown forces, to believe in my power of self-release. Towards my own destiny I had become entirely passive; for my one ardent desire had spent itself, and impulse no longer predominated over knowledge. For this reason I never thought of taking any steps towards a complete separation, which would have made our alienation evident to the world. Why should I rush for help to a new course, when I was only suffering from the consequences of a deed which had been the act of my intensest will? That would have been the logic of one who had desires to gratify, and I had no desires. But Bertha and I lived more and more aloof from each other. The rich find it easy to live married and apart.

That course of our life which I have indicated in a few sentences filled the space of years. So much misery – so slow and hideous a growth of hatred and sin, may be compressed into a sentence! And men judge of each other's lives through this summary medium. They epitomize the experience of their fellow-mortal, and pronounce judgement on him in neat syntax, and feel themselves wise and virtuous – conquerors over the temptations they define in well-selected predicates. Seven years of wretchedness glide glibly over the lips of the man who has never counted them out in moments of chill disappointment, of head and heart throbbings, of dread and vain wrestling, of remorse and despair. We learn *words* by rote, but not their meaning; *that* must be paid for with our life-blood, and printed in the subtle fibres of our nerves.

But I will hasten to finish my story. Brevity is justified at once to those who readily understand, and to those who will never understand.

Some years after my father's death, I was sitting by the dim fire-light in my library one January evening – sitting in the leather chair that used to be my father's – when Bertha appeared at the door, with a candle in her hand, and advanced towards me. I knew the ball-dress she had on – the white ball-dress, with the green jewels, shone upon by the light of the wax candle which lit up the medallion of the dying Cleopatra on the mantelpiece. Why did she come to me before going out? I had not seen her in the library, which was my habitual place for months. Why did she stand before me with the candle in her hand, with her cruel contemptuous eyes fixed on me, and the glittering serpent, like a familiar demon, on her breast? For a moment I thought this fulfilment of my vision at Vienna marked some dreadful crisis in my fate, but I saw nothing in Bertha's mind, as she stood before me, except scorn for the look of overwhelming misery with which I sat before her . . . 'Fool, idiot, why don't you kill yourself, then?' – that was her thought. But at length her thoughts reverted to her errand, and she spoke aloud. The apparently indifferent nature of the errand seemed to make a ridiculous anticlimax to my prevision and my agitation.

'I have had to hire a new maid. Fletcher is going to be married, and she wants me to ask you to let her husband have the public-house and farm at Molton. I wish him to have it. You must give the promise now, because Fletcher is going to-morrow morning – and quickly, because I'm in a hurry.'

'Very well; you may promise her,' I said, indifferently, and Bertha swept out of the library again.

I always shrank from the sight of a new person, and all the more when it was a person whose mental life was likely to weary my reluctant insight with worldly ignorant trivialities. But I shrank especially from the sight of this new maid, because her advent had been announced to me at a moment to which I could not cease to attach some fatality: I had a vague dread that I should find her mixed up with the dreary drama of my life – that some new sickening vision would reveal her to me as an evil genius. When at last I did unavoidably meet her, the vague dread was changed into definite disgust. She was a tall, wiry, dark-eyed woman, this Mrs Archer, with a face handsome enough to give her coarse hard nature the odious finish of bold, self-confident coquetry. That was enough to make me avoid her, quite apart from the contemptuous feeling with which she contemplated me. I seldom saw her; but I perceived that she rapidly became a favourite with her mistress, and, after the lapse of eight or nine months, I began to be aware that there had arisen in Bertha's mind towards this woman a mingled feeling of fear and dependence, and that this feeling was associated with ill-defined images of candle-light scenes in her dressing-room, and the locking-up of something in Bertha's cabinet. My interviews with my wife had become so brief and so rarely solitary, that I had no opportunity of perceiving these images in her mind with more definiteness. The recollections of the past become contracted in the rapidity of thought till they sometimes bear hardly a more distinct resemblance to the external reality than the forms of an oriental alphabet to the objects that suggested them.

Besides, for the last year or more a modification had been going forward in my mental condition, and was growing more and more marked. My insight into the minds of those around me was becoming dimmer and more fitful, and the ideas that crowded my double consciousness became less and less dependent on any personal contact. All that was personal in me seemed to be suffering a gradual death, so that I was losing the organ through which the personal agitations and projects of others could affect me. But along with this relief from wearisome insight, there was a new development of what I concluded – as I have since found rightly – to be a provision of external scenes. It was as if the relation between me and my fellow-men was more and more deadened, and my relation to what we call the inanimate was quickened into new life. The more I lived apart from society, and in proportion as my wretchedness subsided from the violent throb of agonized passion into the dullness of habitual pain, the more frequent and vivid became such visions as that I had had of Prague – of strange cities, of sandy plains, of gigantic ruins, of midnight skies with strange bright constellations, of mountain-passes, of grassy nooks flecked with the afternoon sunshine through the boughs: I was in the midst of such scenes, and in all of them one presence seemed to weigh on me in all these mighty shapes – the presence of something unknown and pitiless. For continual suffering had annihilated religious faith within me: to the utterly miserable – the unloving and the unloved – there is no religion possible, no worship but a worship of devils. And beyond all these, and continually recurring, was the vision of my death – the pangs, the suffocation, the last struggle, when life would be grasped at in vain.

Things were in this state near the end of the seventh year. I had become entirely free from insight, from my abnormal cognizance of any other consciousness than my own, and instead of intruding involuntarily into the world of other minds, was living continually in my own solitary future. Bertha was aware that I was greatly changed. To my surprise she had of late seemed to seek opportunities of remaining in my society, and had cultivated that kind of distant yet familiar talk which is customary between a husband and wife who live in polite and irrevocable alienation. I bore this with languid submission, and without feeling enough interest in her motives to be roused into keen observation; yet I could not help perceiving something triumphant and excited in her carriage and the expression of her face – something too subtle to express itself in words or tones, but giving one the idea that she lived in a state of expectation or hopeful suspense. My chief feeling was satisfaction that her inner self was once more shut out from me; and I almost revelled for the moment in the absent melancholy that made me answer her at cross purposes, and betray utter ignorance of what she had been saying. I remember well the look and the smile with which she one day said, after a mistake of this kind on my part: 'I used to think you were a clairvoyant, and that was the reason why you were so bitter against other clairvoyants, wanting to keep your monopoly; but I see now you have become rather duller than the rest of the world.'

I said nothing in reply. It occurred to me that her recent obtrusion of herself upon me might have been prompted by the wish to test my power of detecting some of her secrets; but I let the thought drop again at once: her motives and her deeds had no interest for me, and whatever pleasures she might be seeking, I had no wish to baulk her. There was still pity in my soul for every living thing, and Bertha was living – was surrounded with possibilities of misery.

Just at this time there occurred an event which roused me somewhat from my inertia, and gave me an interest in the passing moment that I had thought impossible for me. It was a visit from Charles Meunier, who had written me word that he was coming to England for relaxation from too strenuous labour, and would like to see me. Meunier had now a European reputation; but his letter to me expressed that keen remembrance of an early regard, an early debt of sympathy, which is inseparable from nobility of character: and I, too, felt as if his presence would be to me like a transient resurrection into a happier pre-existence.

He came, and as far as possible, I renewed our old pleasure of making *tête-à-tête* excursions, though, instead of mountains and glaciers and the wide blue lake, we had to content ourselves with mere slopes and ponds and artificial plantations. The years had changed us both, but with what different result! Meunier was now a brilliant figure in society, to whom elegant women pretended to listen, and whose acquaintance was boasted of by noblemen ambitious of brains. He repressed with the utmost delicacy all betrayal of the shock which I am sure he must have received from our meeting, or of a desire to penetrate into my condition and circumstances, and sought by the utmost exertion of his charming social powers to make our reunion agreeable. Bertha was much struck by the unexpected fascinations of a visitor whom she had expected to find presentable only on the score of his celebrity, and put forth all her coquetries and accomplishments. Apparently she succeeded in attracting his admiration, for his manner towards her was attentive and flattering. The effect of his presence on me was so benignant, especially in those renewals of our old *tête-à-tête* wanderings, when he poured forth to me wonderful narratives of his professional experience, that more than once, when his talk turned on the psychological relations of disease, the thought crossed my mind that, if his stay with me were long enough, I might possibly bring myself to tell this man the secrets of my lot. Might there not lie some remedy for me, too, in his science? Might there not at least lie some comprehension and sympathy ready for me in his large and susceptible mind? But the thought only flickered feebly now and then, and died out before it could become a wish. The horror I had of again breaking in on the privacy of another soul, made me, by an irrational instinct, draw the shroud of concealment more closely around my own, as we automatically perform the gesture we feel to be wanting in another.

When Meunier's visit was approaching its conclusion, there happened an event which caused some excitement in our household, owing to the surprisingly strong effect it appeared to produce on Bertha – on Bertha, the self-possessed, who usually seemed inaccessible to feminine agitations, and did even her hate in a self-restrained hygienic manner. This event was the sudden severe illness of her maid, Mrs Archer.

I have reserved to this moment the mention of a circumstance which had forced itself on my notice shortly before Meunier's arrival, namely, that there had been some quarrel between Bertha and this maid, apparently during a visit to a distant family, in which she had accompanied her mistress. I had overheard Archer speaking in a tone of bitter insolence, which I should have thought an adequate reason for immediate dismissal. No dismissal followed; on the contrary, Bertha seemed to be silently putting up with personal inconveniences from the exhibitions of this woman's temper. I was the more astonished to observe that her illness seemed a cause of strong solicitude to Bertha; that she was at the bedside night and day, and would allow no one else to officiate as head-nurse.

It happened that our family doctor was out on a holiday, an accident which made Meunier's presence in the house doubly welcome, and he apparently entered into the case with an interest which seemed so much stronger than the ordinary professional feeling, that one day when he had fallen into a long fit of silence after visiting her, I said to him, 'Is this a very peculiar case of disease, Meunier?'

'No,' he answered, 'it is an attack of peritonitis, which will be fatal, but which does not differ physically from many other cases that have come under my observation. But I'll tell you what I have on my mind. I want to make an experiment on this woman, if you will give me permission. It can do her no harm – will give her no pain – for I shall not make it until life is extinct to all purposes of sensation. I want to try the effect of transfusing blood into her arteries after the heart has ceased to beat for some minutes. I have tried the experiment again and again with animals that have died of this disease, with astounding results, and I want to try it on a human subject. I have the small tubes necessary, in a case I have with me, and the rest of the apparatus could be prepared readily. I should use my own blood – take it from my own arm. This woman won't live through the night, I'm convinced, and I want you to promise me your assistance in making the experiment. I can't do without another hand, but it would perhaps not be well to call in a medical assistant from amongst your provincial doctors. A disagreeable foolish version of the thing might get abroad.'

'Have you spoken to my wife on the subject?' I said, 'because she appears to be peculiarly sensitive about this woman: she has been a favourite maid.'

'To tell you the truth,' said Meunier, 'I don't want her to know about it. There are always insuperable difficulties with women in these matters, and the effect on the supposed dead body may be startling. You and I will sit up together, and be in readiness. When certain symptoms appear I shall take you in, and at the right moment we must manage to get everyone else out of the room.'

I need not give our farther conversation on the subject. He entered very fully into the details, and overcame my repulsion from them, by exciting in me a mingled awe and curiosity concerning the possible results of his experiment.

We prepared everything, and he instructed me in my part as assistant. He had not told Bertha of his absolute conviction that Archer would not survive through the night, and endeavoured to persuade her to leave the patient and take a night's rest. But she was obstinate, suspecting the fact that death was at hand, and supposing that he wished merely to save her nerves. She refused to leave the sick-room. Meunier and I sat up together in the library, he making frequent visits to the sick-room, and returning with the information that the case was taking precisely the course he expected. Once he said to me, 'Can you imagine any cause of ill-feeling this woman has against her mistress, who is so devoted to her?'

'I think there was some misunderstanding between them before her illness. Why do you ask?'

'Because I have observed for the last five or six hours – since, I fancy, she has lost all hope of recovery – there seems a strange prompting in her to say something which pain and failing strength forbid her to utter; and there is a look of hideous meaning in her eyes, which she turns continually towards her mistress. In this disease the mind often remains singularly clear to the last.'

'I am not surprised at an indication of malevolent feeling in her,' I said. 'She is a woman who has always inspired me with distrust and dislike, but she managed to insinuate herself into her mistress's favour.' He was silent after this, looking at the fire with an air of absorption, till he went upstairs again. He stayed away longer than usual, and on returning, said to me quietly, 'Come now.'

I followed him to the chamber where death was hovering. The dark hangings of the large bed made a background that gave a strong relief to Bertha's pale face as I entered. She started forward as she saw me enter, and then looked at Meunier with an expression of angry enquiry; but he lifted up his hand as it to impose silence, while he fixed his glance on the dying woman and felt her pulse. The face was pinched and ghastly, a cold perspiration was on the forehead, and the eyelids were lowered so as to conceal the large dark eyes. After a minute or two, Meunier walked round to the other side of the bed where Bertha stood, and with his usual air of gentle politeness towards her begged her to leave the patient under our care – everything should be done for her – she was no longer in a state to be conscious of an affectionate presence. Bertha was hesitating, apparently almost willing to believe his assurance and to comply. She looked round at the ghastly dying face, as if to read the confirmation of that assurance, when for a moment the lowered eyelids were raised again, and it seemed as if the eyes were looking towards Bertha, but blankly. A shudder passed through Bertha's frame, and she returned to her station near the pillow, tacitly implying that she would not leave the room.

The eyelids were lifted no more. Once I looked at Bertha as she watched the face of the dying one. She wore a rich *peignoir*, and her blonde hair was half covered by a lace cap: in her attire she was, as always, an elegant woman, fit to figure in a picture of modern aristocratic life: but I asked myself how that face of hers could ever have seemed to me the face of a woman born of woman, with memories of childhood, capable of pain, needing to be fondled? The features at that moment seemed so preternaturally sharp, the eyes were so hard and eager – she looked like a cruel immortal, finding her spiritual feast in the agonies of a dying race. For across those hard features there came something like a flash when the last hour had been breathed out, and we all felt that the dark veil had completely fallen.

What secret was there between Bertha and this woman? I turned my eyes from her with a horrible dread lest my insight should return, and I should be obliged to see what had been breeding about two unloving women's hearts. I felt that Bertha had been watching for the moment of death as the sealing of her secret: I thanked Heaven it could remain sealed for me.

Meunier said quietly, 'She is gone.' He then gave his arm to Bertha, and she submitted to be led out of the room.

I suppose it was at her order that two female attendants came into the room, and dismissed the younger one who had been present before. When they entered, Meunier had already opened the artery in the long thin neck that lay rigid on the pillow, and I dismissed them, ordering them to remain at a distance till we rang: the doctor, I said, had an operation to perform – he was not sure about the death. For the next twenty minutes I forgot everything but Meunier and the experiment in which he was so absorbed, that I think his senses would have been closed against all sounds or sights which had no relation to it. It was my task at first to keep up the artificial respiration in the body after the transfusion had been effected, but presently Meunier relieved me, and I could see the wondrous slow return of life; the breast began to heave, the inspirations became stronger, the eyelids quivered, and the soul seemed to have returned beneath them. The artificial respiration was withdrawn: still the breathing continued, and there was a movement of the lips.

Just then I heard the handle of the door moving: I suppose Bertha had heard from the women that they had been dismissed: probably a vague fear had arisen in her mind, for she entered with a look of alarm. She came to the foot of the bed and gave a stifled cry.

The dead woman's eyes were wide open, and met hers in full recognition – the recognition of hate. With a sudden strong effort, the hand that Bertha had thought for ever still was pointed towards her, and the haggard face moved. The gasping eager voice said: 'You mean to poison your husband . . . the poison is in the black cabinet . . . I got it for you . . . you laughed at me, and told lies about me behind my back, to make me disgusting . . . because you were jealous . . . are you sorry . . . now?'

The lips continued to murmur, but the sounds were no longer distinct. Soon there was no sound – only a slight movement: the flame had leapt out, and was being extinguished the faster. The wretched woman's heart-strings had been set to hatred and vengeance; the spirit of life had swept the chords for an instant, and was gone again for ever. Great God! Is this what it is to live again . . . to wake up with our unstilled thirst upon us, with our unuttered curses rising to our lips, with our muscles ready to act out their half-committed sins?

Bertha stood pale at the foot of the bed, quivering and helpless, despairing of devices, like a cunning animal whose hiding-places are surrounded by swift-advancing flame. Even Meunier looked paralysed; life for that moment ceased to be a scientific problem to him. As for me, this scene seemed of one texture with the rest of my existence: horror was my familiar, and this new revelation was only like an old pain recurring with new circumstances.

*

Since then Bertha and I have lived apart – she in her own neighbour-hood, the mistress of half our wealth, I as a wanderer in foreign countries, until I came to this Devonshire nest to die. Bertha lives pitied and admired; for what had I against that charming woman, whom everyone but myself could have been happy with? There had been no witness of the scene in the dying room except Meunier, and while Meunier lived his lips were sealed by a promise to me.

Once or twice, weary of wandering, I rested in a favourite spot, and my heart went out towards the men and women and children whose faces were becoming familiar to me; but I was driven away again in terror at the approach of my old insight – driven away to live continually with the one Unknown Presence revealed and yet hidden by the moving curtain of the earth and sky. Till at last disease took hold of me and forced me to rest here – forced me to live in dependence on my servants. And then the curse of insight – of my double consciousness, came again, and has never left me. I know all their narrow thoughts, their feeble regard, their half-wearied pity.

*

It is the 20th of September, 1850. I know these figures I have just written, as if they were a long familiar inscription. I have seen them on this pace in my desk unnumbered times, when the scene of my dying struggle has opened upon me . . .

Elizabeth Stuart Phelps

THE PRESENCE

Our last story brings us to a final conflict between life and death power-fully portrayed by the American writer Elizabeth Stuart Phelps (1844–1911). Phelps was an extremely popular writer in her day chiefly because of the phenomenal success of her spiritualist novel, The Gates Ajar *(1868). Written during the American Civil War, where many thousands had died, it gave a glimpse of the afterlife and provided solace to all those who had lost loved ones. Phelps wrote two sequels of lesser value but sufficient to cement her reputation. Though she wrote many stories that might be defined as supernatural, such as those col-lected in* Men, Women and Ghosts *(1869), few would be defined as traditional, as they are dominated by mood and atmosphere rather than people and events. She had a long and productive career, writing almost up to the day of her death in January 1911. This story comes from her final collection,* The Empty House *(1910).*

The Presence

THERE IT IS again. No – no. The fire flared; or the screen jarred in the draught – I don't see where that draught comes from! Everything is close, and shut; even the door behind the portières; I drew the curtains myself, because these long, low windows are so treacherous on winter nights. I think everything is colder to a person who sits alone in a room – I don't mean seems to be colder, but is actually so. I suppose human beings are like horses in a barn; several, warm the place and are comfortable, but one will shiver. To-night I am cold to the soul.

I am glad that portière is just the dull gold that it is; it fights with firelight so sturdily, and yields so graciously; it has a lambent softness, neither glow nor gleam; he liked it from the day it was hung. His tawny, splendid, blond colouring made it akin to him, I always said. He stood against it like a Viking when he came in and looked about the room for me. Sometimes I hid, to tease him. I often teased him – too often, I am afraid. He was not a teasable person; it never amused him, and it sometimes tried him. I begin to see that – now. I begin to see –

There again! Surely, yes! No – ah-h, no. I don't know whether I am most sorry or most glad. If I should *really* see him I might die of fright, I think. And yet, I would sell my soul, my poor, petty, exacting soul, that never has given a blessed thing worth having been created for, to this world – nor to him – alas, never even to him! Sell it? I would throw it away like rubbish on a river if I could know, if I could be perfectly sure, that he were in this room. And if I could know, 'past all doubting, truly', that he could understand how I feel *now;* if I could speak, and have any reason to believe that he could hear. But I haven't any – not any at all. I cannot fool myself; I care

235

too much about it. Nor I can't cheat him. A woman may torment a live husband if she wants to. She can't deceive a dead one. He is not any longer at my command. He has escaped me.

Is life deaf? Or is death dumb? What sign language must I learn, to reach him? He was so acute and studious–such a scholar; and I was an ignorant girl – frivolous, foolish. I don't think it would occur to him that I would take the trouble to learn any kind of an unknown language for his sake. Why should it? I never did. What billows of affliction he went through trying to teach me a little Spanish the year we thought of going to Madrid! I acted like a fire-fly moth; and I know perfectly well what I mean by that, while I am perfectly conscious that nobody else would know. It is not of the least consequence whether there are such things as firefly moths, either.

But he was patient. He was so patient I could have *screamed* . . . I never was patient in my life.

. . . Oh, there! Yes – No – Yes, *yes*. The outline forms against the screen; just so I saw it that other night, and once besides; but then it blurred and was not. And now it blurs and will not be. And I shall sit here and stretch my arms out for him, and cry my heart out for him, but it will not form; it will only struggle to be an outline; and it will not succeed. I shall not see him. I must not expect anything, and so I shall not have the disappointment to bear. I am not used to bearing disappointment, and I do it very badly. No, he will not come into this room. I need not look for him, nor call him . . .

Antone? Antone? Are you there, Antone? Is it you – after all? How still you are, how stony still! How vague you are, like a mist-man – *you!* Why, you were all man – if you did learn languages and study books – and had that dreadful patience; live, warm, real man, every nerve and muscle of you, everything you thought, and felt, and did – you were all real, Antone . . . Impossible! This wreath of gray shadow cannot be you. I won't believe it. I won't insult you so. You would be the livest ghost that ever had died. You would –

Strange, it is very strange. It does not melt at all. It is like a sea-fog when the sun shines through it. The power of it persists and holds against the screen, and brightens a little, all the time. The outline sharpens slowly – tall, broad in the shoulders, regal about the head, with that high look you had, and your brown-gold hair and beard . . . your eyes; searching for me? Your arms, oh, your dear arms, groping for me . . . Antone! *Antone!*

So it is you. It *is* you. And I sit here, and you stand there – I the living, you the dead – with the width of the room between us. But I am not frightened, not at all. I said a minute ago that I should be afraid of you if you actually came. No – no. I am not afraid, Antone. I would not hurt your feelings so much as that – now. I have hurt them too much more than that too many times, Tony, dear. Oh, I know. I understand now. And the very first thing of all, I want to tell you so. I want to tell you – Don't you hear? Can't you speak? Can't you move? Just a little nearer? This is a pretty large room; I never thought how wide it was before. Who turned down the gas? And the fire – how low it has fallen! There is moonlight – I thought I drew every curtain there is. But, yes, there is moonlight from one of the long windows, and it flows between us like a river . . . Antone? Why don't you cross it? How do you think I can talk over here – so far from you, Tony? Come! I promise not to be afraid. I feel quite brave, and calm. Antone! Can't you come to me? . . . How slowly, how solemnly he shakes his head. It is plain that he cannot speak; or else I cannot hear. Which of the two is it? I suppose God, who made ghosts, must know. Clearly, nobody else does . . .

Then I shall go to you, Antone. See. I stand, and walk quite steadily. I will cross the river of moonlight – so – and I will come to you. I am not in the least afraid. Remember it of your firefly moth, she was not afraid of her dead husband. Some greater, better women might be. You used to call me your little devil. Remember, Antone? If I'd been a big saint I might scream, and get on my knees to say my prayers. But your little devil stands on her feet – to go to you, Antone. I won't stay over here, so far from you . . . *Antone!*

I think the river drowned me. That was it. The river of moonlight was too deep for me. I could not cross it, and that is sure. It let me through like a trap, and tossed me back, and then it rose to the flood again, and now it runs between us, as it did before – a stream of pearl – it has that solemn look. It is like an altar, or a communion table. It is too sacred for devils, big or little. Perhaps the other kind of woman, the sort that says prayers, might have crossed it, and got over. I can't do it . . . It wasn't the river altogether, either. Something else prevented. It felt like hands, or arms; as if I had been pushed away, or turned face about.

Antone! Was it you did that? Did you keep me off? Your great strong arms, so true, so warm, forgiving always, ready always – why, I thought they were created to hold me, Antone! I thought they would hold me for ever . . . Does dying do that kind of thing to people? . . . How disagreeable it must be to be dead . . . Well, then. I can't help it. I'm a live woman, you see, Antone, and I must act as live people do, and *any* firefly-moth woman that I know of would get as near her dead husband as she possibly could. I won't go back to the fire. I shall stand right here, close to the moon river that has been put between us. Pearl, silver, opal, tourmaline – it is made of them all; but they are all jewels and metals, and so they had to melt to make a river. Before they were a moon river, they were solid. And so am I. I don't know whether you are or not. I can't get near enough to find out, Antone . . . I think if I could – if I could reach you, if I could touch you . . . but I cannot do it . . . I cannot forget things, either; not the things I want to forget. I remember all the things I don't want to remember. They trouble me, Antone. They torment me . . .

I am going to tell you because I've got to. I've got to do it, or else go mad myself. I don't know what I am speaking to, nor whether it will do the least good in the world – the dead world, or the live one – but speak I will, because I must. I don't know any ghost-language, only woman-language; I don't understand ghost-laws, only love-laws. Yes, and firefly-laws, and moth-laws. I don't know whether you are mist or matter, whether you are deaf or dumb, whether you are blind or whether you can see, whether you want me or don't want me – Oh, and I can't help it, I don't care. I only know you are my husband because you were my husband. Deaf or listening, blind or seeing, warm or cold, loving or not loving – Antone! Because I was your wife, because I am your wife – listen to me.

I never was fit for you, Antone, from the very beginning – never. But I never knew that till now. It was the way it is with girls who have been admired a good deal, and spoiled a little – I suppose I thought I was worth any trouble on the part of any man. I really believed it. It never occurred to me how much *you* were worth. It did not seem to me as if I had anything to do about it – about our married life. I never once thought that I should do a mortal thing to keep us happy, Antone! I left all that to you, just as I did business, and income, and newspapers, and writing books, and paying bills, and all those troublesome things. Antone, I left everything to you. I asked everything of you. I leant on you like a heavy baby. I clutched at you like a person in the water when another person dives to save him from drowning. I believe I strangled you. Sometimes I have a dreadful thought. I wonder if I tired you out. I think perhaps I took your strength and weakened your pluck. When you had that accident, it seems to me you didn't try so hard to get well as you might. Antone! It looks to me now as if you didn't care enough. How do I know that wasn't my fault? There's a thought I have. It is a cold thought, and crawls across me, the way a snake crawls upon warm flesh. I cannot crush it nor throttle it. This is the way it looks to me: Perhaps I was so much to blame that I never even knew I was to blame. Perhaps I did you nothing but harm, and brought you nothing but evil.

Antone! I don't believe I ever understood you any more than I understood your Chinese grammar. I see now – persons who are ignorant don't know they are ignorant, and people who don't understand don't understand that they don't understand. And that is what makes it so hard – yes, hard on both sides. But listen to me, Antone! See. I want you to know it. Now it does not seem to me as if there ever *were* two sides to the troubles we had. It does not look to me now as if I had any 'side.' It seems to me that I was almost always in the wrong. As I look back on it, you were almost always right. And that is the dreadful part of it – now. Sometimes I think it will kill me. But I know better. I know it won't do any such thing. I am young and well, and live, and my blood leaps, and my heart beats and fights in me, and I shall last – oh, I shall last till I am a very old woman. And I shall sit here evenings alone in this great room, this lonely house, and I shall cry myself sick on your empty pillow, for I loved you – oh, I did love you, Antone, whether you believed it or not, whether you forgive me or not, whether you love me or not . . . I did. I do. But you are a dead man. You are so dead you cannot speak. How do I know you will care whether I love you or not – now? I don't know the first thing about you – now. You might as well be a star, ten million miles away. Or you might be a character from the Bible – something three or four thousand years off – some strange, old, cold person that wouldn't notice a poor girl like me.

. . . How bright and fine the outline grows! Like drawing turning to painting, or colour changing to form. Hush! I am talking too loud; or I am saying too much. His noble head lifts and leans a little, backward, and I see the shape of his chin; it is just the same as it was; he had such a high-minded chin. Now the features begin to take on their old lines and looks – his dear eyes, his lips that curved and quivered so easily, so exquisitely. I can see them move, I am sure.

. . . Antone! I can't keep still. I must speak while I have the chance. How do I know I shall ever have it again? Ghost-laws are not like woman-laws, and life, I see it plainly, is the servant or the prisoner of death.

Hark! I want to tell you two things. There are a hundred things – they pour over me, torrents of them, but there are two I must say if I do not say another word. These two rise above all the others like the foam from a cascade or a wave; they may be less solid than the wave; but they are easier to see; they dash higher – Antone! I must tell you, I will tell you how I feel now about that wretched business of Rob Acres. I was always a little fool about such things – but I never cared two Roman pearls for him. I was born a silly thing, – half moth, half firefly, – but I never forgot that I didn't love any of them the least little bit; never, after I had seen you, Antone – never! You were so patient – too patient with me. You reasoned with me as gently as a man-angel; you should have shaken me and locked me up in a closet on educated crackers and water till I came to my senses, such as I had. I hadn't many in those days. I flitted and floated about – and Rob did like me very much – and I went sizzling into that feeling he had, as if it had been a kerosene burner, a bright, hot, staring light, where you get caught between the chimney and the shade; and then, when it scorched a little, just a little, I flew to you. And *you* – oh, Antone, you made me feel so ashamed of myself, and Rob. You held it all up to me, so quietly – not ten words – as if you held up a Claude Lorrain glass to a glaring sunset that I had been looking at, and showed me that it was all set in black. Antone, I want to tell you. If I don't I shall die of the shame of remembering how it was. Antone, there never was a minute I didn't care more for one eyelash of yours than for Rob Acre's whole soul and body. I loved you – I love you, Antone, just you, nobody else. And Antone! Listen! It is true, and you've got to believe it, he never touched me, not so much as to hold my silly hand. He never came too near me, except his eyes did – and his thoughts, I suppose. That was bad enough. But it never was any worse. And then that day I said to him: 'Rob Acres, I want all this to stop. Look at that.' I held up my wedding-ring, with your diamond above it, blazing. 'I love my husband, Rob,' I said; 'I don't care for you. I don't care for any man but him. We've treated him very badly. I am going to ask his pardon, and behave myself. I am the most to blame, because I'm married and you're not,' I said. 'But I won't be to blame any more. Go away, Rob,' I said. 'I never want to see you again. Go off on a fishing trip, or something. I shall tell my husband every mortal thing I've said and done. He'll forgive me – he is made that way – but I never shall forgive myself.' And I never have. And here it is, Antone – the whole story. I am telling the holy truth . . . the unholy truth, if you want to call it so. I won't deny that, either. Antone, there are times it crucifies me . . .

Now, quick! Listen, while you can. The other one is that day when you were sick, and I went to the Frasers' and left you. Out of half a thousand matters that happened in our married life, why that one? Just that one to come back, and persist, and corrode the same spot in me, like a spatter of vitriol. No, it has never healed over. It's just the way you looked, that's all. I see it; I see it, till I think I'd rather go blind way back in the optic nerve if I needn't ever see it again. But that wouldn't make any difference, would it? See just the same, wouldn't you? You'll know. I don't. You used to know everything. I don't have anybody to ask about things now.

It was the look about your mouth I minded most, more than your eyes; and you didn't speak. You turned your face away upon the pillow. You were so hurt you couldn't say a word. And I went and left you – so. I went and danced and fooled till midnight. When I came back you were worse – feverish, and coughing hard. I said some silly thing, I remember – making light of what ailed you, the way well people do. That was one of the troubles with me. I was too well – did not understand. I never knew what it was not to be comfortable. I was not sensitive. You were. I hadn't nerves enough. You had too many – all that studying and writing. I treated you as if you had been a rough person. I never discounted anything for what you were or what you did. I never understood you – never. Now that it is too late, I am beginning to. And that is the cruel part of it.

. . . Antone! Don't *go!* Not *yet!* Oh, stay! Wait a little. Listen to me. I haven't finished. I must say something more. Antone!

. . . He shakes his head so determinedly, so silently, that it frightens me. Is it that he cannot stay? Or that he will not? Antone! . . .

See the grey breath between us. Now it is a cloud – purple – almost black – it mounts, and darkens. He yields to it, and it takes him. He melts, and is not. The river of moonlight has dwindled to a sickly brook. The great room is so still that I could shriek into it. The curtains stir, the screen thrills . . . as if it had absorbed him. Perhaps he has not gone beyond it. Who knows? I have never been a spirit; how can I tell what spirits are capable of? Who knows what things contain them? Or thoughts? Perhaps thoughts contain them. It might be . . . Antone! Don't stay hiding over there. Come to me. Come into my thoughts, Antone. They can't hold anything but you.

Oh, come into my heart! It aches for you, as if it had been gashed and emptied. I am *all you*, Antone. Come back to me, I say. If you were alive, and I were dead, I'd go to *you*. Heaven nor earth nor hell shouldn't prevent me . . . not if you wanted me. Antone!

. . . I believe it is coming back, after all . . . but so new, so different from the other. This is not so real as the other. It is like a photograph. I see it quite distinctly – small, like a figure on a negative. Am I the camera? Has my heart photographed him? Or my will? He stands as he stood in that picture of his I like best – in his rough, tweed suit; just his everyday look, his dear look. He regards me straight and steadily. As I watch, the picture slowly grows; as if the photographer were enlarging it . . . the noble head, the strong attitude, the whole man of him.

There, Antone! I knew you would come back to me. I meant you should. I didn't believe you could refuse me – now. It doesn't seem much for a live wife to ask of a dead husband – just stay long enough to hear her through. So! Listen again, Antone . . .

It's just as I told you, I was too well. I had always been too comfortable. I was dulled by health and happiness, and having my own way. And when I first began to know what discomfort was, and what it meant not to do things, and what it was like to bear anything unpleasant – I think I must have been a perfect little devil. I wonder you put up with me at all, Antone. I can't see how you bore with it, or why you were so patient . . . never scolded once; never a cross word, not one in all that time . . .

Now this is what I'm coming to. Of all the hatefulness I ever did by you, the hatefulest was the way I acted about the baby. Why in the world girls marry, and then are so surprised, and act so wronged, and are so wretched – I can't see. But they do. And I did. And I went through all that stage; I went through it like an imp. I was fairly vicious. I believe I was malignant. I fretted and fumed and fussed. I complained and blamed – oh, I believe I blamed you. I was capable of it. And I did everything I could, short of murdering. You never knew the half of it, Antone. I never quite went so far as to be willing to kill it; but I wanted it to die. Oh, yes, I wanted the baby to die.

I'll own to that . . . the poor little miserable, helpless thing . . . my baby . . . our baby. I never wanted it, and when I found it was going to be, I hoped it never would be at all. I did, I did! I confess to you, Antone. Listen to me.

Confess again! Confess again! When it really happened, the poor little fellow did die, then I wanted him to live. While I lay there, weak and wretched, broken and brought to myself, I longed for him to live. If I'd known how to pray, I should have prayed for the baby to go on living. But he couldn't – how could he? After all there was of me had set against him for so many months – like something smothering fire – the poor little spark went out. It had to. It never had the chance to be a living flame. And when I saw the way you looked – and trying not to let me know how you felt, for fear it should trouble me or hurt me – Antone! Tony – *dear* Tony! Oh, forgive me, can't you? Won't you try?

You are a great white ghost, and I am so small and so miserable – nobody but you in this world or any other. Antone, I say, you *shall* forgive me! I will come – I don't care if I die for it, too – I will come into your arms, and take the consequences. I don't care how dead you are, nor I don't care what happens to me. Where should a live wife go if not to her husband's heart? Dear ghost! Dear Tony! Take me – see – take me this very minute. Hold out your arms – so – Now keep me, Antone . . .

There, I knew you would. Hold fast, darling. Don't let any of your cold, old angels pull me away. I don't belong to angels – no, nor to devils, either. I belong to you. Keep hold of me, I say.

What? I don't understand. Antone? *Not dead?* Live, and warm and strong – the same as ever – just you, dear, after all? . . . I can't seem to sit up. Don't let me go. I feel pretty weak and strange. Slip your arm under my shoulder – so – and never let me go again. Didn't die? Are you sure you didn't die, after all? . . . Are you sure you didn't die, at all? . . . You live, strong, warm, real man, you! . . . Oh, hush! Tony, Tony, *Tony!* . . .

Was I so sick as all that? Oh, I see. And that accounts for it. I must have been . . . Yes, I see. It blunted the pain of my body and sharpened the pain of my mind. And it took that form, Tony – just you, you . . . nobody else . . . But such a little time? And eternities happened . . . That little dead baby – I don't think I want to see him. I might feel badly, after all.

How curious this is! Don't let me slip away again. I mustn't see those sights I saw any more . . . What is that over there on the other side of this big bed? It lies so still. I am afraid of it. I'm too weak to look at any more ghosts. And this would be such a tiny one – it would make your heart sick to look at it.

Why, it moves, Antone! It is warm. It is warm to my fingers, now they touch it. It is a living thing. It never died. Nobody died at all. Why, you poor little, blessed, breathing baby! Lift it up, Antone, and put it in my arms.

THE GHOST-FEELER
Stories of Terror and the Supernatural
Edith Wharton

Edited and introduced by Peter Haining

978-0-7206-1152-6 • paperback • 190pp • £9.95

'Wharton's ghost stories are among the best in their genre.' – *All Hallows*, Journal of the Ghost Story Society

'Wharton is rich in implication . . . the selection here is an excellent one.'
– *Daily Telegraph*

'This dark new anthology is no narrow collection of standard Victorian ghost stories . . . A delightful compendium.'
– *Glasgow Herald*

Diagnosed with typhoid fever at age of nine, Edith Wharton was beginning a long convalescence when she was given a book of ghost tales to read. Not only setting back her recovery, this reading opened up her fevered imagination to 'a world haunted by formless horrors'. So chronic was this paranoia that she was unable to sleep in a room with any book containing a ghost story – she was even moved to burn such volumes – and these fears persisted until her late twenties. She outgrew them but retained a heightened or 'celtic' (her term) sense of the supernatural. Wharton considered herself not a 'ghost-seer' – the term applied to those people who have claimed to have witnessed apparitions – but rather a 'ghost-feeler', someone who senses what cannot be seen.

This experience and ability enabled Edith Wharton to write chilling tales that objectify this sense of unease. Far removed from the comfort and urbane elegance associated with the author's famous novels, the stories in this volume were praised by Henry James, L.P. Hartley, Graham Greene and many others.

Peter Owen books can be purchased from:
Central Books, 99 Wallis Road, London E9 5LN, UK
Tel: +44 (0)845 458 9911 Fax: + 44 (0)845 458 9912
e-mail: orders@centralbooks.com

www.peterowen.com

THE DEMANDING DEAD
More Stories of Terror and the Supernatural
Edith Wharton

Edited and introduced by Peter Haining

978-0-7206-1272-1 • paperback • 222pp • £10.95

'It is in the warm darkness of the pre-natal fluid far below our conscious reason that the faculty dwells with which we apprehend the ghosts we may not be endowed with the gift of seeing.' – Edith Wharton

'Elegant, chilling tales.' – *Goodreads.com*

'A master of the ghost story.'
– Jack Sullivan, author of the *Penguin Encyclopaedia of Horror and the Supernatural*, on Edith Wharton

Eight outstanding ghost stories by one of the finest writers in the genre, *The Demanding Dead* is an absorbing collection of tales from Edith Wharton's fertile imagination. Like her mentor Henry James, Wharton had the ability to switch genres seemingly without effort. *The Demanding Dead* highlights a lesser-known side of Wharton's writing. The same literary genius evident in such famous works as *The Age of Innocence*, *Ethan Frome* and *The House of Mirth* is here dedicated to giving the reader a damned good scare. Stories such as 'Kerfol' (considered by aficionados to be Wharton's best ghost story) and 'Pomegranate Seed' are perfect illustrations of consummately crafted horror fiction. Wharton's vivid sense of the supernatural betrayed her deeper anxieties about the claustrophobia of domestic life and the pain of a failing relationship.

Taut, suspenseful and surprising, these stories, together with those in their companion volume *The Ghost-Feeler*, establish Wharton as one of the greatest proponents of suspense fiction.

Peter Owen books can be purchased from:
Central Books, 99 Wallis Road, London E9 5LN, UK
Tel: +44 (0)845 458 9911 Fax: + 44 (0)845 458 9912
e-mail: orders@centralbooks.com

www.peterowen.com

HUNTED DOWN
The Detective Stories of Charles Dickens
Charles Dickens

Edited and introduced by Peter Haining

978-0-7206-1265-3 • paperback • 224 pp • £9.95

'A fascinating anthology.' – *Independent*

'One of the great pioneers of detective fiction . . . This collection will be of great interest and is thoroughly enjoyable.'
– *The Good Book Guide*

The detective stories of England's greatest Victorian novelist

Charles Dickens was a pioneer of detective fiction, and *Hunted Down* assembles a fascinating selection of his work in which the men of the law make their mark. Their working methods were based on Dickens's observations of the fledgling police detective force when he was a solicitor's clerk and reporter and witnessed the workings of police stations and accompanied detectives on their nightly street patrols; he also attended magistrates' courts and was present at murder trials and public executions.

This first-hand experience runs throughout the stories in this superb collection – much admired by contemporary crime writers – and includes 'The Edwin Drood Syndicate' and 'Hunted Down' itself. Here we meet a compelling cast of crimefighters, including an amateur detective, a river policeman and all manner of undercover cops.

Peter Owen books can be purchased from:
Central Books, 99 Wallis Road, London E9 5LN, UK
Tel: +44 (0)845 458 9911 Fax: + 44 (0)845 458 9912
e-mail: orders@centralbooks.com

www.peterowen.com

Also published by Peter Owen

SENSATION STORIES
Wilkie Collins

Edited and introduced by Peter Haining

978-0-7206-1220-2 • paperback • 288 pp • £12.50

'Wilkie Collins is the one man of unmistakable genius who has an affinity with Dickens . . . there were no two men who could touch them at a ghost story.'
– G.K. Chesterton

'To Mr Collins belongs the credit of having introduced into fiction those most mysterious of mysteries, the mysteries which are at our own doors.'
– Henry James

'A master of plot and situation.'
– T.S. Eliot

The arrival of *The Woman in White* in 1860 is said to have ushered in the modern mystery genre. But, as Peter Haining reveals in this collection, Collins had actually been writing sensation stories for almost a decade previously. With dramatic plots that revolve around hidden secrets, bloody crimes, villainous schemes and clever detective work, Wilkie Collins helped to invent a genre worlds away from anything written by his contemporaries – one that was to have a far-reaching influence.

Originally published in various periodicals, many of these pieces have not been in print for more than a century. All ten stories are thrilling reads, and each shows Wilkie Collins's towering contribution to the development of the mystery genre, so much so that he is now commonly regarded as one of the chief forefathers of the detective story.

Peter Owen books can be purchased from:
Central Books, 99 Wallis Road, London E9 5LN, UK
Tel: +44 (0)845 458 9911 Fax: + 44 (0)845 458 9912
e-mail: orders@centralbooks.com

www.peterowen.com